WHITE TREASURE

A novel by R. Jack Punch

iUniverse, Inc.
New York Lincoln Shanghai

White Treasure

Copyright © 2006 by R. Jack Punch

All rights reserved. No part of this book may be used or reproduced by any means, graphic, electronic, or mechanical, including photocopying, recording, taping or by any information storage retrieval system without the written permission of the publisher except in the case of brief quotations embodied in critical articles and reviews.

iUniverse books may be ordered through booksellers or by contacting:

iUniverse
2021 Pine Lake Road, Suite 100
Lincoln, NE 68512
www.iuniverse.com
1-800-Authors (1-800-288-4677)

This is a work of fiction. The names, characters, and places exist purely in the mind of the author and are used fictitiously. Any similarities to actual events, places, or persons, dead or living, is entirely coincidental.

ISBN-13: 978-0-595-36575-3 (pbk)
ISBN-13: 978-0-595-67393-3 (cloth)
ISBN-13: 978-0-595-81006-2 (ebk)
ISBN-10: 0-595-36575-2 (pbk)
ISBN-10: 0-595-67393-7 (cloth)
ISBN-10: 0-595-81006-3 (ebk)

Printed in the United States of America

Special thanks to my instructors Tom and Debora Coveny, Elby Benton, Joe Plano, Dennis Lesslie, Paul King, Steve Stevenson, Rob Wellman, and several others that have helped me gain diving knowledge. I want to express a sincere thanks to all the divers and diving students that I have worked with; I hope that we will ascend safely from the serenity of the deep blue together again. Also, thanks to my wife, Jane, and my son, Ryan, who had to listen to me orate this story as I put the words on paper. And to my sister, Kathy, for her guidance.

A Man to Remember

It would take all my inner strength to control my emotions that Saturday morning. I was driving my lifelong best friend, Michael Moresby, to the airport for the last time. Glaring, blinding sunlight flooded the car. I couldn't see the road clearly. Perhaps it was the sun that made my eyes water as Mike sat silently in the seat next to me.

By the end of his life, Michael Moresby was a somewhat miserable man with three ex-wives who probably still loved him but just could not stand to live with his perfectionism. At a young age, I had observed Mike's kindness and strength. We were good friends throughout high school. Mike joined the Army after high school, and I went to college. Shortly after Mike came home from Vietnam, I finished college and started teaching high-school English. Mike found a job at a local factory but worked his way into a management position, and eventually bought the business. Despite the different paths we had taken, we always found some time to get together and share the happenings in our lives.

Six years ago, when I was fifty-six years old, I retired from teaching high-school English. I enjoyed a good retirement package, while Mike went broke. I really felt bad when Mike lost his business. He had been losing interest in the factory for quite awhile, even before new technology phased out the products it produced, but the closing was still a hard thing to take. Yet he bounced back and was enthusiastic about returning to school. I was surprised by how eagerly he studied to get a college degree and even a master's degree in physical education. Mike told me that he felt like he was nineteen years old again, and I saw his energy climb. Still, at his age, the only job he could get was a part-time job teaching a scuba diving class at the community college. Last year, Mike lost his house and moved into his boat, the *Gold Hunter*.

The small grass runway came into view, allowing a right turn, away from the sun's glare. The pilot stood next to the shiny white-and-red Cessna that would deliver Mike to his final destination. I got out of the car and walked over to the pilot. He was over six feet tall with a brown monk-style haircut, bald in the middle, and he had bright blue eyes that smiled contagiously.

"Hi! My name is Peter Digs. You must be Wilbur Bone," the pilot said with a smile.

Peter knew Mike, which made me feel a little better about the occasion. I walked to the passenger side of the car. I was surprised to see the smile on my face in my reflection in the window. My hazel eyes were glossy from the tears that I was fighting to hide.

I opened the door and felt as though Mike were smiling back at me. Despite his miserable attitude, Mike had always enjoyed making people laugh. I was sure that he would approve of some joking today. I reached in and picked up the waxy cardboard box that contained Mike's final remains.

Peter had the passenger door open on the small two-seat airplane, and he held the box as I climbed in. I told Peter, "It's a good thing Mike fit into such a small box." Mike had been a large man who weighed over two hundred and fifty pounds. Peter and I had a little bit of a laugh together then, which eased the tension as we left the ground and headed for Shadigee, a small hamlet on the southern shore of Lake Ontario.

Mike grew up loving the lake and became an expert on its history, especially any history involving sunken ships. It was his wish to have his ashes scattered along the stretch of Lake Ontario where he had spent most of his life searching the bottom for sunken ships.

I pulled out Mike's letter with the instructions for today's events. I had contacted his family and friends, telling them to gather at ten o'clock in the morning at Shadigee, where a plane would deliver his ashes to the lake. Peter had studied a copy of the instructions before we met that morning, and he knew exactly what to do.

In the air, the sun was to my right but high enough to light up the beautiful August morning. The ground was a gorgeous blanket of green trees, golden wheat fields, and colorful red-and-green rooftops. The foreground showed an unusually blue Lake Ontario that blended with the sky in the far-off distance. Puffy white clouds decorated the sky over the lake.

Peter said, "Here we go!" as he pulled the throttle back, leaving us in utter silence except for the sound of the plane's engine. As we began to drop down, Peter pointed out the array of different-colored vehicles on the shoreline right in front of us. I watched the cars get closer and saw a lot of people standing in front of the cars. Per Mike's instructions, we descended from the south to a point fifty feet above the crowd. We were close enough to recognize Mike's children and some of the other mourners when Peter pushed the throttle all the way into the dash. I was happy to see such a large number of people present at Mike's wake. I could see startled people jump from the noise of the airplane, and the box on my lap seemed to jiggle, as if Mike were laughing.

Then the plane rose once more into the sky for a minute before turning left, and Peter pulled the throttle back, leveled off, and added flaps to slow us down. Peter told me to wait for him to give the command before opening the door and dumping out the ashes. The plane made a right turn and followed the shoreline back to the group. I half expected a giant spring-loaded worm to jump out when I opened the box, but the box contained only dark gray ashes.

I looked at the ashes and thought to myself, *Mike, old boy, you always did like to make things grand.* Peter yelled, "Now!" and I opened the door. The wind sucked most of the ashes out before I had even tipped the box out the door. With the box empty, the door closed hard as the plane ascended again toward the heavens. I looked back and saw the dark ashes hitting the water, as if a windstorm had left a spray of black water in a line over the lake. I looked back to the sky and said, "Michael is yours now, God. Enjoy him!"

Peter landed the plane and taxied up to my car. We shook hands before I got out. Then Peter rolled down the runway and left for Batavia, where he had to give a flying lesson to a student. I stood there and watched as the plane shrank in size and disappeared before I got into my car. An hour later, I would have to meet with Mike's children at the lawyer's office in Lockport.

Although it was a busy day for me, I was happy to be helping my old friend. On the drive to Lockport, I thought about how dull my life was. Mike had always added excitement to my simple life. I had learned to scuba dive with Mike a long time before, even though I had not spent much time in the water over the last several years. My first airplane ride had been as Mike's first passenger when he'd earned his private pilot's license. My first date had been a double date with Mike and his girlfriend's cousin from California. I remembered thinking that she would be ugly; however, I was thrilled to find that she was a beautiful blond with a wild sense of adventure. Everything I did with Mike was utterly adventurous and truly did fulfill a void in my life.

I felt a bit guilty realizing that my memories were focused more on the fun that Mike and I had shared rather than on anything in particular about his personality, but a smile came to my face because I knew that Mike would want me to remember the good times. Still, it would be hard for me to see his five children at the reading of the will. I was certain that the will would be an extension of Mike's humor because he had no money left.

I was the first to arrive at the office of Mike's attorney, John Carski, a short man half my age. Mike had chosen him because John was a religious man who had offered to simply pray for him when no attorney's acumen could help Mike through a difficult divorce. Mike had told me, "An attorney that will pray for a client must be a good man, and a good man is better than a great attorney." Although I knew that John Carski had built up a reputation as a really good lawyer, I appreciated Mike's fundamental approach to describing people by their ethical points of view.

"Hello! I am Dolores, Mr. Carski's secretary. You must be Mr. Bone." The secretary's warm welcome eased my nervousness. She led me down a hall to a large conference room where John Carski was eagerly waiting. Mr. Carski's handshake was professionally firm, but his eyes were comforting. His secretary left, saying, "I will bring the rest when they are all here."

John Carski pulled a chair out from the grand conference table and asked me to sit down. Then he sat next to me and began talking about Mike. "Mike was certainly a man who knew how to enjoy life…and how to make other people laugh. Do you remember that time at the New Year's Eve party when he showed up in a tuxedo with a clown nose?" I did remember, and I had to chuckle, even after all those years. I thought about the many times I had laughed because of Mike's sense of humor and his outlook on life. Sharing some memories with John Carski was a relaxing beginning to the meeting, and I was grateful for that.

We heard voices coming from down the hall. Mr. Carski stood up, looking toward the door, and said, "Time to begin." One of the voices sounded like Mike's, which startled me until I saw Jason Moresby enter the room. At twenty-eight, Jason was the spitting image of a younger Michael before he had lost his hair and gained weight: a large, short, solidly built guy. I stood up as Jason extended his hand. I shook hands with him but was at a loss for words. Paula, an elegant woman in her thirties with long dark hair and a slim figure, and Jackie, a short, perky twenty-year-old, were Mike's oldest and youngest daughters. I remembered them all as small children. They came over and gave me a group hug. Patrick, a big guy already at twenty-four, and Mike, Jr., two years younger, followed the girls and shook my hand and exchanged cheerful greetings with me.

John Carski told us all to sit down. He wasted no time in getting into his speech, which obviously had been prepared by Mike. When Mike lost his house shortly after the factory folded, he had already divided up most of his possessions among the children. Mr. Carski summed it up, saying, "You know, don't you, that Mike asked me to say that there was nothing else, but at least that way you could all share it?" Mike's children laughed at their father's postmortem attempt at humor.

Then Mr. Carski handed them envelopes marked with their names and instructed them not to open them yet. They talked about how they had probably just received one of their dad's favorite jokes. Mike was very close to his children, even as adults, and ever since they had learned of his heart condition, they all had felt the loss and dealt with it in their own ways. Now they had mutually decided to shelve their grief and celebrate the lovable jokester father they remembered so well. Mr. Carski told them that Michael had requested that they all act as equal members of the Moresby Foundation. Mike had set aside an investment portfolio to provide college educations for his grandchildren, and for others, if the members of the foundation agreed.

Mike's children just chuckled, assuming that this was another joke their dad had asked John Carski to play on them to cheer them up a bit. They knew as well as I did that Mike had been broke when he died. Mr. Carski understood the disbelief and was well prepared. He held up a folder to quiet the giggles in the room, and said, "The portfolio was started three months ago with exactly two million dollars and has earned approximately two and one-half percent so far, bringing its value to two million, two hundred and sixty thousand dollars. All five of you, as Michael Moresby's children, are the officers of the foundation. This is not a joke."

Without hesitation, Mr. Carski added that Mike figured there would be plenty of money when his first grandchild started college in ten years. "Now you can open your envelopes," Mr. Carski said, sitting down and looking at me with a smile.

The faces in the room expressed varying degrees of astonishment, surprise, skepticism, or delight, sometimes all at once. Jason was the first to speak, saying in a mock-disappointed tone, "Just a check? No joke or dumb story?"

The others laughed for awhile. Then Paula, sounding truly bewildered, said, "Five times a hundred is half a million dollars. Where did Dad get that kind of money?"

Mike Jr. grinned and added, "I have no clue, but it's sure gonna make my life a lot easier."

Jackie patted him on the back. "Congratulations, Mr. Mike, Jr., to you and to all of us. Dad was evidently very good at keeping a secret, wasn't he, though?"

Patrick, always more serious than his siblings, sighed deeply and wondered aloud, "Yes, but should we really believe all this or not?"

Mr. Carski assured them that the money and the foundation were real, before he added that there was one more item to discuss, which involved Mr. Bone. He opened a large manila folder, removed some papers, and handed them to me, saying, "However, I am not so sure what this is all about." The mysterious pile of assorted papers included some text and drawings, as well as photographs of sunken ships: sixteen in all.

I was surprised to realize that the background of all the photographs looked familiar to me; I recognized it as Lake Ontario. I thought to myself, *What wrecks are these?* There were old wooden ships labeled "Sloop of War" and "Galleon," and one that was clearly a Viking ship, and one that appeared to be a submarine. Each photograph was attached to a short paragraph with some history on the ship. We passed the papers around for Mike's children to look at before Mr. Carski asked for them back.

Carski put them back in the folder, looked up at the group with a sterner expression on his face, and announced that Michael Moresby had left all of his personal belongings to Wilbur Bone. These only consisted of Mike's thirty-two-foot scuba diving boat, the *Gold Hunter,* and the items that were on board. Then Carski told Mike's children that Michael had left sixteen "chapters" (information packets concerning the shipwrecks in the photos), and that a list has been compiled and sent to potential bidders for an auction to be held next Friday.

Mr. Carski went on, "It was your father's wish that his children not be involved in the auction, but that half the proceeds from the auction be divided up equally among you. The other half will go to Wilbur. In fact, Wilbur, I have a letter for you from Mike regarding the proceeds of the auction and what Mike would like you to do with the money. He asked me to give you the letter three days after the auction." He looked at me and asked, "Will you be here Friday at noon?"

I said, "Yes, I'll be here," but I wasn't really sure what it was all about or why I was involved.

Mr. Carski wrapped up the meeting, and we all stood to leave. I couldn't tell precisely why Mike's children were so agitated as we left the lawyer's office. Of course, it could have been the hundred thousand dollars they each had received; or maybe they were thinking about the two-million-dollar foundation that would assure their children a chance for a college education; or maybe, like me, they were just baffled about the mystery of the shipwrecks.

As I drove home, I could not stop thinking about Mike. The images of the airplane ride earlier that day came to mind. I think I must have dozed off at the wheel because all of a sudden Mike's ghost was flying the plane, and he was laughing. He pointed down to show me something, and it was as though the lake were drained of water, exposing an array of ships from different periods of history. They were scattered in no particular pattern, and brightly colored, as if freshly painted.

One ship in particular sparkled like a golden sun. We were flying down closer to the wreck when I suddenly came to and realized that a fast-moving deer had stopped its run and was looking at me through the windshield. I slammed on the brakes, screeching to a halt. The deer calmly crossed the road and disappeared into the woods on the other side. I was back to reality, but I felt startled by the daydream. It was unusual for my mind to wander.

Trisha was sitting on the front porch waiting for me when I pulled into the driveway. She was ten years younger than me, but she looked almost as young as when we were married forty years before because she took such good care of herself. Trisha exercised regularly to keep her trim figure, dressed nicely, and maintained her soft, pale skin, and silky, long blond hair. She stood up gracefully and eagerly and walked over to the porch steps, moving like a young, sexy woman. Since retiring, I had become lackadaisically content, and sadly, I was just not that interested in sex anymore. I thought it must be difficult for Trisha, but I was embarrassed about my lack of energy, and so I was reluctant to talk about it very directly. But she was such an understanding person that I imagined she knew somehow that I wished things between us were still the way they once were.

Trisha, with her normal gentleness, took my hand and silently led me to the glider on the front porch. We sat down, and she let me tell her of the day's events. A mist filled my eyes as I relived the airplane ride. Trisha had been there, watching with Mike's family and friends at Shadigee, and they had all talked about Mike's sense of humor, his adventurous attitude toward life, and his love of doing outrageous and goofy things. I guess I still looked a bit sad, so she stopped me to remind me that I had been with Mike whenever I had done something stupid but hilarious. A slight smile sparkled in her eyes when she described how everyone had been watching the lake when the plane had come from behind, startling everyone when its engine roared right above the spectators.

I saved telling Trisha about the will until last. "Believe it or not, he actually left each of the five kids a hundred thousand bucks and set up a two-million-dollar foundation for their children's education."

She was as shocked as I had been. "But I thought Mike was broke! He lost his factory, he lost his house, and he lived on his diving boat until he got really sick, didn't he?"

"Yeah, I know. It's a huge surprise that he had all this money that nobody ever knew anything about. By the way, Trish, I should tell you that Mike left his boat to me."

She looked concerned for a minute, as though she were a little worried about whether I could handle a boat. Then she said, in her straightforward but kind way, "Gee, honey, do you think you're up to running a dive boat these days?"

"Well, I don't know, Trish, but don't worry about it at this point. You know, actually, I'll probably sell it anyway. Maybe that's even something I should just go ahead with right away. What do you think?"

Trisha said, "I think it's up to you, sweetheart. He was a dear friend, and his boat means something to you, I'm sure, but do whatever you think is best."

"Well, I've spent enough time putting things off and puttering around since I retired. Maybe I'd better put some of the energy Mike was so famous for into making arrangements. I think I'll go to the marina right away," I said.

The very next thing I did was to make a *FOR SALE* sign for the boat; then I drove to the marina to check on the boat before the day ended. Trisha offered to go with me, but I told her that it was something I needed to do alone. She gave me a peck on the cheek, and I put the sign in the car and left, despite an urge to stay in the comfort of home.

The sun was still pretty bright, demanding the use of sunglasses, which gave the puffy white clouds a darker contrast against a blue-green sky. The marina was busy, as would be expected on a Saturday evening in August. I felt strange when I pulled into the parking spot beside the sign that read *GOLD HUNTER*.

Bill Reed, who owned the marina, must have seen me pull in. Before I could get out of the car, he was walking briskly toward me, smiling, with his hand extended in a friendly wave. Bill's white hair glowed on top of his lean frame and dark, suntanned face.

"Been waiting for you, Wilbur," the jolly mariner said. I wondered why Bill would be waiting for me, but he answered my question before I could ask.

"Mike told me that you'd be here after the funeral." Well, that made sense. After all, Mike had carefully planned his own funeral and the reading of the will, so naturally he would have informed Bill in advance that I was inheriting the boat.

"In fact, I've just come to check on the boat, Bill. Maybe you could help me out a bit. I'm going to need some detailed information so I can put it up for sale."

Bill laughed, "That's very efficient of you, Wilbur, but you might want to think it over more first. Don't be too hasty to sell that boat. You know, the marina has been getting several calls inquiring about scuba diving boats for hire. As a matter of fact, like Mike suggested, I saved some phone numbers to give to you. You see, the *Gold Hunter* is the only dive boat around for a hundred miles. You might even want to run a few diving trips yourself before selling her."

I turned my head toward Mike's boat. I just wanted to sell the boat and go on with my simple life. But I felt a longing for the excitement Mike had added when Trisha and I had joined him on his excursions.

Looking back at Bill Reed, I simply said, "I'll think it over."

Bill looked a bit surprised, but said, "Okay, but don't take too long." Bill left for the marina's office, and I walked down the small grassy hill to the boat.

The *Gold Hunter* was a thirty-two-foot lobster boat, built in Maine. Mike had bought it twelve years back and converted it into a dive boat. The forward cabin, where Mike had been living, was very small, leaving a large deck for divers and their gear. A huge aluminum ladder stuck up from the open transom; it rotated into the water so that divers could get back in the boat easily after a dive. The helm station was on the right—or starboard, as Mike would have said—and it took up little space next to the door leading down to the cabin.

I stepped onto the deck and looked at the row of scuba tanks lined up in a wire holder down the center of the boat. A lockbox behind the helm offered storage, as well as a seat for the skipper. A small two-foot roof covered the helm station but left the rest of the boat's deck open to the sky.

A fleet of small fishing boats filled the docks on both sides, with numerous fishing poles reaching for the sky and big downriggers, used for salmon and lake-trout fishing, extending astern from each boat. People were cleaning off their boats, and I noticed some inquisitive glances as I boarded the *Gold Hunter*.

Not in the mood for company, I decided to take the *Gold Hunter* out for a ride. I was used to driving boats, as Mike and I had always shared a love for the water, and Mike used to let me drive the boat when he took Trisha and me for evening rides to have cocktails and watch the sunset. John Carski had given me the keys to the boat, so I started the starboard diesel engine. A familiar roar broke the serenity of dock life in the marina. The port engine did not seem to make any noise, but I knew it was running from the movement of the tachometer on the dash.

With the engines idling, I untied the neatly flemished deck lines, noting the way Mike had tied them so that I could tie them the same way when I came back. Watching a row of cabin cruisers pass by, I waited for a good opportunity to leave the dock and enter Oak Orchard River, which led to Lake Ontario.

Across the river, the bank was higher, about forty feet, and I noticed the nice homes overlooking the river. People were on their front porches or decks, watching the boats come and go. Nested among the homes were maples, birches, and pines, but directly in front of me, towering into the sky and starting to hide the sun, was a massive oak tree.

I looked back down toward the river and saw no boats nearby, so I eased both engines into forward, and the heavy lobster boat eased out along the dock and into the river channel. Once away from the dock, I pulled the starboard engine into reverse, and the vessel rotated to the right. Once I was facing the direction I wanted to travel, I shifted back to forward. I traversed the half-mile stretch of river to the lake with a peaceful feeling of comfort.

On each side of the river, a breakwall extended about two hundred yards out, with another breakwall extending perpendicular to it, preventing waves from rolling into the harbor. The cool breeze felt good as the *Gold Hunter* rounded the left breakwall and headed west, following the shoreline away from the harbor.

Earlier waves had settled into a calm sea with a mirrorlike finish that reflected the sun, so that it appeared to shine from below the bow as well as from the sky above. The green shoreline was decorated with blue, gray, and white cottages and was separated from the silver lake with a tan layer of lake stones. A feeling of loneliness enveloped me as I took in the familiar scenery. I missed Mike and thought about the times we'd spent on the lake when he was teaching me to scuba dive long ago, and maybe I felt a melancholy sort of nostalgia for my younger self as well.

As I pushed the throttles forward, the boat dug into the lake water, pushing a huge wake out from its sides before gaining enough speed to rise to the top of the water and shoot forward at twenty-five knots. The refreshing, cool breeze was welcome on the hot August evening. I hugged the shoreline for a couple of miles before I slowed the vessel down and let it settle back to displacement speed.

A picturesque cove just ahead was filled with rafted boats, anchored, with occupants enjoying the cool lake breeze. I put the engines in neutral to avoid the congested area. I needed some serenity. When the boat stopped moving, I dropped the anchor into about twenty feet of water and went below to check out Mike's former onboard home. I was surprised to see how neat everything was, but at the same time I wondered how Mike had managed to fit on the small sleeping berth.

Across from the berth was Mike's diving gear. His dry suit bag, regulator, mask, and fins appeared to be lined up and ready to use. I looked back and saw Mike's form. Startled, I realized that it was Mike's quarter-inch wet suit hanging on a hook by the cabin door. The wet suit had even retained the shape of Mike's round belly. I left the cabin and went back on deck, where I sat, looking at the water.

What I did next will remain a mystery to me. I had always loved the water, but even when I was younger and learning to dive with Mike, I never had gotten completely comfortable with the unnamed fears that seemed to overtake me when I went below the surface. Mike was a great scuba diving teacher and was very reassuring, but my fears had never gone away. I went back down to the cabin and changed into Mike's wet suit. Mike was shorter and much wider in the gut, but his wet suit stretched to fit my taller frame.

I brought his equipment up on deck and started assembling a scuba unit, just as Mike had taught me twenty years ago. Thinking that I wasn't going to actually use it, I pulled a tank out from the rack and grabbed Mike's buoyancy compensating vest, or BCD. I lowered the dive ladder into the water and leaned over to soak the vest in the water. The vest slid over the tank and was tightened on by ratcheting the strap buckle, followed by slipping the regulator yoke over the valve. The regulator was on the right side. I fastened the low pressure inflator hose to the BCD and turned the valve on. The submersible pressure gauge read three thousand pounds.

I laid the unit down on the deck and put on a weight belt and fins. The scuba unit seemed heavier than I remembered, but somehow I managed to get it on my back and adjust the straps. I was remembering what I had learned from Mike when he'd given me lessons and certified me back in the eighties. It was hard to bend over and pick up my mask off the bench seat; the act revealed an extra twenty years of age since my last dive.

With the mask on, I slowly moved to the back of the boat. I took a breath or two from the regulator and realized how foolish I must have looked standing at the back of the boat, wearing a full set of dive equipment, clinging to the hand railing, and looking at the lake. I did not enjoy diving when I was younger, and there was no way I was going to get into the water now! I was too exhausted from putting the gear on, and I was starting to overheat from wearing the dry, hot dive suit.

Standing at the stern of the boat, petrified to death and realizing that I was too old and inexperienced, there was no way that I was going to step off that boat and get into the water. I knew how important it was to follow the recommendation of experienced scuba divers never to dive alone. I decided to turn around and remove the scuba gear, but something stronger—perhaps courage that I didn't know I possessed—lifted my right hand to hold my mask and mouthpiece. My left hand grabbed the weight belt, and as if Mike were in the water in front of me, my left foot seemed to be beckoned forward, followed by the rest of me.

One foolish moment of courage plunged my overheated and anxious self into an intense fear for my life. Cold water rushed into the back of the badly fitting wet suit with a chill that made me gasp for more air. I turned and struggled, out of control. The distance of three feet to the boat's ladder seemed like a mile. Somehow I got there and held on. I was too tired to climb up to safety.

I spit the regulator out of my mouth and briefly let one hand leave the ladder to pull the mask off of my face. Sweat was stinging my eyes and the cold water felt like needles pricking my back. All I could do was to hang on and rest until I had the energy to climb up. I thought I was about to die. In my mind, I heard the words, "Stop, think, rest, and just take it easy; I am here." I looked around, expecting to see Mike's easy smile, but I was totally alone and helpless. Still, feeling Mike's presence relaxed me, and I was eventually able to regain some sense of control in the water.

Wilbur Dives Again

I was breathing better and the cold Lake Ontario water was getting warmer inside the wet suit. A few more minutes, and I would be able to climb onto the boat and feel safe once more. I looked around for another boat but saw no one. I gulped some lake water and had to cough it out. I remembered Mike saying to leave the mask on and the snorkel in your mouth.

Where was my mask? I let go with one hand and found it on top of my head, which is a distress signal for divers. I figured that was okay because I was in distress. I put the mask on and started taking deep, slow breaths through my snorkel. With both hands on the ladder, I put my face into the water and felt refreshed as the cool water surrounded my head.

I was relaxed and feeling ready to climb up the ladder when I saw the lake bottom. It was right below me and in plain sight. A large bass swam under me and headed toward the front of the boat. As I watched the bass, I realized that I had let go of the ladder. I looked up, and the ladder was right in front of me. Suddenly, I was filled with the same irrational terror I had known years before during my first dive. I had never understood the source of it, but I knew I shouldn't panic; I should just breathe and let it calm me down. As it finally subsided to a simple fear, I started swimming along the side of the boat, following the bass before it swam off in another direction. I looked up and found myself in front of the boat, by the anchor line.

I turned around and mentally measured the distance to the back of the boat, and although I was relaxed, a bit of anxiety returned. Mike's voice rang out in my head again, saying, "Once you are three feet down the anchor line, you will feel like you are in heaven." I snorkeled the four feet to the anchor line and held on firmly to the line. Anxiety was creeping back into my head, but somehow I managed to spit out my snorkel and replace it with the regulator. I felt for the power-inflator hose, and raising it over my head, I squeezed the release valve and sank beneath the surface. Not sure if I was going any further down, I looked up and found security in seeing the boat.

Hanging onto the line, I could see clearly to the bottom, and it was more inviting. I let my hand slide along the anchor line until I reached the bottom. I was instantly more relaxed than I could remember from previous dives. The bass came back and looked at me as if to say hello. I noticed a crayfish hiding from the bass under a thin layer of green seaweed. Smaller fish were swimming closer to the bottom. I left the anchor line to look around but made certain that it was always in sight.

Neither cold nor heat tormented my body as I floated weightlessly along the bottom. I conversed mentally with Mike. I told him that I really did understand his addiction to the sport of scuba diving, that I wished that I had spent more time underwater with him, and that he truly had made my life more adventurous.

I was enjoying the one-sided conversation and the tranquility of the calm underwater realm when a voice inside my head spoke to me. It was Mike reminding me to check my pressure gauge. I held it in front of me; it read fifteen hundred pounds. I had used half of my air, and as Mike would have said, it was time to head for the boat.

The anchor line was nowhere in sight as I turned in a circle to look for it.

Oh well, I thought, *I can't be too far away from the boat.* I looked at my depth gauge and saw that I was only eighteen feet from the surface. I found my power-inflator hose, raised it above my head, and dumped air out of the buoyancy compensator as I swam slowly up to the surface, leaving the tranquility of the bottom behind.

My right hand was extended upward to save me from hitting the boat when I came up, but my hand just reached for the sky, lonesome, touching nothing. The boat was not there. I started to kick my feet harder to rise up out of the water as I turned. A familiar anxiety once again filled me.

The boat was a hundred and eighty degrees behind me. It looked so much smaller and farther away. I held out my compass, and struggling to stay afloat, I took a bearing to the boat. Following the compass, I descended and saw the bottom again. Serenity and relaxation returned. Without sinking all the way to the bottom, I grabbed my inflator hose and swam back to the surface. This time I inflated my BCD to float comfortably on the surface, and managed to stay calm.

I headed for the boat, looking up occasionally to make sure that I was headed in the right direction. I kept my regulator in my mouth, because I wanted to sink back down and avoid the long surface swim. I was getting hot and feeling increasing anxiety by the time I reached the ladder. I left my mask on and the regulator in my mouth so that I would be able to breathe if I fell back into the water. I struggled up the ladder, feeling all of my sixty-one years of age. Despite the encumbrance of the heavy equipment, I made it up the ladder.

Once I was safely on deck, I removed my mask and spit out the regulator. The scuba unit (tank, BCD, and regulator) came off next. I stood up to catch my breath. All anxiety was gone, and a feeling of youthful energy overwhelmed me as I removed the weight belt and fins. I looked around the boat, as though someone might be there to talk to about the dive. I found only loneliness, which made me wonder how Mike used to do so much diving alone.

I unzipped the front of my wet suit and felt relief as the hot water evaporated and rose in a mist of steam from my clammy skin and was replaced with cooler air. I pulled my arms free from the confines of the suit, and my energy grew as I spryly put the diving equipment away.

I was about to start the engines when I noticed the sun twinkling above the horizon. It was like a devilish wink from Mike. With everything put back in order except for the wet suit, which was hanging over the tanks to dry, I fired up the engines and idled back toward Oak Orchard River and the hustle and bustle of the busy marina.

Feeling twenty years younger now, I thought about and understood Mike's energy. Even after he had told me that he had a heart disease called cardiomyopathy, his energy and passion for diving had increased until almost the end of his life, when congestive heart failure had filled his lungs with fluid. I had thought he should quit diving sooner, but he'd shrugged it off when I mentioned it to him, saying, "I live in two worlds: our world and my private underwater realm. I imagine heaven to be exactly like my underwater world, with the exception that you can smoke cigars there."

It was then that I noticed the cigar box sitting next to the radio. I opened the box and saw an envelope on top of the cigars. I picked up the envelope and read the inscription on the front: *Wilbur, have a cigar and relax before you read this.* The only time I ever smoked was on rare occasions with Mike. I put the boat in neutral, unwrapped a cigar, and lit it with a lighter that I found in the cigar box. I climbed up on the bow and watched the sun set as I puffed away on the cigar.

The cigar smoke rose straight up, as there was no evening breeze at all. It was so quiet on the lake that I could have sworn I heard the sun make a sizzling sound as it started to disappear from the horizon and into the lake. Watching the sunset was something that Trisha and I had shared with Mike and other guests aboard the *Gold Hunter* on several occasions. This time it felt extremely lonesome, but the beauty of the sunset's color and the lake's serenity cleared my head, and I felt happy as the day ended. The serenity of the moment transformed when a colorful vision filled my head: Mike was swimming, unencumbered by any heavy equipment and smoking a cigar *underwater*. It was time to head back to port.

The trick was to guess the current in the river and compensate for it by backing the boat into the slip. The lack of wind made the maneuver easy and a young man with a dark blue pinstriped suit was waiting on the dock. He helped me with the lines. He just held onto them until I tied them to the cleats.

"Wilbur Bone?" the young man said inquisitively. He was a small man with dark hair and a white complexion, like someone who spent his days inside an office. In a businesslike tone, the well-dressed man said, "My name is Abraham Buffield. I have been waiting for you. Can I have five minutes of your time?"

Still feeling my increased energy, I was anxious to get home to Trisha, but I was intrigued enough to find out what this rather formal-looking man wanted. "Sure! Climb aboard," I invited.

The young Abraham gracefully climbed aboard, stepping down onto the deck and offering me his hand. He had a much firmer handshake than I expected from such a small man. Standing in front of me, he was much shorter than I was (about five foot eight), but strength seemed to exude from his dark eyes.

He told me that he was in the jewelry business and that he wanted to hire out the *Gold Hunter*, starting the next Friday, to bring three or four scuba divers up from New York City. I was not very interested, but he said that he would pay me ten thousand dollars for a week to take his group diving, exclusively.

Even though I had halfway planned to sell the boat, Bill's words had triggered something in my mind. I'm not a person who makes quick decisions, but I found myself deciding to give running the dive boat a try. So I agreed to his request, but I had a strange feeling about the job—just an intuition, really—that something here wasn't what it seemed to be, that this man wasn't what he seemed to be.

I did not have the experience that Mike had running a dive boat, so I added, "But I am not too knowledgeable about running a dive operation." Abraham assured me that his divers would be able to show me what I needed to do and told me that he foresaw no problem with my lack of experience.

I remembered the auction and the fact that I still didn't know Mike's instructions about what I was to do with the proceeds, so I told Abraham that I didn't want to use the boat commercially until after the auction. With a straight face, he said, "I know. I will see you at the auction and we can start immediately after." Abraham Buffield left the boat, walked up the hill and got into a black Mercedes-Benz. I recognized the car from a magazine photo and thought it was strange to see such a car around this part of the state.

There was something about Abraham Buffield that I did not like. Perhaps it was just his cockiness, or maybe it was the unfriendly, businesslike manner in which he had just cornswaggled me into a week's work, even though it was at a high price. I wondered what Abraham knew that I didn't.

Something piqued my interest when I thought about the photos of shipwrecks that I had seen at the lawyer's office. Now an out-of-towner wanted to rent the boat. Then the big question once again hit me like a brick. Where had Mike gotten the two-and-a-half million dollars he had left to his children?

Other boaters and Mike's friends used to laugh at Mike for diving so close to home, when any treasure would certainly be found in the ocean, where old ships carrying gold taken from the Aztecs back to Europe had sunk somewhere on the way. Mike had even admitted that there was no treasure in the Great Lakes other than the tremendous historical value related to the thirty-five hundred ships that had sunk and never been found. Was Mike hiding something? Maybe he had found a valuable treasure in Lake Ontario and kept it a secret—a secret that might be unveiled at the attorney's office during the auction next week.

I stopped into the marina's office and saw Bill. I asked if Mike owed him any money. Bill said that Mike had paid up for the slip for the season and that his fuel bill was paid. Mike owed nothing. Bill pulled a note from the wall behind the cash register and gave it to me, saying they were messages about the boat that had been left for Mike. I put them in my pocket with the envelope from Mike's cigar box and left.

It was starting to get dark earlier, and it was only nine o'clock when I got home. Trisha was inside, waiting for me. The house seemed extra-quiet, even though it had been years since our own children had grown up and left the nest. At fifty-one, Trisha still looked great in the pair of tight-fitting jeans she was wearing. With my newfound energy, I wrapped my arms around her and kissed her gently. An old skill came back to me, and with a simple twist of my hand on her back, her bra was undone. She pushed away from me, smiling, and asked, "What's gotten into you?" No answer was needed as she pulled me back with her arms around my neck.

The next morning, I told Trisha about the dive. I held back telling her about the fear I had felt. She sounded angry, and said, "With Mike gone, I do not expect you to do such dangerous things." I assured her that it had been a one-time adventure and that I would not do it again. Still, a strong desire tugged at me to go straight to the lake and dive again.

I took a cup of coffee with me to the front porch and opened the envelope from Mike. All it contained was a single piece of paper with a poem written on it in Mike's handwriting. I thought it was strange, because Mike was no poet. The poem read:

Forward the sun sets
An opposing zenith
Bigger the oak gets
All my secrets
Treasure begets
From beneath

I read the poem over and over but gained no understanding of the words. Maybe Mike was just saying good-bye in some strange way. I put the note in my pocket and sat back, enjoying the morning sun's warmth.

I looked at the list of phone numbers from Bill at the marina. They were all from out of the area except one belonging to Bernie Kloch. I met Bernie at one of Mike's after-dive barbeques. He had a dive shop in Batavia and brought in a lot of customers for Captain Mike's charter business. I thought that maybe I would call Bernie and leave the rest for Monday.

"Bernie's Dive Shop," the voice on the other end of the phone answered hastily.

"This is Wilbur Bone, returning your call."

The voice raised an octave in obvious excitement and shot back, "Boy, am I glad you called. I have a group of divers who want to do a lakeshore dive, and if it is in any way possible for you to take us out in Mike's boat, we sure would appreciate it."

Since Bernie was local and an old friend of Mike's, I decided it would be okay to handle this lakeshore dive before the auction. Besides, I was eager to get back out on the lake. I agreed to meet Bernie at the boat, then I went inside to tell Trisha that I was going to the boat to take out some divers.

"Not without me!" Trisha shot back enthusiastically. I put on some shorts and a pair of old deck shoes, and Trisha put on her bathing suit under a pair of shorts and a blue button-down blouse, tied in the front instead of buttoned up. I felt something stir once again when I looked at her, but I was in a hurry to leave for the marina.

Most of the fishing boats were out on the lake when we arrived at the marina, leaving the *Gold Hunter* alone at the docks. I parked the car and boarded the boat. I took the keys out and opened the electronics box that was mounted above the helm, suspended from the short ceiling. Trisha walked over to the marina and bought some sodas and bottled water and a bag of ice, which I helped her put into the boat's cooler. I was looking forward to spending some time on the water with Trisha.

Bernie rolled his pickup truck up to the edge of the parking area and began unloading equipment. Other cars pulled into the parking area and unloaded more equipment. People were carrying bags to the boat. They were talking excitedly, anticipating the scuba diving. I introduced Trisha and myself as our passengers handed us bags from the dock. We stuffed dive bags under the bench seats and put dry bags in the cabin.

Bernie was about thirty-five years old and very muscular. He climbed onto the boat and helped stow gear as he introduced each diver. Six couples were going to Tobermory, Ontario the next weekend, and this was a checkout dive for them. Bernie handed me a clipboard with their names on it and an envelope containing six hundred dollars. He asked if I would charge the same as Mike, or if I wanted more. Six hundred seemed like a lot of money, so I agreed to keep things the same.

With everyone on board, I started the engines. Bernie cast off the lines, and the *Gold Hunter* left the dock. Bernie asked, "Do you know how to get to the Saddle?"

I told him, "I do not have a clue." Bernie reached up into the electronics box and flipped some switches on. A screen lit up, and Bernie pushed some buttons. He showed me the global positioning satellite (GPS) system and how it worked. He pushed a button that read "Waypoints," and a list came up with the Saddle as the number twelve waypoint. Bernie highlighted number twelve and pushed the "Go to" button, changing the screen to one giving me directions and the distance to the dive site called the Saddle.

Then Bernie went down into the cabin, opened an electronics door, and started another diesel engine that operated a compressor somewhere under the deck. He then checked and filled any empty tanks that were in the rack that ran down the center of the deck.

The passengers were assembling gear. An array of multicolored dive gear covered the deck of the boat. The lake was a little rougher than it had been the last evening, with waves reaching about a foot and a half. I was thinking about how calm it had been the night before, and I was thankful that I wasn't diving today.

Bernie talked me to the waypoint and helped set the anchor. Bernie was a dive instructor and an experienced diver. His skills were evident as members of his group asked questions while they geared up. Trisha, as usual, found a friend to talk to on the ride to the Saddle. Watching her fit in with the other people gave me a feeling that somehow I was responsible for the safety of these people. After all, that had been Mike's job!

I felt bad that I had failed to remember the divers' names. As a schoolteacher, I always made an effort to memorize students' names. My mind was somewhere else, following the beckoning of a smallmouth bass that led to the peaceful serenity found underwater. A powerful urge to return to that haven was overcoming me when a voice inside said, "Share the experience."

It was Mike's voice again, and I looked at the divers, realizing that for the first time since my retirement, I had a purpose. Making my way astern through the smiling faces, I found the first couple ready to enter the water. I reached up and made sure that their air was turned on and asked them their names, which they happily gave me. Checking to see that they had air in their BCDs, I helped them as they took giant strides off the back of the boat into the beckoning cool weightlessness of the lake.

I did this for each couple as they approached the rear of the deck, making sure that they gave the okay signal once they were in the water. Some faces were absolutely cheerful, but others had reluctant eyes. Remembering the high anxiety I had felt the night before, I gave the divers encouragement.

As the last couple approached me, Bernie hollered that he was going to get in if I had everything under control. I looked forward to seeing Bernie throw his scuba unit over his head and onto his back. He did up his BCD, put his mask on, and rolled backward over the gunwale. I watched for a moment until he popped upright on the surface and gave me the okay signal.

With the last couple in the water, all I could do was watch Bernie lead them around the side of the boat to the anchor line. Trisha and I stood watching until all that remained was white foamy water where bubbles broke the surface. As the bubbles drifted away from the boat in the direction of the anchor line, I told Trisha, "You know what? I really wish that I could be down there with the divers right now. I think I've needed some sense of purpose since I retired. Working with divers would be different from teaching school, of course, but it would be a way to help people and enjoy myself at the same time."

To my surprise, Trisha smiled broadly and said, "Well, Wilbur, I'm glad to hear you talk this way. Diving might be a really good thing for you. I was worried about your diving alone, but I wouldn't be concerned if you were diving with Bernie. Maybe you'll wind up keeping the boat after all."

A tinge of anxiety crept into me as I thought about my lone dive the day before. Still, I felt excited when I thought about Bernie taking me on a dive. I grinned back and said, "Yeah, maybe I will keep the boat."

The names on the diver roster now had faces to go with them. As I held the roster and counted the divers, I remembered hints of the different personalities of the divers I had talked to briefly. Twelve plus Bernie had descended, and I was wishing that there was one more—myself! I set the roster on the dash, and noticing the cigar box, I took a cigar. I lit it and joined Trisha, who was sitting on the roof. Together we watched the bubbles traverse in a rectangular pattern that started west, turned north, then east, and then moved south, coming back toward the boat.

The lake offered a different kind of serenity, with waves making a gentle lapping noise and rocking the boat up and down in a slow motion that relaxed the two of us, the only remaining passengers on board. The sun was high in the bright blue sky, but it provided heat that balanced the cool westerly breeze. The divers' bubbles disappeared in the waves for a while, but Trisha spotted them right next to the boat in another moment.

We watched the bubbles disappear under the boat and reappear on the other side. They continued to move south about twenty feet from the boat, where they seemed to grow, making the water churn in a spot above the divers. Trisha stayed on the roof as I climbed down onto the deck. The first pair of heads appeared in the churning bubbles. They seemed surprised and happy to see the boat so close. I touched my hand to the top of my head, making the okay signal, which was immediately returned by the divers.

The divers started swimming toward the back of the boat as heads starting popping up to the surface all around them. Trisha announced the number of heads that appeared on the water's surface as I helped the divers into the boat. As each diver made his or her way onto the deck to remove equipment, the boat hummed with increased activity, until just Bernie was at the back of the boat.

When I told Bernie that everyone was back on board, he agilely scampered up the ladder, handing me his fins as he held the railing. Bernie stood at the back of the boat, counting people to double-check that everyone was on board. Once satisfied, Bernie removed his gear and helped me pull up the ladder.

We sat at anchor for another half hour as divers stowed some gear, while leaving the gunwales and the row of tanks decorated with black wet suits and other more colorful diving gear. Bottled water and bags of carrots, celery sticks, and some corn chips were passed among the still-excited divers. They had seen a large salmon and several white perch on the dive. A pair of drum fish had joined their rectangular journey until their air supplies had demanded a return to the surface.

Earlier anxieties had all disappeared. I went back up onto the roof with Trisha to watch the commotion on the deck and to enjoy her company. The diver Trisha had befriended on the way out climbed up on the roof with us and brought some chocolate chip cookies to share. I grabbed two cookies before the bag was handed back down to the divers, who resembled hungry wolves when they heard the words "chocolate chip cookies." I remembered how much energy I had used after diving last night, and how hungry I had been.

Bernie looked at me and made a swirling motion with his hand above his head. It was time to "head 'em up and move 'em out," as the signal signified. Bernie's familiarity with the boat was helpful. He had the engines running and the anchor on its way up by the time I got down from the roof.

The *Gold Hunter* must have resembled an old third world country houseboat as it entered the harbor with wet suits flapping in the wind and bright yellow, blue, and green equipment hanging from every available protrusion. I could not help smiling as other boaters watched us maneuver into the dock.

I was surprised at the speed at which the divers packed their belongings into their dive bags. Within a short five minutes the boat was cleared of clutter, and divers were loading gear into their cars. Bernie helped the divers carry gear to their cars before picking up his own gear. It was the first chance that I had to talk to Bernie.

Bernie showed me how to run the compressor as we filled the air tanks. "Hey, Bernie," I said, "can you believe it? After twenty years of not diving, I got on this boat last night and had the urge to go down."

"So what happened, Wilbur? You didn't dive alone, did you?"

I said, "Well, I know it's not recommended, but yes, I did. Not for long or anything. I was nervous, but basically okay. But it was great to be back in the water again."

Bernie said, "What do you say we turn around right now and go back out on the lake and take a dive together?"

I felt a combination of excitement and anxiety. Bernie seemed to sense my apprehension. He looked out over the breakwall at the growing waves and suggested, "On the other hand, it's getting a little rough out there, so maybe tomorrow morning would be better."

Bernie was the same age as my son, but he was very different. My son worked for a bank in Pennsylvania and was working on a master's degree in finance. Bernie's motivation was diving. He ran a dive shop but lived for the dive trips in which he guided people in the Caribbean during the winter season. Bernie understood people and saw my fear right through me.

Bernie was verbally testing my dive knowledge when a voice rang out, "Could one of you guys do me a big favor?" I turned around to see a gray-haired man with a salt-and-pepper beard, holding a boat hook in his hands. He was the captain from the fishing boat next to the *Gold Hunter*. His shorts were old and stained with a season's worth of boat grease, and he wore a button-down plaid shirt with the sleeves ripped off at the shoulders.

He introduced himself as Captain Jack and explained that he had dropped his cooling system's water filter when he was cleaning it. It had gone into the water next to his boat. Bernie was happy to help, and he grabbed his gear bag and took out his mask. Then he looked at me and said, "Why don't we do a dive right here? It's only ten feet deep at the end of the dock, but it will give us a chance to get wet." I agreed, wondering what it would be like in the river.

The anxiety came back immediately as Bernie helped me suit up with Mike's diving gear. I wanted so badly to dive that I tried hiding my fear from Bernie. I was successful at hiding it from Trisha, who climbed up to the bow to lie in the sun, but I saw in Bernie's eyes his understanding of my hesitation. Just having Bernie with me lessened my nervousness as I back-rolled off the side of the boat.

The water in the river was much warmer than the lake, giving me more comfort in the water. Also, the shore was only fifteen feet away from the side of the boat. I gave Bernie a lethargic okay signal, and an instant later he joined me with a loud splash. I was surprised at how much more comfortable I was in the water with Bernie at my side. We snorkeled around the boat to the end of the dock, where Captain Jack was waiting.

Bernie told Captain Jack to put one end of the aluminum boat hook into the water and bang it with a coin or another metal object five times if a boat came within fifty feet of our bubbles. This would create a sound that we could hear underwater to warn us of danger. Bernie looked at his watch, and then, facing me, he gave the thumbs-down signal. We simultaneously raised our buoyancy compensator release valves, letting air escape until the scene of clear blue sky and bright white boat hulls turned into the murky brown area that filled my mind with anxiety once more.

We could barely see each other, but Bernie's face was right in front of me, giving me a sense of comfort amidst the darkening murk. Then the bottom appeared, and visibility seemed to increase significantly. My fins hit the bottom, creating a brown cloud of mud that slowly followed the weak current, to be replaced with clearer water again. I added air to my BCD so that I could swim along without stirring up the bottom.

Bernie held my arm and turned to the left about forty-five degrees, and we started moving slowly up the riverbed. The shadow from Captain Jack's boat made a dark forbidden area right in front of us. Bernie produced a flashlight from somewhere, giving me an added sense of security as he maneuvered the beam slowly from side to side about two feet ahead of us.

As I relaxed more, I began to notice the small minnows that appeared in Bernie's underwater light. My eyes were glued to the clear area of his beam when suddenly it illuminated a shiny object that did not belong to the surrounding river life: a stainless steel form the size of a coffee cup.

I felt the bubbles race around my head as a burst of triumphant excitement left my lungs and ascended to the eagerly watched bubbles somewhere above us. I watched my own hand, as if it were somebody else's, reach in front of me and grab the shiny filter.

My instinct was to head for the surface with the treasure, but Bernie stopped me by holding my arm and shining the light at my vest pocket. He helped me put the filter in my pocket and turned me around, motioning for me to follow his light. Understanding that he wanted me to stay underwater and finish the dive, I obediently followed the beam of light down the riverbed to deeper water.

Pressure in my ears let me know that we were going deeper, and I imagined we were moving away from the boats. The water changed temperature, and a current of chilled frigid water hit my head and hands. The cold was only a slight discomfort compared to the relaxation that I was feeling. A small fish swam up to my mask and wriggled a greeting. I was back in a different, more peaceful world again and loving it.

We came out of the cold water and the murkiness lessened. An old rope led us to a lost anchor, which Bernie dug out of the mud. He'd pulled up old anchors before and he knew they were worth something. We each had one hand on the anchor as we lifted it up, shoved it forward, and let it splat down, stirring up more mud. We performed the maneuver several times before an unnatural sound reached my ears.

It was a metallic sound. Then I realized that it was the danger signal from Captain Jack. A boat was coming. But underwater, I felt safe. Bernie pointed to his ear to ask if I had heard the signal. I nodded yes, and he made a fist and shook it toward the anchor. I grabbed the anchor tight and shook it to let him know that I understood that he wanted me to hold on tightly to the anchor.

Three more mud-thumping moves, and a wooden pylon appeared in front of us. Bernie signaled to ascend. I looked up through the mud and saw some faint light. Keeping my grip on the anchor, I reached for my BCD deflator hose and raised it above my head.

The sound of a boat engine getting closer did not seem to concern me as I headed for the surface, following the pylon that would most certainly lead to the dock. Although I was ready to release air from my BCD, I did not. I felt the weight of the anchor hold me down, and I left a forbidding cloud of mud on the bottom. I looked upward until the growing circle of light brought me back to the real world. I heard Bernie's air hissing as he added air to his BCD so he could float more easily on the surface, and I did the same.

Captain Jack was lying on the dock with his hand reaching down. Moving together, Bernie and I brought the anchor to the surface, where it met Jack's hand. The anchor disappeared upward and I felt myself bounce on the water from having too much air in my vest. By the time I had let a little air out, Bernie had his mask off of his face and around his neck, so that he would not lose it. His smile met mine; we turned and watched a boat pass by about thirty feet away.

Captain Jack's voice took us back to our purpose when we heard him ask, "Did you find it?" Bernie looked up at him. Smiling, he raised his hands above the water, showing them to be empty. Jack's eyes quickly turned to me as I carefully felt for my vest pocket and slowly brought the shiny filter to the surface.

Jack's grin was a welcome sign, and I felt proud to hand him the filter. We took off our gear and passed it up to Jack and Trisha. Bernie climbed onto the wharf easily, but I needed a little help, despite the energy the dive had given me. Captain Jack told us that a replacement filter would have cost him eighty-five dollars. The real problem was having one express-shipped, leaving Captain Jack unable to take his customers out fishing for a couple of days.

"So what do I owe ya?" Captain Jack asked.

Bernie looked at me and I just shrugged, so he told Captain Jack, "A couple of drinks would be fine."

A smile that seemed to extend from ear to ear came across the captain's face, and I knew that I had just made a new friend. He asked, "How about a giney?" Not sure what a giney was, I accepted anyway and we started peeling off our wet suits. Our new friend helped us load the gear into the boat before inviting us onto his boat, the *Sea Dog*, for the drink.

A narrow entrance led us between an array of neatly hung deep sea fishing poles and the transom-mounted downriggers to a small aft cockpit. Captain Jack beckoned us to follow him below, then he disappeared down some stairs through a door from the crowded cockpit. Once we were inside, we found that the combination lounge and galley was very roomy and decorated in well-polished teakwood.

Captain Jack talked his way through making the drinks, demonstrating a certain ritual in the making of a giney. He cut a lime in quarters, put just the right amount of ice in each of the four glasses, and mentally measured the gin as he poured it from the bottle into the glasses. Then he squeezed the lime quarters on top of the gin before topping off the glasses with tonic water.

Captain Jack handed Trisha her giney first, then me, and finally Bernie. Then he picked up his own and added his final touch: three stirs as he swirled the ice cubes around with his finger. We all followed suit and laughed when Trisha licked her finger.

We made a toast to the lake and sat down to enjoy some friendly conversation as we sipped the welcome drinks. Captain Jack smiled and reminisced a bit. "Yup, a drink on a boat's a fine thing. Me and Mike often had gineys together at the end of a day. I live on my boat in the summer, you see, and after he lost his house, Mike lived on the *Gold Hunter* himself, so we were wharf-side neighbors for the past three years. I'll miss his company, I will."

We finished our drinks and thanked Jack, turning down his offer for a second giney. Back on the dock, I asked Bernie what we should do with the anchor. He told me that Mike used to give them to Bill to resell at the marina. I told Bernie that I would do the same, and picked up the ten-pound navy-style anchor and headed for the marina.

When I got back to the boat, Bernie had finished topping off the air tanks. Bernie looked up at me and asked if I wanted to go diving in the morning. I looked at Trisha, who said, "As long as Bernie's with you, it's okay with me."

I was a little surprised when Bernie said, "How about six o'clock? It's usually calmer in the morning." I agreed, hiding the sudden rush of nerves that came over me.

A normal night for me includes getting up to pee a couple of times. I was up before the alarm, so I reset it for when Trisha got up to go to work at the craft store. I got dressed quietly and had some cinnamon toast and orange juice.

It was still dark outside and chilly enough for a jacket. I was not used to getting out of bed until the sun was up and had warmed the air. This morning gave me a mix of excitement, welcome anticipation, and growing anxiety, all at the same time. As I drove to the marina, I was more awake than I had been for a long time.

The marina was a busy place, even on a Monday morning. Fishermen were boarding boats to get on the lake before sunrise. Bill Reed was inside the marina, selling everything from extra-warm sweatshirts to coffee. Bernie was already there, drinking a cup of coffee. Bernie greeted me on my way over to the self-serve coffee station. I dug into my pocket to pay, but Bill waved his hand, saying, "Coffee's on me this morning. Thanks for the anchor." I realized that the old barter system was alive and well at the marina.

Captain Jack was already leaving the dock with a group of six fishermen stuffed in his cockpit. His smile was lit by the dash lights as he waved to me while maneuvering his boat carefully away from the dock. I waved back as he disappeared down the dark river.

When we boarded, Bernie's gear was already on the boat and set up. Bernie asked if he could drive the boat so I could set up my gear on our way out to the lake. I nodded and Bernie stepped up to the helm and fired the engines up. I cast off the lines and marveled at Bernie's skill in maneuvering the boat away from the dock and into the river.

I went below and brought out Mike's diving gear to set it up for the dive. Bernie started telling me what we were going to do on the first of our two dives. "The plan is to go to the cove and do a SCUBA review in shallow water. That way, I can evaluate your skills and enhance your comfort level. Does that sound okay to you, Wilbur?"

I was somewhat embarrassed, yet happy at the same time, to know that Bernie had recognized my fear during the previous evening's dive for Captain Jack's water filter. Memories of removing my mask and gear underwater resurfaced uncontrollably from many years ago when I had taken the diver certification course from Mike. Yet, I knew a review was imperative if I was going to dive.

I knew Bernie was concentrating on navigating the dark river, but I could feel him watch my nervous hands fumble as I put the scuba unit together. I turned on my air, checked my pressure gauge, and neatly wrapped my vest's cummerbund backward around the tank, tucking the hoses inside to protect them from damage as I placed the unit in the rack behind the bench seat.

As I headed back down below to get the wet suit, Bernie asked if I had ever worn a dry suit. "No," I said, remembering Mike telling me that he loved his dry suit.

Bernie told me, "Grab the red-and-black bag. I will give you a lesson on dry suit diving as we do your review."

I brought the bag up as we passed the breakwall. A bright area to the east signaled that the sun was about to appear. Still, a cold breeze came off the lake, chilling me and adding to my growing discomfort. I thought that maybe I shouldn't finish the coffee because I didn't want to have to pee during the dive, but I held onto the cup anyway to warm myself up. Bernie took a final swig from his cup and turned west from the channel. A feeling of dismay came to me from the slight waves already on the lake. I had been hoping for perfect weather.

Bernie said, "Take the helm while I put my suit on to keep warm." I finished my coffee as we idled away from the point. Bernie showed me how to put on a dry suit as I drove the boat. Then it was my turn. Bernie took the helm so I could suit up. It was cold, so I did not have to worry about overheating like I had on Saturday.

"It's cold enough today. I got really overheated when I did that lone dive on Saturday night," I said to Bernie. "I told you I was nervous, but I have to admit it was really more like truly afraid and maybe a little bit panicked."

Bernie said, "Gee, I didn't realize. Of course, part of the problem was that you were diving alone; as I said, that's asking for trouble. But you don't have to do that, Wilbur. If you ever want to dive again, just let me know and I can always find someone who will want to go with you."

I admitted to myself that it had been dumb of me to go diving alone, especially after not diving for so many years and with the fear that I felt. "You're right, Bernie. From now on, I promise not to dive alone." I realized that the conversation had relaxed me. "I appreciate what you said, Bernie. Now I'm thinking about the dive we're going to take without feeling so much anxiety."

I put on a pair of thin cotton coveralls right over my clothes and stepped into the bright orange dry suit. The sun appeared, but it didn't warm us up like we had hoped, so the dry suit felt pretty good. Bernie had brought the boat into the small cove and was headed for shore. When the depth on the sonar read ten feet, he dropped the anchor and shut off the engines.

It was less windy in the cove, which alleviated some of my stress. Bernie fixed my dry suit's neck seal so that it would not leak. He had me wear a hood that worked like a wet suit hood, but was made to cover the neck seal. He put a pair of wet suit gloves in my dry suit pocket so that I could put them on in the water.

We dropped the ladder into the water and let out a safety line with a faded orange ball at the end. This would give us something to hang onto while we were at the back of the boat. We donned our gear and stood at the back of the boat. Before we could step into the water, Bernie went through the predive safety check, making sure our BCDs had air in them and our weight belts had right-hand releases, and he made an informed guess as to how much weight we needed. Then Bernie double-checked to make sure our air was turned on. He did this by having me look at the pressure gauge and take three breaths. If the gauge did not move, the air was turned on. I also felt him reach up and grab the valve while I was looking at my gauge. Then he said, "Final okay," and looked at the water.

I only felt a hint of anxiety as I stepped off the stern. Instead of a rush of cold water, this time I felt the air in the dry suit race up to my shoulders, making me sit comfortably high in the water. I touched the top of my head to let Bernie know that I was okay. Bernie's fin protruded from the back of the boat, followed by a splash. I looked at the area where Bernie had entered the water and saw Bernie give me the okay signal as he switched from his regulator to his snorkel.

The sun filled the air with light as I followed Bernie around the boat to the anchor. He removed his snorkel and asked me how I was doing. To my surprise, I was very comfortable, both physically and mentally. I took my snorkel out of my mouth and answered by saying, "Boy, this dry suit is comfortable."

Bernie looked at his watch, signaled to go down, switched from snorkel to regulator, and left the surface, with me right next to him. It felt strange having to hold my left arm up with the BCD deflator valve and have the air leave the dry suit through a valve in the sleeve. Slowly, we descended to the bottom of the lake. Once on the bottom, we emptied all the air out of our BCDs and suits, which left us kneeling on the bottom, next to the anchor.

The small waves on the surface didn't bother me, but as I watched the anchor chain move up and down I realized that the boat was bobbing in the water above. Still, I felt relaxed diving with Bernie next to me.

Bernie had me remove and replace my mask, regulator, and scuba unit, one at a time. As I practiced these skills, my confidence rebounded. I took my mask off and a rush of cold water hit my face, but the cold water did not bother me as much as I thought it would. With my thumb in the nose section of the mask to make sure I had it right side up, I pulled the mask full of water back over my head. I tucked it into the hood, and looking up, I exhaled air from my nose, forcing the water out the bottom of the mask. As the water drained out of my mask and I could see clearly again, I was filled with a sense of accomplishment.

Bernie had to help me with putting the scuba unit back on, but I was happy to have progressed this far without any fear. Next, Bernie had me do a fin pivot by lying on the bottom, removing my regulator from my mouth, and blowing air into my BCD until my body rose up from the bottom, leaving only my fins resting on the rocky bottom. This allowed me to rise as I inhaled air and drop back down after I exhaled.

After the fin pivot, I dumped the air out of my BCD and did another fin pivot using the power inflator on the dry suit. Once I had established the neutral buoyancy needed for a comfortable dive, I was able to follow Bernie along the lake's bottom. Bernie was doing one of his rectangular patterns along the bottom of the lake.

I was anticipating seeing the anchor again when Bernie turned to me and ran his hand across his throat, signaling that he was out of air. Then he motioned back and forth, asking to share my regulator. The thought of Bernie running out of air heightened my anxiety, but I was glad that I could share my regulator with him.

Global Positioning

I wondered how Bernie had managed to use up his air. Then I thought that maybe this was part of the dive review, so I calmly took another breath of air and removed my regulator, extending it to Bernie. Bernie took a breath and held up one finger. Then he took another breath and held up two fingers. Bernie handed me the regulator. I was starving for air, and I took a deep breath and then another. Feeling a bit more relaxed, I moved the regulator back to Bernie. We did this exchange several times, and Bernie adjusted the way I held the regulator in my hand. Finally, Bernie signaled to ascend. Holding on to each other's vests with our left hands and sharing the precious air with our right hands, we slowly left for the surface.

As the light circle overhead grew, I knew we were nearing the surface of the water. At the surface, I tried to fill my BCD with the power-inflator button. Any mental relief that I had been expecting at the surface left me when Bernie would not let me use the power inflator.

I had to get buoyant by gasping for a breath of air and sinking back down, blowing the air into the valve on the power inflator. Then I kicked back up to the surface to gasp for another breath of air. It took three times before I was floating enough to keep my head above water. A final long breath filled my BCD, so that I was resting high on the surface, staring at the smiling eyes of my instructor.

Another feeling of accomplishment removed the moment of panic I had felt trying to get buoyant on the surface. Bernie assured me that we were in control, and explained that the regulator sharing and the decision not to allow the power-inflator button had just been part of the testing for my dive review.

We were only twenty feet from the back of the boat. Bernie pulled his mask down around his neck and swam backward toward the boat. I planned to follow with my snorkel in my mouth and my mask on, but decided to tough it out and mimic Bernie, swimming toward the boat with my mask around my neck. I found that swimming backward made it quite comfortable to both swim and talk to Bernie.

The thirty-year age difference between us dissipated as we climbed up the ladder to the boat. I had not taken any tests for a long time, especially a physical one. I felt a great sense of accomplishment from the dive, and Bernie's praise boosted my pride.

Removing my weight belt first, then the scuba unit, I felt younger than I had felt in a long time. Bernie chose that moment of exuberance to ask, "Are you ready for another dive?" Even though it surprised me a little bit, I agreed to another dive.

Bernie continued to comment and give recommendations on how to conduct myself underwater and on the surface. He assured me, saying, "After a few more dives, Wilbur, my friend, you will be comfortable enough to really enjoy diving!"

I thought about how much I really did enjoy diving already. The trouble was that my irrational fears got in the way and sometimes kept me from wanting to dive more. But Bernie had a point and I told him so. "Maybe you're right, Bernie. More dives should increase my confidence overall."

We changed tanks and prepared our equipment for the next dive. The sun was starting to warm things up, and the wind and wave height were increasing. I left the dry suit on, but unzipped the zipper, letting a rush of warm air escape from within it. I had not overheated or panicked, and I felt really good about myself.

It was only seven o'clock when we dropped anchor in sixty feet of water. I thought about Trisha just reaching over to turn off the alarm clock. I would usually be lying in bed, waiting for her to leave for work before I got up. Usually I would spend my day reading or puttering around the house. Picturing myself like that made me feel like a younger version of the person I had become. I was starting to like the younger version of myself more.

Before we suited up for the next dive, Bernie showed me how to use the underwater dive computer that was mounted on Mike's gauge console. Fear had completely left my mind by the time I back-rolled over the gunwale of the boat, followed by my new friend. My ears had become accustomed to the tactics used to equalize pressure during the descent. A bit of anxiety came to me when we were thirty feet down, following the anchor line into a white underwater cloud. Another ten feet down, the anxiety quickly left, because on the other side of the cloudy layer of water was a truly unique and clear world.

It was cold under the thermocline, but the water was very clear. I could see the bottom; it felt as though I were flying in air above ground. The lake bottom was filled with the usual small lake stones, but in this spot there were larger underwater boulders that resembled small mountains. We descended between them. Jack perch and bass floated around the miniature world that I felt privileged to visit.

A brown eel peeked out of a crack in one of the mountain-shaped rocks, displaying itself to us deliberately. It seemed as though the eel was actually talking, warning the divers to stay away. Bernie pointed out a school of elwaies swimming off to the east. It look like a wall of symmetrically stacked fish separated us from another world that was only a few fin-strokes away. A moment later, the wall of fish disappeared, leaving more lake bottom to explore.

I adjusted the air in my dry suit to keep me off the bottom. I could see much more about eight feet above the bottom. I felt like I belonged in that place at that time, and actually, I did belong there. Bernie was moving small rocks and peeking into every crevice he found. I enjoyed watching the fish watch Bernie stir up a cloud of lake dust. Occasionally a small fish would swoop into Bernie's cloud and find something floating there to eat.

After stirring up a large cloud by moving several rocks, Bernie came up next to me and watched as some rock bass fed on whatever it was he had stirred up. He held his hand out in front of me, showing me a crawfish that he'd captured. I followed Bernie to another group of rocks in an area that wasn't clouded. Behind a rock that rose about five feet above the lake bottom, a large bass was hiding; it was probably waiting for dinner.

Seeing the bass, Bernie made the crawfish dance closer and closer to the hiding hunter. The bass stared at the crawfish and cautiously moved about an inch closer, but then backed away, as if trying to communicate with Bernie. The crawfish was trapped in sheer torment between two rubber-clad fingers. In a flash, the bass attacked and made a meal of the crawfish, ending its torture.

The bass disappeared into the distance, but we saw it circle back in front of us. The bass looked at Bernie's hands to see if he had more food, and Bernie held his fingers out, showing the fish that they were empty. I watched the bass go around and settle next to the same rock he had been hiding behind when we'd first spotted him.

The lake bottom sloped downward as we moved north. I looked at my computer, and I was only mildly surprised that the incline had taken us from the original sixty feet to eighty feet deep. I looked up and noticed Bernie watching me. He signaled for me to follow him.

We ascended to the bottom of the thermocline at forty feet. We could still see the bottom clearly. It seemed to rise up to meet the white cloud of water that was changing temperature. We could see our bright white anchor chain bouncing up and down just before the water turned to murk.

The anchor was a welcome sight, and I realized that I was getting tired. I followed Bernie up though the layer of underwater clouds, impressed by his underwater navigational skill as we ascended above the cloud to thirty feet. We were only five feet away from the anchor line.

We followed the anchor line up until we reached fifteen feet and the light from above was more dominant than the lure of the bottom. Bernie made me wait at fifteen feet for the next three minutes, completing a safety stop. I remembered from the diver certification class how our bodies build up nitrogen bubbles in the blood, and that those bubbles could expand and do damage if proper procedures were not followed. A safety stop was one such procedure.

I was thinking about reading up on dive tables when Bernie looked at my computer and signaled to ascend. I was tired, but I comfortably ascended the next fifteen feet to the surface. On the way up, I could see the silhouette of the boat, and the light from above grew brighter. But the surface had changed. The expected sunrise had not taken place. A black and white background of threatening clouds covered the above-water world, and three-foot waves were tossing the boat up and down.

Bernie's smile put a stop to the sudden fear that threatened to enter my psyche. With my regulator still in my mouth, I traversed the waves to the back of the boat; while Bernie waited, I tried to gauge the best time to step onto the ladder. The ladder was rising with the waves and falling quickly back into the water. When the ladder was all the way down in the water, I grabbed it and stuck one foot onto it. The next wave brought the ladder back up into the air, with me on it. As the boat dropped back down with the next wave, I easily climbed on board.

Holding tightly onto the railing, I turned to see how Bernie was doing. He was already on the ladder, and a moment later, he was standing right next to me. I pulled my foggy mask down, and the whole world seemed to be in place.

We took off our gear while talking about the dive. I was energized, transformed into a young man again, and ready for anything that might come my way—except for what I saw next.

A streak of lightning appeared to hit the water a few hundred feet south of the boat. We left our gear on the deck, and still wearing our dry suits, Bernie and I pulled the ladder up and brought in the aft line and anchor, then Bernie started the engines. We pointed the *Gold Hunter* for the harbor, wondering whether or not we would make it to port. It took a while before the boat rose up on plane, and in less than ten minutes, the storm had passed by and we were idling down to turn into the Oak Orchard River and safe port.

By the time we were tying up the boat at the dock, the sun was out again. Bernie looked at his watch and said, "Good; it's only eight-thirty and I have plenty of time to get to work." We stowed gear, and I hung up the dry suit over the roof to dry before putting it away. For the first time, I was getting warm. I took off the cotton coveralls and stowed them in the dive bag.

Bernie did not have to ask how I felt; I was still grinning from the dive. Bernie told me that he could dive any morning, and that if I wanted to dive the next day, he could probably scrounge up another diver or two. I told him that it sounded great to me, and it really did sound great. We planned to meet on the boat at six again the next morning.

By the time I finished cleaning up the boat, the gray sky had turned bright blue and the hot August sun was glaring. It was as hot as it had been the day of my Saturday dive. I rubbed food-grade oil into the rubber seals on the dry suit and packed it in its bag. I was thinking about the lake's bottom, and the storm that had just missed us on the surface.

I filled the tanks that we had just used with compressed air. I continued to run the compressor until the two air-storage tanks were back up to forty-five hundred pounds. Convinced that the boat was ready for another dive trip, I walked over to the marina's store and had another cup of coffee. Bill Reed asked how I had made out in returning the calls.

I told Bill that the only call I had made had been to Bernie, and that I planned to wait until after the weekend to return the rest of the calls. "That's just today, and it's still early," I added. Bill had the anchor all cleaned up, and he told me that he would get about fifty dollars for it after a second coat of paint.

"Half that money goes into the account for the *Gold Hunter*," Bill told me. I thanked Bill as I left, with coffee in hand, to go home and make the phone calls.

The first call was to a Chicago number belonging to a Richard Bailey. A woman's voice answered the phone, "Bailey Fine Metals."

I told her who I was, and said that I was returning a call from Richard Bailey. A moment later, a husky voice said, "Hello, this is Mr. Bailey. What can I do for you?"

I began explaining that I had gotten the message he had left with Bill at the marina, but he cut me off and asked, "Are you the one that owns the dive boat?" His voice sounded excited, but became annoyed when I told him that I'd already chartered the boat for that week to Abraham Buffield. Richard Bailey offered me twice as much as Buffield was paying me, but when I told him that I had already shaken hands on the deal with Buffield, he simply hung up. I didn't even have a chance to ask him if he also knew about the auction.

I did not feel like making any more calls, but I was hoping to figure out what Mike had been up to before he died. The next call, to a James Donahue, was closer to home. A machine answered with "Trinity Foundry" and led me through a series of digital choices. Finally a raspy voice said, "Donahue." Again I explained the reason for the call, but this time the reaction was different; James Donahue seemed like a real gentleman. He said that his company was a precious-metals business, and he sounded only somewhat disappointed when I told him about the boat being booked for the week. When I asked if he would be interested in the following week, he said maybe, but asked whether I knew of any other captains around Oak Orchard that might be able to take out divers.

I thought of Captain Jack, but told Donahue that if I found one, I would have him call. He was thankful, but before he hung up the phone, I asked if he could explain the sudden interest in diving in Lake Ontario. He said that he could not divulge any information—at least not until after Friday's auction. I thanked him and hung up.

It was more than curiosity that made me wonder what Mike had found. Mike must have stumbled onto something that made him a fortune. And so far, Abraham in the jewelry business and now James Donahue in the precious metals business were planning to attend the auction. I became certain that Mike must have found *gold* after all his research and years of searching in Lake Ontario.

The last call I had to return was to Shirley Tempest from New Orleans. "Tempest Investments," she answered the phone. Interested in obtaining some information about Mike's hidden life underwater, I tried to feel her out by not giving her much information.

"This is Wilbur Bone," I said coyly into the phone.

Her feminine, youthful voice went up an octave. "I've been waiting to hear from you. Is it too late to hire your boat for next week?" I told her that the boat was available until Friday morning, but that it was booked for a week after that.

Shirley Tempest could not hide the disappointment in her voice. Like the others, Shirley asked about other boats that might be available for divers. When I told her there were only fishing boats in the area, she politely thanked me and hung up. Shirley had been pleasant to talk to, but lacked the accent of a New Orleans girl, and I thought that was strange.

It was only ten o'clock in the morning. Usually I wandered into town for coffee with some old retired buddies at this time, and then we would play a round of golf. With my mind beginning to grasp the mysterious wealth that Mike had left his children—and the treasure that must still be in the lake—I decided to skip my golf game. I was a bit reluctant to talk to Trisha about diving for treasure, at least until I knew more about what was really down there, since a hunt for some mysterious sunken fortune sounded like something fanciful and maybe even foolhardy. I decided to drive to Bernie's Dive Shop in Batavia and skip my ritual coffee shop visit.

The dive shop, on a side street in Batavia, had a large sign reading *Bernie's Dive Shop* above the door. It was a one-room store in a small business complex with ample parking. A sign indicating the store was open hung in the glass window of the entrance. The shop looked nothing like the prosperous shops Mike took me too in Florida.

Bernie was both surprised and happy to see me. He was showing a customer how to use a dive computer the customer had just bought. Bernie looked up and said hi, but continued to take care of his customer. Not wanting to bother Bernie, I looked around the shop. I found a book for beginning divers by PADI, the Professional Association for Diving Instructors, and decided to buy it.

When Bernie finished explaining the computer to the customer, he sold him a bottle of "sea drops" (for defogging masks) and a small underwater flashlight for use as a backup light for night diving. Before the customer left, Bernie introduced him to me as Joe Diamante, a fellow diver. I shook hands with Joe, saying that I hoped to see him on the lake sometime. He agreed and left the shop.

I asked, "Bernie, how much do you know about the diving Mike was doing before he was hospitalized?"

Bernie said, "Gee, Wilbur, I don't really know. Mike would come into the shop, of course, and we'd joke around and all. Maybe we'd talk about the weather on the lake that day, or what boats were out, or gossip about other divers we knew. But he never really said much about where he was diving or what he was looking for. Why do you ask?"

"Well, I have a few suspicions, is all." I felt that I could trust Bernie, and heaven knew how much I wanted to talk to someone about Mike's hidden wealth. "The thing is, Bernie, Mike left a lot of money to his children—money I, for one, didn't realize he had, and that raises some questions."

Bernie's eyebrows rose in surprise. "But I thought Mike was broke and that's why he lived on his boat. How much did he leave them, anyway?"

"One hundred thousand dollars for each of the five of them, and two and a half million in a foundation for the grandkids' college money. And there's an auction on Friday with these photos of shipwrecks."

Bernie was flabbergasted, and then he started talking ninety miles an hour. "The only wreck Mike ever took us to was an old barge near Rochester. He talked about all kinds of historic events that might have left wrecks in the area, but he only admitted to finding the unidentified sloop-of-war ship near Thirty Mile Point." I had no doubt that Mike had kept Bernie as much in the dark as he had me.

Then Bernie's eyes lit up like the landing lights on a 747 breaking out of a Buffalo snowstorm. He said, "Mike must have the locations of the wrecks on his GPS on board the boat."

Bernie had showed me how to use the GPS (or global positioning satellite system) the day before, and I was certain that I could bring up the waypoint list on the screen. Bernie took out a piece of paper and wrote out some instructions for me to follow, then he asked me to call as soon as I found the location of the wrecks.

I told Bernie that I didn't have one of those new cell phones everyone was using, so he agreed to call the marina in one hour. We figured that would give me enough time to get the information from the GPS after driving back up to the lake.

As I drove north toward the lake, the blue sky gradually transformed through shades of gray until rain blocked out my view of anything more than fifty feet in front of me. I found my way to the marina despite the downpour, which changed into a slight drizzle when my car pulled up to the sign reading *Gold Hunter*.

I unlocked the electronics box above the helm on the boat and turned on the GPS. The unit was searching for satellites when a strange ringing came from the bottom of the electronics box. At first I backed away, but then I reached up and felt around in the bottom of the box. I pulled out a cell phone. It was ringing.

I looked at the device with the obnoxious ringing coming from it, and found a button labeled *TALK*. I pushed the button and recognized Bernie's voice. I put the phone to my ear and said, "Bernie?"

Bernie simply asked, "Is the GPS on?"

Looking up at the GPS screen, I asked Bernie, "Whose phone am I using?" He explained that he had taken a chance that Mike's phone was still on the boat, and that he had simply called Mike's number, hoping I would answer.

He asked me again excitedly if the GPS was on, and when I said that it was, he proceeded to talk me through the process to bring up the waypoint list. Once the list appeared, I read the twelve waypoints to Bernie.

Disappointed, Bernie told me that he recognized all the waypoints and had dived on each site that was listed. Bernie suggested that the wreck sites must be hidden somewhere on the boat. I was baffled. Why hadn't Mike told me about any wrecks? He knew I liked history. Bernie interrupted my thoughts when he asked, "Can you imagine the historical value of any wreck that Mike might have known about?"

I guess the idea of finding treasure had loomed so large in my mind that I hadn't thought about the historical side of the picture, which was equally intriguing. I told Bernie that we could check the boat for hidden compartments in the morning, before our dive. Satisfied that we could do no more over the phone, Bernie asked me to call him if I found anything. I agreed and tried to figure out how to hang up the phone. I pushed the button marked *END*, and it went quiet.

It began raining again, so I grabbed the diving book and went below to read it. I found a light over the bunk and lay down to read. I did not even start reading, because my mind took a journey to another world.

Trisha was riding on the bow of a large wooden ship similar to the *Mayflower*, with a jewel-trimmed gold crown on her head. Too many gold chains and necklaces adorned her chest. She had rings of gold with bright green emeralds, rubies that looked like red emergency lights, and multicolored diamonds. There was a storm all around, but the glow from Trisha seemed to open the sea to a glowing calm that the ship traversed through safely.

I had not felt myself fall asleep. When the clattering of metal against metal woke me up, I was not sure where I was. I sat up and banged my head on the cupboard above the berth, which must have knocked the realization into my mind that I was on the boat.

I crawled out of the berth and started up the stairs to the deck. When I opened the door and stepped out, the figure of a man came toward me. I looked up and raised my arm to protect my face as a black crowbar came at me and sliced the air in front of me. I let go of the doorway and grabbed the arm that held the crowbar as I let myself fall back. My attacker gasped as he hit the door frame and slid down into view.

Attempted Theft

I caught my balance on the cabin floor, and braced myself to fend off the attacker. I had not been in a fight since grade school, but the courage to defend myself came from someplace in my subconscious. I wrenched the crowbar out of my attacker's hand and aimed it for his already-bloodied face.

I saw intense fear in the man's face, and the use of deadly force seemed unnecessary. I crouched down, placing the crowbar over my attacker's throat, applying enough pressure to hold him there without choking him.

His nose was bloody, and he had blood trickling down his forehead from a cut the shape of the cabin-door hinge. The man was about half my age, with a wiry frame and dark brown eyes that showed his fear. I was surprised by how calm my voice was when I asked, "Who are you, and what are you doing on this boat?"

He seemed ready to answer me, but just then the boat rocked and Bill Reed's voice yelled out, "Wilbur!" The split second I looked up through the doorway, a knee came up, hitting me in the forehead. I fell back with the crowbar still in my hands. My attacker leaped to his feet and dashed out the door before I knew what had hit me.

I got up, holding my painful noggin, and climbed up the stairs, following the attacker with his crowbar in my hand. Bill Reed was lying on the deck, and the attacker was running up the wet hill in an athletic gait that made the thought of chasing after him impossible. I offered Bill my hand, and helped him to his feet. Fortunately, Bill was unharmed, but he was shaken up. The attacker had hit him with his shoulder, sending Bill to the deck.

Bill and I made our way toward the marina's store, where Bill explained how he had watched the attacker attempt to steel my electronics with the crowbar. A voice came through the steady rain from the river. "Anyone hurt?"

Bill explained, "It's Deputy Bruce." He said into the rain, "An attempted robbery turned into an assault, but we seem to be okay."

The deputy said, "I'll meet you at the marina's store in a minute."

The pain in my forehead was gone, but I accepted a couple of aspirin when Bill offered them to me. While we waited for the deputy, I thought about the electronics box with the GPS in it. Was the robber after Mike's waypoints? Fear increased my adrenaline rush from the fight. *Trouble is brewing*, I thought to myself.

Bruce O'Connor stood six feet four inches tall and he spryly carried his two-hundred-pound frame through the door. I recognized him at once from the high-school class I had taught; he had been a star football player. A soft-spoken and friendly guy, his easygoing manner was amplified by a pale, freckled face and red hair. However, his amiable appearance in no way diminished the sense of physical authority his size and build implied.

Bill explained to Bruce, "The sky had gotten real dark, even though it was daytime, but I saw something moving over near where the *Gold Hunter* was docked, so I took a closer look. Then I saw a man step onto the boat. He moved over to the electronics box, and I saw he had a crowbar in his hand! That really surprised me, you know, because I always watch over the boats at my marina. Most of my boaters don't even feel the need to lock up their boats. Nothing has ever come up missing around here. We've got a reputation as a safe and friendly marina."

Living in a rural farm area, everybody pretty much knew everybody else. This was a friendly community and neither Bill nor I had ever seen the robber before. It was pretty obvious that he was not from around here. Deputy Bruce agreed.

Bill offered the deputy a cup of coffee. "After I take a look at the scene of the crime. You guys wait here," Deputy Bruce said, and headed back out in the rain for the *Gold Hunter*. Bill poured me a cup of decaf and apologized for the incident at his marina, as if it were his fault.

I thought about how Mike's leaving his boat to me had stirred up trouble in my otherwise calm life, and I wondered about those people from Mike's phone messages, the people that were looking to hire the dive boat. I was thinking about what they really wanted. I knew it was connected to the waypoints that might be stored in the GPS. In a way, I wanted to tell Bill that it was the waypoints the robber was after, but that was just my suspicion, without proof, and it might be better to keep it to myself for the time being.

Deputy Bruce came back in with a surprised look on his face and said, "There is quite a bit of blood around the door and on the floor below. Who got hurt?" I explained how I had fallen asleep below until the noise had awakened me, and told him about my struggle with the assailant.

Deputy Bruce O'Connor was less cheerful on the phone as he requested an investigator to come to the crime scene. He also asked them to check the local hospital to see if anyone had come in with head injuries. His cheerfulness returned as he turned to me and said, "I dove with Mike on the county underwater rescue team, and I noticed some changes in him before he died. Is there something more I should know about?"

I felt my face turn bright red, and I knew that the explanation I owed Bill was about to be revealed to this trustworthy former student of mine. "At the reading of Mike's will, the lawyer brought out a big envelope with sixteen information packets in it. Each one had photos of a shipwreck."

Bill was wide-eyed when he asked, "Were they all wrecks sunk in Lake Ontario?"

I answered, "Yes, they were. There were notes and other written information to go with each sunken ship."

Bruce had a look of concern when he asked, "Do you think these boats went down recently, Wilbur? I would have been informed about something like that."

"No, Bruce. We're talking about history here. These were photos of big ships that looked to be very old in some cases. I know this sounds like a fantasy, but they were the kinds of sunken ships that looked like they held treasure chests."

Bruce interrupted to say, "Wait a minute. This could explain why Mike seemed more secretive than usual. If we're really talking about something of value in those sunken ships, maybe this whole thing needs to be kept under wraps until we know more about it."

I said, "I agree, Bruce, particularly since the attack seems to be connected. You know, several of the people who called about dive boat trips worked for companies involved with precious metals."

"Do you mean gold?" asked Bill.

"That's what I'm thinking," I replied with a smile. "The sixteen packets are to be auctioned off on Friday, so we'll know more then."

"In that case," Bruce suggested, "I'd better take the GPS and lock it up at the sheriff's office until Friday." Reluctantly, I agreed. When I told Bruce that Bernie was the only one I had confided in, he assured me that Bernie would not stoop to any treachery. Bernie was Bruce's dive instructor, and he worked as a trainer for the county dive team, which explained Bruce's trust in him.

I told my attentive audience, "I should call Bernie and let him know what is going on. He's coming up in the morning to dive with me."

Bruce produced a cell phone, which had Bernie's number in its speed dial. In a completely friendly voice, Bruce said, "Bernie, this is Bruce at Oak Orchard." Bruce explained what he knew before divulging any information about the attempted robbery over the phone, then listened for a minute.

Bruce agreed with whatever Bernie said, then handed me the phone. Bernie told me that he closed the shop at eight and would come up to spend the night on the *Gold Hunter*. "We can still dive at six in the morning," Bernie said. I thought this was a bit overcautious, but I agreed to Bernie's offer.

The sheriff's investigator arrived, and Bruce took him to the boat. Bill and I had another cup of coffee while the investigator took photos of the boat and blood samples. After a while, Bruce came in and said that it was all right to clean up the boat. I found a mop under the port gunwale and scrubbed the blood off the door frame and the floor of the cabin.

The robber had broken the bracket that held the GPS inside the electronics box, making it easy to remove the GPS unit. Bruce gave the GPS to the investigator to take back to the sheriff's office. Bruce left downstream on his boat, and I locked up the boat and gave the keys to Bill, so that he could give them to Bernie when he got there. It was almost four o'clock in the afternoon, and Trisha would be home from work in an hour. I was exhausted when I left. I wanted to beat her home.

On the way home I stopped at the market and bought a nice filet of salmon, some fresh lemons, and the makings of a salad. When Trisha pulled in the driveway, I had the salmon cooking on the grill on the back porch. Through the kitchen window, I saw Trisha stop and take a deep breath by the grill. She was smiling when she came through the back door. She looked puzzled when she glanced at the lit candles on the table, the two champagne glasses filled with ginger ale, and the salads I was making on the kitchen counter.

"Okay, what have you done?" she said as she sat her purse down and looked at the table.

The microwave oven's bell rang, letting me know that the baked potatoes were ready. "Just in time," I said as she sat at the table, waiting for an answer. I put the salads on the table and told her that I had to check on the salmon.

The salmon was done just the way she liked it, so I put it on the platter and took it back inside. Her suspicions seemed to diminish as I set the platter of her favorite meal on the table. I took the hot potatoes out of the microwave and put one on each of our plates. Trisha was still waiting for an answer to her question when I sat down. I raised my glass of ginger ale and simply said, "To Mike."

Trisha understood that I was having trouble with my friend's early death, and she smiled and raised her glass, repeating, "To Mike," without saying anything more. It had been a while since I had done anything special for Trisha, and I found a real joy as she expressed her childlike appreciation for the meal.

Conversation was basic, and pertained to how well the salmon was cooked and how nice it was to come home to a special dinner. After dinner, I stopped Trisha from clearing off the table and told her to go relax in the living room while I cleaned up the kitchen. She gave me a peck on the cheek and left the room.

Her lips were warm, and I felt something stir in me from her kiss. I had not had the feeling of desire for her in a long time, until just a few days ago, but it was evident that I felt it now, and I thought that Trisha sensed it. I finished cleaning up after dinner and met Trisha in the living room.

The weather report was on the television, and I heard that the rain was ending and tomorrow would be a sunny day. Trisha asked me if I was getting up early to go diving again in the morning, and I said yes. She suggested that I must be tired and should go to bed early. I was exhausted from the day's activity, but I did not feel sleepy. I looked at Trisha's smile, and my desire for her stirred again. I stood up and said, "Are you tired too?" Trisha stood up, grabbed my hand, and led me to the bedroom.

I did not get up all night long. I had a great night's sleep, then awakened from a dream of an underwater paradise when the alarm clock went off. I slipped into the bathroom quietly, so that I would not wake Trisha. After a welcome hot shower, I came back into the bedroom to get dressed. Trisha was not in the bed.

I found Trisha in the kitchen, cooking scrambled eggs and toast. We ate breakfast together for the first time on a work day in years. When I left for the marina, Trisha said, "Be careful today." It was a dark Tuesday morning when I walked out the back door, but it was warmer than the previous mornings had been.

Dampness filled the air around the marina, along with the southern warmth delivered by the morning's strong winds. Yesterday's low-pressure system was going to be replaced with a clear high pressure that would bring back bright blue skies. The strong wind was the gradient wind caused by the merging of the two weather systems. Bernie was having coffee with Captain Jack when I parked the car at the marina.

The attempt to steal the GPS was big news around the marina. Captain Jack seemed to think the buzz around the marina showed a concern for the expensive fishing gear on the boats. Still, the whole story had not been let out, and I was happy to avoid any further conversation about Mike's mysterious wrecks.

Another topic of discussion was whether or not the fishing boats were going out that morning. It was rough, with five- to six-foot waves on the lake, so fishing captains were giving their customers the option of canceling instead of braving the waves. Of course, the captains downplayed the extent of the problems caused by rough waves. They could always come back if the passengers got too seasick to stay on the lake. Captain Jack left with his trusting passengers.

Five-foot waves made me think there was no way I was going to dive today, but Bernie did not seem to care about waves. "Ocean surge may bash you against some coral, but waves don't hurt you. They're fun!" Bernie said, with a smile. *Maybe forty years ago*, I thought. Bernie continued, "Besides, Mark Swan is already on his way here, and he is planning to dive with us."

I followed Bernie onto the boat. Bernie had the VHF radio on, and he was listening to the charter-fishing captains talk about the waves. The sun was rising, giving us enough light to see the white waves breaking over the breakwall and spraying into the air in sheets of water that made Captain Jack's boat disappear. The entrance to the lake seemed as forbidding as crossing a four-lane highway during rush hour.

With no ears listening but Bernie's, I asked him how he had slept, and whether any problems had arisen in the night. Bernie told me how peaceful it was to sleep on the boat, and he assured me that no one had come near the boat during the night.

Our conversation was interrupted by a young man's voice that hollered out, "We aren't going out in this weather, are we?" I looked up and saw a young man wearing a pair of shorts with a diving T-shirt and a baseball cap.

"Leave your gear in the car and come on down. We are going for a boat ride," Bernie said to the terrified-looking youth.

"I drove out to the point and saw the waves on my way here, and there is no way I'm going out on the lake today," said Mark Swan as he walked down the hill to the dock.

Bernie was smiling devilishly as he introduced the young diver to me. I shook Mark's hand, and noticed that his blue eyes were fearless. His tiny, muscular body seemed ready for any adventure that might unfold during the day.

We were interrupted by the sound of the radio. "*Gold Hunter! Gold Hunter! Gold Hunter!* This is *Sea Dog* on six-eight!"

Bernie was closest to the helm, and he picked up the microphone connected to one of the radios. He held it up for me. "Go ahead!" I said, letting Bernie answer Captain Jack's voice.

"*Sea Dog*, this is *Gold Hunter*. Over!"

"Yeah! Um, *Gold Hunter*, we are headed back. Too much out here. Over!"

"*Sea Dog!* I will talk to the skipper and see you when you get to the dock. Over!"

"*Gold Hunter*, thanks much! *Sea Dog* out!"

"*Gold Hunter*, clear six-eight! Out!"

Bernie looked at me and explained that Captain Jack had asked if he could use the *Gold Hunter* to let his passengers fish off the back if it was too rough out. "Certainly!" I said, in an overzealous tone that showed my relief not to be going out on the rough lake.

We needed to turn the boat around, so they would be able to fish off the back. Bernie started the engines, and Mark, who also seemed relieved, undid the dock lines, I moved the fenders to the other side of the boat as Bernie directed the boat out into the river. Bernie skillfully turned the boat a hundred and eighty degrees, then backed into the slip as quickly as Mark and I were able to switch the lines and fenders to the other side.

After we tied the boat securely, we looked up and watched the top of the *Sea Dog* appear through the breaking waves at the end of the channel. The up-and-down motion seemed intense before the vessel settled down on the calm river.

Jack pulled in bow first, to keep his transom facing the river, and we helped him tie his boat to his dock. Captain Jack's passengers were having a good time as they walked off the dock and joked about kissing dry land. Smiling, Jack said to us, "At least they got to go out for a ride." The passengers quickly made the decision to cancel the salmon fishing and fish for panfish at the dock.

Bernie was smiling too. He admitted that the anchor probably would not have held in the rough water, and that there was no way we could dive in the raging Lake Ontario. But he explained that Mike had a spot above the dam, in Lake Alice, where he had taken divers on days like this.

I was very familiar with Lake Alice, and I remembered Mike talking about some old buildings in only eighteen feet of water. They had been left there when the power company built the dam and flooded the area. My curiosity about this underwater town added to my newfound eagerness to explore. Mark quickly agreed to dive the dam as well.

We transferred our diving gear from the boat to Bernie's pickup truck, and Mark threw in his gear too. Bernie said, "Let's all ride over there together. That parking lot at Lake Alice can be a problem, so we're better off just having the one vehicle."

I asked Mark, "So how do you happen to know Bernie here?"

"Well, I'm a student, so I'm always broke. Bernie lets me help him out at the dive shop." He grinned and went on, "I really like hanging out at the shop, and I'm crazy about diving, so Bernie took me along on some dives. After a while, we started going diving together regularly."

The three-mile ride to Lake Alice led us along the winding river road. The rage of Lake Ontario receded in the distance, leaving the bright sunrise that showed nature's neatly choreographed dance of different shades of green. Trees swayed, slow-moving white clouds above them. The clear, light blue sky was a background that magnified small, brightly colored birds that added decoration to the beauty of the day. Occasional glimpses of the river between the trees added a silvery depth to the scene.

Lake Alice had small waves that seemed to move fast, adding some whitecaps to the scenery. Bernie pulled up to a spot on the east side of the lake. Surprisingly, there were no waves there. Getting out of the truck, we were delighted with the protection the trees gave us from the wind. This was going to be a calm dive.

Mark suited up with a wet suit, while Bernie and I slipped into our comfortable dry suits. We lined up our gear on the rocky beach and easily donned the equipment, then we walked down the gentle slope of the lake's bank and into the water. Bernie produced a piece of bright yellow polypropylene rope about ten feet long with a loop tied on each end, which he called a "buddy line."

Bernie explained, "Due to yesterday's rain, the visibility might not be so good at the bottom of the lake. The buddy line will keep us together, even if we can't see each other." I thought that it could not be that bad, and that carrying a piece of rope would be a nuisance.

This time, I had no fear or anxiety as we entered the water. Bernie was in the middle, with Mark and me at each end of the rope. We could reach out and touch each other, but as soon as we ducked our heads under the water, I realized that the buddy line was more than necessary.

I could barely see Bernie when I bumped into him as we got horizontal on the bottom. Still, I saw his hand make the okay signal right in front of my face. I could see the bottom about two feet in front of me, and made the okay signal with my hand stretched out in the direction that I thought Bernie's face was.

Holding onto the buddy line, I followed Bernie through the brown murk, looking at brown mud with small brown rocks scattered over it. I felt a bit uncomfortable not being able to see Bernie, who was less than five feet from me, and I wondered how Mark was doing on the opposite end of the line.

I was just getting used to moving with the line and not jerking it all the time, when we literally hit a brick wall. It was one of the buildings that we had heard Mike talk about. A sense of accomplishment filled my mind. I was happy we had found it, even in such poor visibility.

We followed the wall around each corner, seeing abundant fish, crabs, and clams everywhere we looked around the structure. Large windows without any glass made interesting hiding places for the fish.

I swam right next to Mark; Bernie was somewhere just above us. I could see Mark in the two feet of visibility, and both of our buddy lines pointed up to Bernie, whose hand would appear from above once in a while to point out a sign on the building that said "Built in 1886" or a large carp that was swimming along beside us.

When we got back to the spot where we had first encountered the building, a cloud of mud we had stirred up remained around the building. Bernie eased his way between us, and using his compass, he led us away from the mud cloud. We swam north for about fifty feet before coming to another building.

This second building had nothing more than a foundation on two sides and large stone pillars that extended upward and ended about six feet high. It was darker, and in about twenty feet of depth, but it had more fish than the first building.

Mark held up the line for a minute, making me wonder if he was okay. When Bernie brought Mark's hand in front of my face, I saw the reason for the stop: Mark had found a small perch-colored fishing lure. I decided to be a little more observant, so that I too might find some kind of underwater treasure to take home as a trophy.

It did not take long. Four feet ahead of us, stuck into the stone wall, was another fishing lure. This one was smaller than Mark's, but it was painted bright yellow and looked like a cricket. I held it out for Bernie to see, and he took my arm and stretched it over toward Mark. I saw Mark's hand form the okay signal, showing his approval of my treasure.

Bernie led us away from the structure. I looked at my depth gauge and compass, and figured that we were heading for shore. To my surprise, my submersible pressure gauge read twelve hundred pounds, and it did not seem like we had been down long enough to use that much air. I had not felt the serenity that I felt on my previous dive in Lake Ontario, but I found satisfaction in my minute treasure as we broke the surface in the exact same place we had entered the water.

Mark was holding his fishing lure up and saying, "Treasure."

I surprised myself by holding up my prize and repeating the word "treasure."

Mark said, "But mine is bigger."

As we back-stepped onto the beach, I said, "Mine is prettier," and we both laughed.

Then Bernie's hand released a whole handful of lures, which landed on the rocks in front of him. He said, "I left some for the next time!"

Mark and I were humbled, but still we were pleased that we had found some treasure.

All of a sudden, I understood Mike's obsession with diving. I wondered who had lost the fishing lure I held in my hand. Was it a young child on a fishing trip with his dad? Had they caught anything? What else was out there? Mike had talked about the history of the wars fought on Lake Ontario, and obviously had studied the history, since he knew that ships had disappeared in the lake. Answers to the questions Mike must have had could only be answered by finding the wrecks.

As we took off our gear, I imagined piles of gold in a sunken ship, and I could imagine thousands of people smiling as they learned the resting place of their beloved ancestors.

The ride back to the marina was enjoyable. We no longer noticed the wind or the gorgeous scenery, but instead talked about our dive. As it turned out, Mark did not have a lot of experience, and he shared my displeasure in diving the murky waters of Lake Alice. Bernie explained that whenever Mike had taken divers to Lake Alice, it was because the conditions in Lake Ontario were too extreme for diving. Unfortunately, when Lake Ontario was bad, so was Lake Alice.

Bernie said, "I went on a dive once in Lake Alice when there was twelve feet of visibility. We really ought to dive there again sometime in the future when the weather is acceptable."

Mark said, "Yeah, that's a good idea."

I agreed, but added, "I still like the boat-diving out in the big lake."

Bernie dropped Mark and me off at the marina, where we unloaded our gear onto the ground. Bernie apologized for not helping me carry my cumbersome gear back to the boat, but told us that he needed to get to work and open the dive shop. Mark worked as a fireman in Batavia, and today was his day off. He agreed to help me with the gear.

Mark hung his wet suit on top of his car and set gear out over the car's hood to dry. I carried my lighter gear to the boat and hung it over the boat's roof. Captain Jack's people were fishing off the back of the two boats, and they were having some luck. They thanked me for letting them use the boat, and poked fun at the cramped cockpits in the fishing boats as they enjoyed the roomy deck and seats in the back of the *Gold Hunter*.

Mark helped me carry the rest of my gear to the boat. He eagerly accepted my invitation for a cup of coffee at the marina. He poured a cup of regular coffee, but added so much cream and sugar that I joked that he should just have a cup of hot chocolate instead. "I need my caffeine," Mark replied as I poured a cup of black decaffeinated coffee for myself.

Bill Reed was busy with the fishing captains that could not venture out onto the lake. They were buying oil and boat parts. Stormy weather provided them with an opportunity to maintain their boats, as customers either canceled or fished in the river instead. Bill said, "Coffee is on me, but don't leave the marina until I get a chance to talk with you."

Mark and I walked outside and joined a couple of boat captains at the picnic table in front of the marina. They were watching the waves by the breakwall and commenting on their decreasing size. I noticed that the waves no longer came over the breakwall, and that the wind seemed to have died down greatly.

Mark was eager to ask about my diving experience. Surprisingly, I was just as willing to tell him about my limited experience. We both agreed, though, that we wanted to dive more. We talked about the murky water we had just experienced, comparing it to pictures of the Caribbean. I had snorkeled in the Caribbean, but it was long ago. I assured Mark that if I went again, I certainly would go scuba diving there.

Mark finished his coffee and told me, "I really enjoyed diving with you, Wilbur. I've got to get back home now and get something done on assignments for class. But let's dive together again sometime soon, okay?"

"You bet, Mark," I replied, "Now that I've started diving again, I don't know why I ever stopped! We'll dive together again for sure."

After Mark left, my mind went back to Mike's pictures of the wrecks, then to the assault from the day before. Bill was still busy in the marina, so I went down to the boat, where the fishermen were catching some perch and bass and an occasional sunfish.

I unlocked the hatches that covered the engines. The oil levels were right on the mark, and the engine compartments were as clean as could be. I checked the oil in the compressor engine and in the compressor itself. When I looked at the dive compressor, I noticed the two cascade tanks for filling the air tanks, but I was shocked to see a third tank with a green top. The third tank was marked O_2. I knew that pure oxygen was dangerously flammable. Mike had taught me that oxygen was never used by divers, and I could not imagine why Mike would have a tank of oxygen on the boat.

I closed everything up and decided to open the lock box behind the helm. Inside I found green tanks marked "Nitrox" and a green equipment bag labeled "Enriched Air". I had read about technical diving that used different gases, and I decided to ask Bernie if Mike could have been using something other than compressed air, especially taking into account Mike's deteriorated health.

I locked the box again, and my mind began to wander back to the man that had tried stealing the GPS. One of the fishermen broke my thought as he offered me a beer. It was only ten o'clock in the morning, and I was not a big drinker. I declined the offer, but went over to sit next to the guys fishing on the back of the boat.

They had a whole bucket of panfish and they were thinking of calling it an early day. Half an hour later, they left to drive back to Pennsylvania.

Captain Jack had been working below, cleaning his cabin. I decided to tell him that he could have any of the phone numbers of the people looking to hire a dive boat. Jack declined, saying he was booked up with fishing people for the whole week. I did not tell Jack how much I was getting paid for the week, because I didn't want to involve him with the kind of people that I would probably be dealing with.

I went below and started reading my dive book. I learned that enriched-air diving was using air with a certain amount of oxygen added; this gave the diver more bottom time with less chance of decompression sickness. Details of how to use the mixture would have to be learned in a separate course by an instructor—another question for Bernie.

The familiar voice of Captain Jack speaking with a voice I had only heard once, and not too long ago, woke me from an accidental midday nap. I came up from the cabin to see Captain Jack on the bridge of the *Sea Dog*, talking to a young, blond-haired woman of no more than twenty-five years of age, who was standing on the dock between our boats. Captain Jack told the young girl that I was on board, and grinned and pointed at me as I appeared on the deck. "See?" he said.

The young temptress was of medium height, suntanned, and as cute as any young girl would want to be. She wore a pair of cutoff blue jeans that had gone out of style with Daisy Duke, and she had a white blouse that was tied in a knot under her small breasts, exposing an athletic waist. She carried a small, tan leather purse that did not match her barefoot, casual look.

She hopped on the boat and said hello, which I thought was bold of her. She walked toward me, raising her hand in a limp position that implied more me kissing her hand than shaking it. I shook her hand. She flirtatiously held on and said, "Hi! I am a PADI dive master, and I'm looking for work."

There was something I did not like about a young girl who would use her sexuality, directed at a married man of my age, to ask for a job. Also, that fact that I recognized her voice as the girl on the phone that had identified herself as Shirley Tempest turned me off, so I said, "I'm not hiring anyone."

As Shirley's smile disappeared, she seemed to age ten years, making her outfit seem more like a costume than a casual style. Her thin face showed strong cheekbones when she spoke in a deeper, more intelligent tone. "I need to talk to you, Mister Bone, in private!" She looked around, as if expecting someone to be listening, before she walked over to the cabin door, opened it, and motioned me down with her cold brown eyes.

Shirley's Investigation

My curiosity made me go below to the cramped cabin, followed by Shirley. "Sit," she said. As I sat down, she opened her purse, exposing a rather large pistol. She must have read the fear on my face when I looked at the gun, because she quickly closed the purse and set it on the bench across from the berth I sat on. Then she sat down on the bench and lowered her voice, saying, "I was just going to show you my badge. I am really with the New York Borough of Criminal Investigation—the BCI." She pointed to her purse, and in a soft, confident voice, she asked, "May I?"

With curious anticipation, all I could muster was a weak okay.

Slowly, she opened her purse and fished out a leather case. She opened it to reveal a shiny badge next to a photo identification card. I accepted the case when she handed it to me, and I looked at the identification, more to see what the BCI was than to confirm her identity. Still leery of this investigator, I handed the identification case back to her. I recognized a kind person behind Shirley's penetrating eyes.

Shirley began to play a mind game to try to gain information from me. Recognizing her form of questioning, I decided to play the game, so that I too could learn more about what was going on. Shirley's first exchange provided some information, but also invited questions. She proclaimed, "I have been investigating Michael Moresby for the past four months."

Not fully trusting Miss Tempest, I said in a surprised voice, "I've known Mike all my life, and I do not believe that he ever would do anything wrong."

A hint of sincerity that could not have been faked came into Shirley's voice as she said, "I would agree. I have dived with Mike several times on his dive charters, by posing as half of a couple with another agent. But I have evidence that proves otherwise."

Digging for more information rather than offering information, I asked, "What do you think the auction will expose?"

Shirley could not hide her emotion, and without thinking, she asked, "What auction?" She had just won the first round, and I was embarrassed, because I had given up more information than was necessary.

I said, "Miss Tempest, I think that I need to talk to the lawyer before I can answer any more questions."

She asked, "What lawyer?"

"Mike's lawyer, Mr. Carski."

"Call him!"

I stood up, thinking our meeting was over, but Miss Tempest held up a finger, then carefully opened her purse, exposing a cell phone. I sat back down. She handed me the phone, saying, "Number seven on the speed dial."

Looking at the phone, I felt myself blush. I admitted that I did not know how to use a speed dial. Shirley shifted her body around so that she was sitting next to me. I was surprised at how easy the process of dialing was.

John Carski's secretary, Dolores, said that he was in a meeting, but he'd be happy to take my call. When he came on the line, I said, "I am sorry to bother you, Mr. Carski, but there is a Miss Shirley Tempest here, and she says that I should give her information about Mike."

John Carski lowered his voice and confirmed that he knew the investigator, before adding that she was very good at her job. The lawyer told me he knew very little about what the auction was all about, and he was curious about why a BCI investigator was interested. He agreed that Mike had been extremely ethical, he doubted any wrongdoing on Mike's part, and he said he would welcome an exchange of information with Miss Tempest.

The lawyer left the decision up to me, but recommended that I cooperate with her to avoid getting involved in any illegal activities. I agreed to cooperate, but asked Mr. Carski one more question. "Could you describe Miss Tempest for me?" I looked at Miss Tempest, and saw an approving smile.

Carski asked, "A physical description or a professional description?"

"Physical!" I answered, watching the young investigator's eyebrows shoot upward as she listened to my side of the conversation. Carski described Miss Tempest in one sentence, and asked if she was with me now. "Yes, she is," I said catching a victorious smile from her.

"With your permission, I will fill her in on what I know," John Carski offered. I handed the phone to Miss Tempest and excused myself to go up on deck, where the air was fresher and where I could be alone to absorb what was going on. Miss Tempest had a childlike "gotcha" smile on her face when she took the phone from my extended hand.

"Hi, John," I heard as I climbed the short flight of stairs to the afternoon sunshine.

A sudden urge to smoke a cigar came over me once I had inhaled a breath of fresh air on deck. The box of cigars on the dash provided temptation to take up the bad habit I had overcome years ago, but I decided that once the box was empty, I would not smoke anymore. Besides, smoking a cigar was like toasting Mike. I could picture Mike, laughing underwater with a gurgling sound, as I lit the cigar and took a long puff.

Miss Temple finished her phone conversation with Mr. Carski and came up from below. "Let's go for a ride!" she said, looking around.

The winds had died down since morning, and I wanted to see how much the lake had calmed down, so I agreed, saying, "Maybe a short one, Miss Tempest."

"Please! Call me Shirley."

"Okay, and I am Will," I answered.

"I need to grab something from my car, and I will be right back."

"I'll start the engines."

By the time the engines were running, Shirley was back on the boat holding a blue travel bag and wearing a blue baseball cap that had the PADI logo and a diver on it. She asked if I was ready to shove off, and when I said yes, she untied the dock lines.

Once we were away from the dock, Shirley disappeared below deck with her bag, but reappeared before we were at the breakwall. She had changed into a more modest pair of shorts and a shirt that covered her tummy. She looked much more dignified, more intelligent, and even prettier. I looked at her and gave an approving smile. It was as though she had read my mind when, holding her arms out, she said, "Sorry for the earlier bimbo outfit. It works most of the time!"

I understood that as a small compliment to my character. I changed the subject by pointing to the waves coming in the channel at the end of the breakwall. "A lot smaller than they were this morning," I said.

Looking over the top of the breakwall at the lake, Shirley said, "No whitecaps." She was right, and the lake looked less threatening, even though it still brought a tinge of the unnamed dread I often felt when I thought about diving again.

My underwater worry was disrupted when Shirley started talking about the auction. "Well, this upcoming auction sounds interesting indeed. I have to admit that I didn't know anything about it until you let the cat out of the bag!"

I was a bit embarrassed by her tone of victory in having caught me out. "Yes, um, I wasn't sure what information you already had."

Her tone changed to one of concern for me as she said, "But I do know about the attempted robbery and the assault on you. I saw the police report. Are you all right?"

A sense of pride made me smile. "It was nothing." In actuality, it had scared the daylights out of me.

The boat became silent as we rounded out the breakwall and entered the lake like a roller coaster leaving the first high point. The waves were chocolate brown and all of eight feet high from the swell to the crest; they moved the boat up and down, giving me a feeling of being out of control. I added some throttle, which brought the bow up a little higher, and I found the boat was able to negotiate the waves comfortably.

I kept the speed slow as we continued our conversation. Shirley asked, "What if, for appearances, you were to hire me as your dive master?"

I wasn't sure that I could disagree even if I wanted to, so I said, "Okay. We'll do that. Actually, I'm curious. How did you happen to be assigned to Mike's case, anyway?"

She explained, "There were various reasons for the assignment, but partly it was because of the diving itself. I'm delighted to take on any case that involves scuba diving. I worked in Grand Cayman as a dive master for two years. While I was there, I earned my instructor's certification and became a technical diver."

I was impressed, and when she suggested that she live on the boat to keep watch at night, I agreed with relief. Someone else, with the authority to do so, would be handling issues that could get me in trouble. I turned the boat north, toward bluer water, and wondered how deep we would have to dive to find clear water.

The brown water turned creamy white as the bow dipped into a wave, bringing water up to the windshield and over the roof. Shirley turned to watch the water run out the open transom of the boat as I made the instant decision to continue turning the boat away from the direction of the waves and back to Oak Orchard.

Images of the shipwrecks filled my mind, and for a moment I even thought that the *Gold Hunter* might join them in a watery grave of its own. It was more difficult piloting the boat with the following waves than it was heading into the waves. The waves were moving faster than the boat, forcing the transom to rise and point the bow down to the water. A wave would move under the boat, raising the bow up into the air, which made it feel like the boat was falling backward down the other side of the wave.

I turned around and saw nothing but a wall of water coming at the boat. I was certain that it would fill the boat's deck, as the boat had only the dive ladder at the back with no transom. I added power to try to outrun the wave that was chasing me, but the eight-foot wave lifted the back of the boat up again. I pulled the throttle back as the wave settled under the boat, making the water in front disappear into a swell that was sure to swallow the boat at a fast speed.

I had not thought of Shirley, because I was too busy trying not to sink the boat. She said, "This is fun, but if you point the boat forty-five degrees to the waves and tack back to the river, it will be easier." After the bow fell, I obediently followed the woman's advice and turned the helm. Adding power again, I felt in control as the boat negotiated the waves with much more ease.

I was thankful for Shirley's advice, and told her so. She reminded me that she was an experienced diver, and like any diver, she'd spent a lot of time on boats. My manhood had been tested too many times this week, and I had not fared well. I was happy to have Shirley Tempest with me, not because she was an investigator, but because she made me feel safe.

In time, the calm river was under us. I looked over my shoulder and recognized a treacherous body of water. Mike had often said, "They don't make a ship large enough that Lake Ontario couldn't claim." I had never really understood that statement until now.

I offered the helm to Shirley, but she declined, saying sarcastically, "Sure, now that the fun is over." I let out a laugh that took out a lot of nervousness with it. Shirley seemed to be memorizing the marina as we made our way to the dock. She handled the lines and tied the knots exactly the way Mike used to tie them. I shut off the engine, realizing that my cigar had gone out and was soaking wet from the waves that had come over the roof of the boat.

I was straightening up some gear that had shifted on the deck when Shirley asked, "Excuse me, Wilbur, could you come down below with me for a few minutes?"

I bent over and stuck my head through the cabin door, saying, "Okay. What can I do for you?"

Shirley had the drawers under the bench open, and she asked, "Do you know whose clothes these are?"

I think my face showed a moment of grief and nostalgia as I recognized my friend's favorite outfits. I told her that they were Mike's, and added, "I haven't really felt ready to do anything with his personal stuff yet, I'm afraid."

In a soft and understanding voice, Shirley offered, "I'd be happy to take care of it for you. After all, if I'm going to stay on the boat, I'll want to keep the cabin tidy. I can easily take these things to Goodwill, if you want me to."

I was flooded with relief as I thanked her. Once more, my appreciation for Shirley grew. I walked to the marina to see if I could get some empty boxes for her.

Bill was enjoying a slow afternoon after his hectic morning at the marina's store. I asked him if he had any empty boxes that I could use. He showed me a pile of empty boxes and said, "Take what you need." I picked out a few boxes and thanked him.

The late-afternoon sun dried the boat off fast. I fumbled with getting on the boat. I started handing the boxes down to Shirley, who quickly filled them with clothes that she had neatly sorted out on the berth. Handing them up to me, she said, "I'll take these to my car and get rid of them later, but I think I have found something you should see."

I stacked the boxes of clothes on the deck and climbed down into the cabin. Shirley opened the drawer that had contained Mike's clothes. Tucked neatly on the bottom was a stack of paper with two large clips on one side. "Underwater Museum" was written in large letters on the top page. Shirley picked it up and opened it, showing me Mike's notes on all the research he had done on shipwrecks in Lake Ontario.

Shirley opened the drawer underneath, and there were two more manuscripts, each about an inch thick. I fanned through the neatly typed and numbered pages. I felt like I had just won the lottery. Then I thought of Mike and how he had lived in poverty in his last years. Somehow he had managed to leave two and a half million dollars to his children, and that puzzled me. I sat down and started to read page one.

I felt Shirley looking at me and looked over at her. She had one of the books in her hand and looked at me with eager eyes. My comfortable retired life had been shattered. I was experiencing moments of sheer fear that haunted me, yet I was sleeping better than ever at night. I imagined myself as a much younger man with an uncertain life ahead of me, and felt a desire for my wife, Trisha, that I had thought was lost forever. I was no longer Wilbur Bone, the retired schoolteacher; I was now Wilbur Bone, the adventurous treasure hunter, the lover, and the detective about to unravel the mysteries of the deep Lake Ontario.

The first ship Mike wrote about was a ship with no name. It was simply referred to as the "Long Ship." According to the description, the wreck was eighty-five feet long and had a seventeen-foot beam. I thought to myself, *How can you hide such a massive vessel?*

I read on. The ship's fifty-foot mast was lying on the bottom, a hundred and ten feet from the stern of the vessel. The ship had twenty-six pairs of oars still attached. A note concluded that the ship must be a warship, because trading ships and "Knerrir" seldom exceeded fifty feet.

Mike estimated that the ship had been built in AD 1100. I thought that was impossible, because America hadn't been discovered by Christopher Columbus until 1492, but then I remembered reading about the Norse explorer, Leif Erikson, who had arrived on the shores of the New World much earlier. Then the text provided a description of a prow (the front end of the ship) with a dragon-snake-like head lying on the bottom, which showed that the ship was on its side.

Realizing that Mike was describing a Viking ship, I flipped through the pages, hoping for a picture. Disappointed that there were no photos, I read on. At one point I gasped out loud, "A Viking ship!" catching Shirley's attention. She leaned over and read some of what I was reading before sharing what she had read.

"Amazing! That wreck could have taken place five hundred years before Columbus! The one I'm reading about is a bit later: an Irish trading ship called *Isolde*, which sank in the mid-1700s." She looked at me inquisitively and asked, "Do you have any idea where that name comes from?"

I knew the name well, and explained proudly, "Isolde was Tristan's lover in an old Arthurian myth that involved a love triangle between a Cornwall king, his nephew Tristan, and the Irish princess Isolde."

Shirley looked surprised and pleased with the new knowledge, but quickly returned to her reading. She was obviously intensely interested in what she was studying. I finished reading about the Viking warship and was beginning to read the next section, about a British frigate, when a knock on the open cabin door startled us. Looking up, I saw Trisha's smiling face appear in the doorway. I tried to stand in the cramped cabin, but had to hunch over a bit, which added to my embarrassment as I introduced Shirley to my wife.

"What are you two doing down here together?" Trisha asked jokingly.

I turned red, banged my head on the cabinet above the berth, and then banged the other side of my head on the cabinets across from the one I had just hit. A strong feeling of claustrophobia made me more uncomfortable and prevented me from answering coherently. Finally, I just flopped back down on the berth next to Shirley.

Trisha and Shirley must have recognized each other's feelings, or used mental telepathy, or said something I could not hear, because they were both looking at me and laughing hysterically. Trisha stepped back from the door, and Shirley said, "Let's go up on deck and get some fresh air."

I was relieved when Trisha offered Shirley her hand and introduced herself. "Hi! I am Clumsy's wife, Trisha."

Shirley smiled and replied, "I'm Shirley. Nice to meet you, Mrs. Bone. Perhaps you might think I'm the type of girl who would be having an affair…and I am." I almost fell overboard, but my head hit the side window next to the helm and saved me. Shirley burst out laughing and continued, "But not with your husband."

Totally humiliated, I moved over to a bench on the side of the boat and sat down. Trisha and Shirley were still laughing at me. I looked at the two women standing on the deck and realized that they were not only dressed alike, but their hair was the same length. Trisha's hair was a bit darker blond and she was about two inches taller than Shirley, but despite the age difference, they looked more like sisters than strangers. In fact, they were both very beautiful women, and the low setting sun was dim compared to the glow radiating from their smiling faces.

Trisha suggested that we go to the Lakeside Restaurant for dinner. The restaurant was just up the road from the marina, and we could easily walk there. I had not eaten since breakfast, and I realized I was hungry. "Dinner sounds good. I'll buy!" I said, trying to save face.

Trisha said, "I know you will." Then she looked at Shirley and asked, "How about it?"

Shirley told Trisha that she was going to be staying on the boat and wanted to get settled, but her stomach growled, making Trisha insist. We locked up the boat, and drove to the restaurant. Inside, Captain Jack and some of the boat people were at the bar.

Captain Jack looked at me when we walked in and said, "Boy! You divers catch all the good ones."

He was talking about Trisha and Shirley, who were standing on either side of me. I introduced them, saying, "Girls, this is our neighbor, Captain Jack.

Captain Jack, this is my wife, Trisha, and my new dive master, Miss Shirley Tempest."

All the guys were looking at the women, and I was proud to have a beautiful blond on each arm as I was led to the back room where the dining tables were.

A hostess seated us at a table near a window with a view of the lake. It was peaceful and allowed us to talk. Shirley told Trisha about being assigned to Mike's case because of her diving experience. "As the dive master, I'm going to live on the boat for a while, and that will give me a chance to watch for problems. We don't know for sure what the attacker was looking for, but there's something of value there."

Trisha replied, "I'm genuinely relieved that Wilbur has your help. I've been a little worried about him being on the boat alone, and I agree that it's not safe to leave the boat unattended at night."

I said, "You know, Trish, how Mike left his things in the cabin below deck and I just didn't know how to deal with it? Well, Shirley's been great about that too. She boxed all of his things up this afternoon."

"Well, it's a small cabin, and I needed to put some things of my own in there anyway," Shirley said, with a modest shrug.

Trisha inquired about the condition of the boat's cabin. "I know Mike wasn't the greatest housekeeper. Why not let me take the bedding for you and wash it at our house? Maybe you'll need some clean curtains and pillows as well."

Shirley was delighted, and the two women chatted about domestic matters while I enjoyed my meal.

We finished dinner as the scene in our window changed from blue-and-white skies over a brown lake to bright orange-red clouds and a purple sky meeting a silvery lake. Outside, we watched the sun finish setting before driving back to the boat. Trisha and Shirley went down and stripped the bedding and curtains, along with anything else that would fit into a washing machine.

I agreed to stay on the boat, because I wanted to read some more about Mike's ships. Shirley left with Trisha and the laundry, saying she would return in a couple of hours. The berth was too hard to sit on and read, so I had to get a couple of life jackets from under the deck benches to form a soft cushion to sit on while I read.

I did not get much reading done. I thought about our two sons, and how much Trisha had always wanted a daughter. She doted over our daughters-in-law, but seemed anxious to have a grandchild. I fell asleep thinking about how energetic Trisha had been tonight.

Shirley's Investigation 63

It was dark when I woke up to loud snoring in the cabin. I fumbled for the light switch, and I was shocked to see Bernie in a sleeping bag on the bench across from me. I got up and went up on deck. The air was chilly. The marina was open, and people were getting on boats. I walked to the marina, gave Bill Reed a quick greeting, and poured myself a cup of coffee.

Bill gave me the Wednesday morning weather report. "Calm winds and hot today." I asked about the waves, and learned that they had been subsiding all night. I wondered what had happened to Shirley and Trisha, and how Bernie had ended up on the boat. It was too early to call home and check on the girls, so I just poured another cup of coffee.

Halfway through my coffee, a grumbling Bernie walked in. He was wearing shorts, a T-shirt, and a pair of socks. He had his sleeping bag around his shoulders and was trying to wrap it around himself to keep warm. His hair stood up in all directions, and his eyes looked half-asleep.

"What is going on?" I asked. Bernie just growled and poured a cup of coffee before mumbling something about cackling hens ruining his dream. "What hens?" I asked.

Bernie walked over and opened the door. He said, "Can't you hear 'em?" I listened for a moment before I recognized Trish's and Shirley's voices.

Bernie muttered, "They threw me out. They said I was in the way." I carried my coffee back to the boat, leaving Bernie with Bill in the marina. The girls were in the cabin, talking and having fun. I noticed that, like me, they were wearing the same clothes they'd had on last night.

I heard a big splash a couple of docks over, followed by someone saying, "Ouch! This water is cold this morning." Some fishermen were standing on the back of a boat, laughing as Bernie swam back to the dock. "Anyone got a bar of soap?" Bernie asked, and one of the boat captains offered him a bottle of dishwashing soap. "That will work!" he replied.

All cleaned up and dripping wet, Bernie was on the dock next to the boat. "Do you think they could hand me my bag, so I can put some dry clothes on?" Before I could answer, a bag came flying up from the cabin. I handed it to Bernie, who walked to the bathroom on the side of the marina. A few minutes later, a normal-looking Bernie appeared.

I too needed to get cleaned up, but I went to the marina's shower room, where I enjoyed a hot shower. Back on the dock, Bernie explained that he had called my home last night to see whether he should stay on the boat, and Trisha had told him it would be a good idea. She had said that she wasn't coming until morning. Bernie held out his hands and said, "You were dead to the world, and

I couldn't wake you, so I climbed on the hard bench and fell asleep in my sleeping bag." Bernie was a character, and his sense of humor and easygoing manner reminded me a lot of Mike. It was good to be on the boat with a friend like that again.

Trisha came up from the cabin, carrying a bucket and wearing rubber gloves. She was satisfied that the place was cleaner and more domesticated. I watched Trisha walk away from us. All of a sudden, Bernie jumped to attention, as though he were in the navy and an officer had entered the area. I turned to look in the direction of Bernie's gaze and saw Shirley in front of the cabin door.

The lights that lit up the dock area seemed to reflect off Shirley's light blond hair. She was wearing a white sweat suit that showed off her athletic shape. I guessed that Bernie was shocked by her good looks, so I had some fun introducing Bernie to "my mistress." Bernie just smiled and said, "Hi, Shirley. How have you been?"

I soon realized that they knew each other from diving with Mike, and it was obvious that there was a mutual attraction between the two divers. Bernie was genuinely happy when I explained that Shirley was going to be our new dive master. Bernie said, "We can use a good dive master." He asked Shirley if she was diving with us this morning.

"Of course!" Shirley answered, with a cheerful smile.

Trisha came back and gave Shirley a hug good-bye, explaining that she had to get ready for work. She told Bernie to take good care of "the old man," referring to me. Then she looked at me with serious eyes and said, "You will be home when I get out of work at five, won't you?"

A bit surprised at her unusually firm tone, I replied, "Of course." Trisha leaned toward my face for her traditional peck on the cheek good-bye. I was ready, but Trisha surprised me by putting her hand around my neck and kissing me on the lips. I felt something stir and watched her disappear as she sashayed away from the boat.

I didn't know if I was more excited about the morning's dive or seeing my wife after work, but I felt lighter as I started getting diving gear together. Bernie had everything ready for his dive and was helping Shirley, who did not need the help, but seemed to enjoy Bernie's attention as they put her dive gear together.

Mark showed up just as I was telling Shirley that I had no secrets from Bernie. They obviously wanted to keep talking, but they greeted Mark and helped him with his diving gear. The local dive community was small, and

Shirley knew Mark as well. "Four of us today," Bernie said, motioning for me to fire up the engines. Shirley took over the task of handling lines, which made me happy, because it gave Bernie a chance to discuss dive locations with me.

After yesterday's rough water, Bernie suggested a deep dive for better visibility. Only a small amount of anxiety crept into my mind, fighting a growing desire for the serenity of diving and the newfound energy I was getting from the exercise. The optimistic side of my mind won, and I agreed. Bernie said, "A deep dive it is."

The air was warmer than usual as the sun announced a new day. Our timing was perfect. We rounded the breakwall, leaving the dawn behind and watching the lake turn from black to silver, then to brown, as the sun made its way upward behind us. We headed west for two miles, barely noticing the rise and fall of the boat on the one-foot-high leftover rolling waves.

Turning north, we approached the line where brown water turned into blue water. The depth gauge read sixty feet, which did not seem too deep for a dive. Bernie had his dry suit on, and he offered to take the helm so that I could suit up as well. By the time I got my dry suit on, Bernie had dropped the anchor in a hundred feet of water. My heart jumped when I looked at the depth gauge.

This time it was Shirley who did the predive briefing. In a firm voice, she explained, "This will be a training dive for Mark and Wilbur. Bernie, you're going to follow the anchor line down with Mark and make sure that the descending and ascending are done at a safe speed. We'll do this by alternating hand over hand on the anchor line, going down and coming back up."

Shirley was going to be my dive buddy, and we would follow about five minutes after Mark and Bernie left the surface. Bernie took his big line reel; he could attach one end of the line to the anchor line, so as not to lose the anchor line if visibility was poor. Shirley and I would take Bernie's line when he and Mark began their ascent.

Bernie tied a tank with a regulator and an octopus hooked up and turned it on. He tied it to a line and lowered it so that it was fifteen feet below the surface of the water. Shirley explained that we would have to do a safety stop at fifteen feet for three minutes before coming up to the boat.

I was a little nervous about having to make a safety decompression stop. I could tell that Shirley noticed my anxiety as we helped Bernie and Mark giant-stride off the back of the boat. Shirley helped me into my scuba unit as she explained that the idea of the dive was to get used to slowly ascending from any dive, and that even if we did not go to the bottom, she would be right with me on the line.

I finished fastening my BCD and turned to help Shirley put on her scuba unit, but I got a glimpse of her unit flying up into the air before her face appeared in front of it. She quickly did up the cummerbund and release on her BCD. I was amazed at her strength and coordination. Shirley suited up in the same time it took me to put on my mask. "Let's go through the buddy check together now, Wilbur. I want to make sure that you get a chance to learn about these integrated weight systems that make the weight belt unnecessary."

When she was ready, Shirley put her regulator in her mouth. I nodded my head and turned to the gentle blue rolling water. A mountain of anxiety stood before me as I began to breathe hard, pondering the thought of drowning in the spot my eyes were glued to. Too hot and scared to care, I managed to bring my left foot out in front of me and lean into it.

The water was dark and cold. My eyes felt like they were growing larger as I tried to see the boat, or even some light. I popped up to the surface after what seemed to be many seconds, but was probably only a single second. I turned around to find the boat. Seeing Shirley with her arm stretched up and her fingers touching the top of her hood, I calmed down and returned the okay signal by touching the top of my head. Shirley entered the water next to me.

The sheer terror I'd felt just a moment ago was replaced by a self-imposed pressure to overcome my fear of diving. I knew that in less than a minute we would be underwater and I would forget all my fear instantly. Shirley recognized the fear in my eyes, and motioned to switch to my snorkel and head for the anchor line.

With my snorkel in my mouth, I was able to swim with my face underwater. Looking up to check my direction occasionally, I made my way to the anchor line. I grabbed hold of it and turned around to see Shirley give the thumbs-down sign. She checked her computer, raised her arm, and let some air out of her BCD. I followed her actions and descended without taking my hand off the anchor line.

Three feet down, the motion from the waves was gone, and I was breathing normally. No longer overheated, I put my hand on the anchor line just above Shirley's hand. We took turns moving our hands on the anchor line, like a couple of kids deciding whose baseball team would bat first.

I was thinking about how people communicate on land and how important it was to choose the right words. Looking at Shirley's eyes reminded me of Bernie. Both of them had an uncanny ability to communicate effectively without words. Shirley's eyes were smiling with a glossy shine that said to me, "Just relax. You're quite safe here. I am right here with you, and we are going to really enjoy this dive." I believed those eyes.

Deep Diving

Too many bubbles! Too many! What's going on? I thought as the water filled with large bubbles that changed shapes and headed upward. Again, Shirley saw my thoughts in my eyes, through my mask. She pointed down with her gloved finger. My eyes followed her finger to see the bright yellow tanks of Bernie and Mark.

Gray stones were all around the first divers. I felt my old, dry eyes glow as I looked at Shirley, who held out her fist. I took my fist and gently punched her fist, giving the underwater "high five" sign, congratulating each other for making it to a hundred feet.

Bernie and Mark made fists and exchanged underwater "high fives" with Shirley and me. Then Bernie gave Shirley the line reel and began his ascent up the anchor line with Mark. Shirley gave me the okay signal by touching her gloved thumb and pointer finger together in a circle, leaving the remaining fingers pointing up. I returned the sign, eager to look around.

It was amazing how clear the bottom was after making a blind descent down the anchor line. With thirty-foot visibility, I watched Shirley play out line as she swam in a northerly direction. All of a sudden she stopped and looked me over, and then took a special slate for underwater communication and verification out of a pocket. She handed it to me, and I read it. It said: *Write name and address.* I was not sure why she wanted me to do it, but I took the pencil attached to a rubber string and wrote my name and address on the slate. Before I had finished, Shirley's hand grabbed the slate and she motioned for us to go back to the anchor.

I released the slate and slowly followed Shirley. We ascended about ten feet off the bottom, and as we headed for the anchor line, she turned the handle to reel in the line. I had a strange feeling, like I had just woken up from a nap. I was extremely relaxed.

I had not noticed that the lake bottom inclined downward as we had swum north, but the incline was obvious as we followed the line south, back to the anchor. I managed to look at my dive computer and saw that we were in a hundred and five feet of water. A hint of fear came over me, but it left just as quickly when I looked up and saw the anchor on an underwater ridge just ahead, above us.

Shirley untied the reel line from the anchor line and hooked the reel to a brass clip on her BCD. She looked at the slate before putting it in her pocket. Shirley turned to me and pointed to her pressure gauge. I looked at mine and signaled by holding all ten fingers up and then just one. This let Shirley know that I had eleven hundred pounds of air left, which was plenty to make to the surface.

Shirley gave the thumbs-up signal, and instead of returning the signal and agreeing to ascend, I pointed to my pressure gauge to find out how much air Shirley had left. I was humbled when she signaled that she had two thousand pounds. We started our ascent up the anchor line. I watched the bottom disappear as we entered the area of nothingness that surrounded the anchor line for the next ninety feet.

Away from the anchor line, it would have been hard to tell which way was up. Our bubbles left us at a forty-five degree angle from the anchor line, and I remembered that the anchor line did not go straight up. The anchor line left the bow of the boat, and although we were in a hundred feet of water, I remembered seeing about three hundred feet of anchor line go out.

The dive book I had read two days before mentioned that divers could follow their bubbles to the surface, but cautioned that they should never pass them. Our bubbles were leaving us for the surface as we continued our hand-over-hand exchange upward.

The water got brighter, but visibility lessened, as there were a lot of floating particles in the water. Shirley was watching both me and her dive computer when she held up her hand in the stop signal. I held firmly onto the anchor line with one hand, let go of my BCD deflator hose, and checked my dive console.

We were at fifteen feet, I had nine hundred pounds of air left, and I was extremely relaxed and having a good time. We waited a while at that level until it was safe to go up further. Shirley looked at her computer and signaled to ascend.

I broke the surface next to Shirley and filled my BCD with enough air to make me float comfortably. I took my regulator out of my mouth, but instead of replacing it with my snorkel, I just pulled my mask down around my neck so that I would not lose it in the waves. I told Shirley, "You know, Shirley, it's amazing. The same waves that were terrorizing me fifteen minutes earlier seem to be fun right now!"

Shirley smiled and said, "I'm glad. Would you like to climb up the ladder first?" It was nice of her to offer, but I declined, saying gallantly, "Ladies first."

Bernie was on the back of the boat with Mark, who helped Shirley up the ladder. Bernie asked me, "How did the dive go for you this time, Wilbur? Did the safety decompression stop give you any trouble?"

I sighed a little and replied, "Thanks, Bernie. Everything went just fine." I floated comfortably in the water behind the boat.

On the boat, Shirley was still talking to me while I floated in the water, and Mark was talking too. Bernie watched us communicate in words all the things that we had wanted to say earlier but hadn't really been able to communicate underwater. Finally, Bernie asked, "Are you going to stay in the water all day, or are you coming on board?" I climbed up the ladder like a healthy forty-year-old and removed my gear. When we were all relaxing on the deck, Bernie looked at Shirley and said, "Ready?"

With a huge smile, Shirley said, "Yep."

Bernie and Shirley dug slates out of their BCD pockets and handed them to Mark and me. I recognized the slate, but where I thought I had written my name and address clearly, I found instead just a penciled line that resembled a lightning streak. Surprised as well, Mark spoke out. "Hey, what gives? I wrote my name and address! Whose scribbling is this?"

All I could say was, "Yeah, me too!"

Bernie became dead serious. He told Mark, "You developed nitrogen narcosis at a hundred and fifteen feet. That was when I asked you to fill out the slate."

"I was narked?" Mark blurted out. Then, after a moment of thought, he said, "I do remember trying to pop my bubbles and wondering why."

Shirley too was dead serious when she looked at me and said, "You were also at a hundred and fifteen feet." I showed Mark my slate and he showed me his. We both laughed. Shirley asked me, "How did you feel on the bottom?"

I could only tell her, "I was very comfortable, but when we started back to the anchor, ten feet above the bottom I felt like I'd just woken up from a nap."

Bernie explained, "Well, even though nitrogen narcosis is fairly harmless in itself, your actions, if you are too comfortable to consider how much time or air you have left, can get you into serious, life-threatening trouble."

Mark and I looked at each other. Mark asked Bernie, "Why didn't you get narked as well?"

Bernie answered, "Because Shirley and I are both used to diving deep. You see, a temporary immunity to nitrogen narcosis is gained with constant exposure to the depth."

Shirley added, "Also, you learn to recognize the symptoms of narcosis after experiencing it once or twice, like you both did today. You know that you need to ascend about ten feet as soon as you feel that way."

"That's right," Bernie confirmed, "and then the symptoms should go away, and you can continue your dive a little higher from the bottom."

"It was a good lesson for today. Now, are you guys ready for another dive?" Shirley asked as Bernie looked at his watch.

Bernie said, "It will have to be a shallow dive, and a quick one."

I looked at the young man, who was a third my age, and said, "How about it, Mark?"

"Absolutely! Positively! Most definitely!" was Mark's enthusiastic reply.

Bernie started the engines and raised the anchor while Shirley pulled up the spare tank and regulators that hung over the side of the boat. Mark and I pulled the dive ladder up, and we sat down as Bernie and Shirley took control of the boat that idled south toward shore.

Mark and I sat in the back of the boat, talking. "That was really a strange feeling, wasn't it?" Mark asked.

"Yeah. I was sort of in a dream world for a while there. What a rude awakening to see what nitrogen narcosis did to my handwriting!" I replied.

"Well, mine's never been good, but that was an all-time low for me too. I think I would be able to recognize the feeling the next time, though. How about you?"

"Yeah, I think so too. It's an unusual and distinct feeling, and I'm pretty alert to any special feelings underwater, because frankly, I get nervous sometimes."

"Well," Mark admitted, "I'm in the midst of working on my PADI advanced certification, and I was a little scared myself today about doing my deep dive. Bernie made me read about deep diving and gave me a written test at the dive shop yesterday."

It must have been a strange sight to see a tall, paunchy sixty-one-year-old sitting next to a muscular twenty-year-old. My experience as an English teacher had lent a dignified air to my speech and mannerisms. Although Mark was a bit rough around the edges, we shared a common love of diving. I sensed that Mark was a little afraid, but I was sure that he did not have the terror that I had to overcome.

Bernie stopped the boat, making Mark and me look up. We were close to shore in the brown muddy water. Simultaneously, Mark and I looked at each other and said, "Not another mud dive!" Bernie laughed as he dropped the anchor. Shirley came back and told us to plan a twenty-foot dive with a thirty-minute surface interval. We would see how much time we could spend on the bottom.

Mark opened his dive bag, pulling out a blue-and-white slate with tables on it. It had been a long time since I'd seen these tables, and although I knew what they were, I had no recollection of how to use them. Mark talked me through the process, showing me that we had a theoretical amount of nitrogen in our systems, noted on the chart as K. Moving over to the second part of the table, he showed me that after thirty minutes, our amount of nitrogen would be reduced to F. Flipping the tables over, Mark showed me that the maximum "bottom time" for a twenty-foot dive was a hundred and sixty-nine minutes.

Shirley told Mark and me to suit up, but I noticed that Bernie and Shirley were still talking. I half-jokingly asked if they were coming with us on the dive. Shirley came over to me and whispered that she wanted to stay on board and talk to Bernie. I understood, and I actually welcomed the idea of just Mark and I diving together. I felt in control and also somewhat responsible for Mark's safety, and I was happy that Mark wanted to dive, even without our dive master and instructor. After we changed tanks and suited up, Bernie handed us his buddy line and said that the dive probably would not be any better than Lake Alice had been the day before.

We did not mind, and we were eager to get in the water. Bernie handed Mark a line reel with a large red rubber float attached to one end of the line. Bernie said, "Because of poor visibility today, you two are going to do a drift dive. You won't have to worry about finding the anchor, because I'll be watching the float, and so I'll know where you'll ascend."

I thought that sounded great, and agreed. Seeing a little fear in Mark's eyes, I added, "Mike used to say that drift diving was the easiest dive to do." We entered the water and dropped into the murk, holding the buddy line close.

I was ecstatic to enter the wavy water, and I descended to the bottom without any anxiety at all. Once on the bottom, we picked a direction and started swimming through the murk. Visibility was not as bad as we had thought it would be. We could see each other from five feet apart. Mark's eyes were happy once we reached the bottom.

About five minutes into the dive, we came to a rocky area. Rocks stuck up about three feet from the normally flat bottom. We played like children around the rocks, then I saw Mark pointing to a face hiding in a crack. The face swam out when Mark moved his hand close, revealing a lake eel about two feet long. It moved impressively with a snakelike motion; a fin on its back extended from the back of its head to the tip of its tail. The eel led us away from the rocks and once again onto the flat, sandy bottom.

I stopped to dig something out of the sand and discovered it to be a pair of sunglasses. Mark made a fist and gave the congratulatory underwater "high five," and we moved on. Mark seemed to move slower, as though looking for his own underwater treasure, but all he found was a beer bottle that he left on the bottom.

I looked at my pressure gauge and saw it was at a thousand pounds. I realized that I was getting tired. Mark looked at his gauge, but when he looked back at me, I had my hands together and on the side of my face, showing the tired sign. Mark signaled to ascend, and I signaled back in agreement. I wondered where the boat would be.

Through the murk, we ascended slowly, until the light let us know that we were about to break the surface. I was tired but comfortable on the surface. I added air to my BCD, switched to my snorkel, and looked at Mark. He had a huge grin on his face. Just then Bernie's voice startled me. "Hey, can you move so I can drop the ladder?" I was shocked and happy to realize that we'd ascended only two feet from the boat. I kicked my fins twice and moved next to Mark, and the ladder came splashing down.

We climbed in and sat down. Shirley pulled the ladder up, and Bernie started the engines. Mark asked how they had known where we would come up, and Bernie just shrugged, saying, "Lucky guess." We accepted that as the boat took off on plane for the harbor.

As we turned upstream into the harbor, I was wearing the sunglasses I had found. They were scratched and dirty, but I displayed them on my face like a trophy. Thoughts of Mike came to my mind as I wondered how many treasures he had found at the lake's bottom.

Bernie was running late for work, and he left before we had a chance to tie the boat up. He said, "Six o'clock tomorrow?"

I replied, "Certainly."

After Bernie was gone and we had the boat secured, Mark said, "I'm starving!" We straightened up our gear, then we all got into my car to go to Lakeside Restaurant for a late breakfast.

The conversation never deviated from diving. When we pulled into the restaurant's parking lot, it was late for breakfast and too early for lunch, so it was fairly empty. We got a good table in the center of the dining room, where we could see out the many windows. Each of the windows had a different view of the lake.

Mark ordered steak and eggs with home-fried potatoes, extra toast, and a large root beer. Shirley and I looked at each other and laughed. Mark said, "What? Diving makes me hungry." Shirley ordered a fruit cup and some coffee. I agreed that diving made us hungry, but ordered scrambled eggs and a single order of toast with decaffeinated coffee, which was more than I usually ate.

"Hey, wasn't that something coming up close to the boat?" Mark asked, grinning and gobbling his breakfast at the same time.

"Yeah, it really took me by surprise," I replied. Shirley didn't say anything, and seemed quiet and pensive. In fact, Mark did most of the talking during breakfast, and I was busy listening to him. Shirley made only a few comments and seemed to be thinking of something else. Suddenly, I remembered that she was not just a diver; she was also diving undercover for a much bigger and more complex reason. Still, I enjoyed diving with her very much and felt safe with her.

Mark finished his meal first, which was puzzling, because he never stopped talking. He ordered a refill of his root beer while Shirley and I enjoyed our food and coffee. When we were ready to leave, Mark started digging in his wallet for some money. I told him, "Let me get breakfast this time. With your appetite, I'm glad I'm not your father, so I don't have to feed you all the time."

We laughed, and Mark said, "Thanks, but I still owe for the dive."

Shirley spoke out and said, "The diving is on me." Shirley was good at reading people and knew that Mark probably could not afford much diving. Then she jokingly said to Mark, "But tomorrow it's your turn to buy breakfast." We left the waitress a good tip before leaving the restaurant in a jovial mood.

Mark packed up his gear and left it on the boat for the next day before he headed home. When he left, I was happy to be able to talk to Shirley alone. Shirley became serious and looked around before talking. "What makes this job so hard is the people," she started.

I said, "But you seem so good with the divers."

Shirley looked at me, a bit puzzled, before she replied, "The diving is fun, and it is why I requested this assignment." Glancing around, she whispered, "I am talking about the investigation."

With the fun of diving and my new friends, I had forgotten that Shirley was actually an undercover investigator with a different agenda. She was such a skilled dive master that it was difficult to imagine her as anything else. We took the boat back out in the lake, where Shirley drove and I filled dive tanks. We idled for about an hour before the tanks were full, and decided to let the compressor run to fill the cascade system below the deck.

Shirley looked at home behind the helm with the wind blowing her hair. With a serious expression on her face, she explained, "You see, Mike was suspected of selling gold on the black market. Mike was never approached for selling the gold, but the Bureau just wanted to watch him. There are problems that could evolve if Mike really did find gold in the lake. The state, the federal government, and possibly Canada would all claim any precious metals found in Lake Ontario. The country owning a ship that sank in international waters would also have claim to gold found on that ship. To make the claiming of found gold even more difficult, any descendant of a sailor who lost his life on the sunken ship could also hire a lawyer and place a claim."

I said, "I had no idea it was that complicated, Shirley. But I see what you mean. So many different parties could be involved."

"Yes," she agreed, "and there are too many other difficulties to mention, but the reason that I volunteered for this case is the historical value of shipwrecks. The Viking ship, for example, would prove that Norsemen were here four hundred years before Columbus discovered America." Shirley concluded her explanation by saying, "Wilbur, could I ask you to handle any press that might get involved?" I happily agreed, realizing that I had not thought about the media interest the ships might provoke, but I didn't mind talking to reporters, answering their questions, and giving them some historical background. After all, a retired teacher is used to answering questions and giving out information.

Shirley's face went from serious back to glowing. She looked at me with a smile growing across her face, and eased the throttles forward. The boat lurched forward and climbed up on plane. "What'll she do?" asked the woman that had transformed back into a fun-loving girl again. I had no idea how fast the *Gold Hunter* could go, and I did not really care, but I knew I was about to find out. I reached up and grabbed the hand rail above the cabin door. That was all it took for Shirley to run the boat wide open.

The motion of the waves lost their effect on the boat as we gained speed. The speedometer read forty knots before it quit climbing. The harbor came up fast, and Shirley said, "Oops," and pulled the throttle back. I saw nothing in front of us that meant danger, but followed Shirley's eyes aft, where I saw our backwash about to swallow the transom.

Shirley added just enough power to keep ahead of the dangerous wake until we turned around the breakwall, letting the wake splash the fishermen standing along the breakwall. Shirley quietly apologized to the now-wet fishermen. A few hand signals and moving lips were aimed at us as we moved up the river.

Shirley offered me the helm when we got to the dock. She was a bit apprehensive of her ability to bring the heavy boat in reverse to the dock. This was the first time she had showed any form of ineptitude, and I found a certain childish pleasure in the situation. I refused the helm and sat back on the diver's bench with my feet up and my hands behind my head, prepared for some entertainment.

Shirley piloted the boat to the deep side of the river, where the bank was high and there was no boat traffic. She played the controls to turn the boat to port and then back to starboard as she practiced backing up to an imaginary dock. Seeing Shirley play the boat was like watching a young father teach his son to play ball. She was developing a skill not just to have the skill, but to be impressive with it.

Following Shirley's eyes up and down the river, I knew she was about to cross the river to dock the boat for real. I got up and stood next to her, in case she got nervous and needed my help. She was planning to let the current move the boat to the north, but the current was much weaker by the dock.

Patiently, Shirley idled in neutral a few feet from the docks. The current moved just the bow north, so that when the boat was in a position to back into our slip, it was not straight. Shirley put the port engine in reverse and backed up to the slip. She was too far to the south, and I thought she was going to hit the boat docked on our left. I was just about to tell her to try again when she put the starboard engine in forward, added power to the reversing port engine, and straightening out the boat, she backed perfectly into the slip.

"Are you going to get the lines?" Shirley asked, with a triumphant smirk. I hurried over and tied a stern line. Shirley tied the forward spring line before getting out and tying the bow. She swung back into the boat and cut the engines. She looked at me, as if waiting for a grade after being tested. "Impressive," I said, knowing that I would have pulled back out into the river and tried to back up perfectly. She seemed to accept my approval contentedly.

I checked the pressure gauge on the cascade system, and it read forty-four hundred and fifty pounds. It was close enough to the forty-five-hundred maximum, so I opened the cabin door and stepped down to turn off the dive compressor. Shirley was right behind me, and she wondered aloud what I thought about the transformation of the cabin.

We stepped down so Shirley could show me what Trisha had helped her do the previous night. The brown curtains were gone, replaced with bright yellow ones that Shirley said were the same curtains with the smoke and dirt washed out of them.

The berth cushion had matched the curtains, but it had been stained with coffee and food. Shirley said that she and Trisha had stayed up until two in the morning making a whole new cushion for the berth. I was about to sit on the bright green cushion that looked two inches thicker than the old one, but Shirley grabbed my arm, stopping me. With a big smile, she said, "Trisha told me to make sure you keep your muddy butt off my bed!"

I blushed a bit, but following Shirley's eyes, I remembered that I was wearing the same clothes I had worn the day before, and that they had dirt and grease on them from the boat. Noticing that the wood in the cabin sparkled and that I could smell the same Lemon Pledge that Trisha used at home, I turned around and headed up the stairs to the deck. Shirley followed me up and told me that she wanted to read the rest of Mike's underwater journals.

It was too late for me to go and have coffee with my buddies, because they would be leaving the coffee shop about now to go to the golf course for the late-morning tee-off. Realizing that Shirley was probably tired and needed some "alone time," I told her that I was going to my Wednesday golf game with my buddies.

She reached into the electronics cabinet and unhooked Mike's cell phone, telling me to keep it with me so that if she needed to get in touch with me, she could. Shirley went below as soon as I stepped on the dock. I had to hustle to meet the guys at the golf course. I checked to see that my golf bag was still in the trunk before heading off to play golf.

The guys joked about me not being at the coffee shop for a while. They even asked if I had a mistress. I told them that I had two mistresses, thinking it was quite true: scuba diving and Mike's shipwrecks lured me like mistresses. My golf buddies stopped joking when I teed off with a swing that sent my ball high and straight, landing it farther down the fairway than any drive I could remember.

I played like that all day, which resulted in destroying my club handicap. I was more than hungry after doing two dives, discussing Shirley's role as dive master out on a boat ride, and playing eighteen holes of golf. As my stomach growled for dinner, I felt a little thinner, my back was straighter, and surprisingly, I was not ready for a nap.

The marina was on my way home from the golf course, and I thought I should stop in to check on any unusual activity, but the sun was low in the sky, and I remembered my promise to Trisha to be home when she got out of work.

Remembering Shirley telling me that they had been up until two in the morning, I figured that Trisha would be tired and miserable tonight. I decided to head straight home without stopping at the marina. After all, Shirley was a big girl, and capable of taking care of herself.

The ten-minute ride home seemed a lot longer as my eyes became sleepy. My mind was on the tan couch in my living room at home. I made it home just in time. Trisha's car was just turning the corner up the street when I got out of my car. I sneaked in the back door and tried to think about how I would explain my day's activities. I poured a glass of water and drank it.

Trisha was not so tired or miserable when she came in the back door as I was putting the glass in the sink. She had some Chinese take-home with her. She looked at me with a smile that quickly turned to mock horror. "Your clothes are filthy, and you need a shave," she said. Trisha leaned close to me and continued, "You even smell like a bum!" Then she calmly said, "Go get cleaned up, and I'll have dinner ready when you are done." I noticed that evil gleam in her eyes that usually meant that after dinner she wanted to convince me to go shopping with her or something equally as boring.

I do look like a bum, I realized as I looked in the mirror and shaved. A tired bum at that, and much too tired to go shopping. I cleaned up, and put some clean "shopping clothes" on before going out to face my wife. Trisha had dinner set up on the coffee table in the living room. I was shocked, because I would get yelled at for bringing a bowl of chips in the living room during a game. I sat down for Chinese, and even took my shoes off.

Dinner was enjoyable. Trisha asked me about my day, "Did you enjoy the deep dive, today, Wilbur? Did it go well?"

I answered, "Yes, it went very well. I tried to write my name on the underwater slate during nitrogen narcosis, though, and my handwriting was worse than the writing on your grocery lists!"

"Very funny. Say, how did you like what Shirley and I did with the boat's cabin?"

I laughed. "It looked so neat and domestic that it was unrecognizable as Mike's last home. You know, Trish, Shirley really seems to like you."

Trisha admitted, "Well, it really was fun to spend some time with a younger woman and to be able to talk a little 'girl talk' with her."

I thought to myself that this was leading into a request to go shopping, but to my surprise, Trisha smiled and said she thought I was probably exhausted. She cleaned up the coffee table, handed me the television remote, and disappeared into the kitchen. It was just time for the news.

I heard water running and figured that Trisha was washing dishes. The news was just ending when Trisha came back into the living room. Obviously, she had not been doing the dishes when I had heard water running; it must have been the shower. Trisha was seductively brushing her hair and wearing one of my white dress shirts. It drove me wild forty years ago when Trisha wore nothing except one of my dress shirts, and she knew it. Seeing her skin through the thin white shirt turned me on. I had not been aroused this easily for years. Her firm nipples pointed at me, attracting me as though I were a hungry beast. I started to sit up from my prone position on the couch, but Trisha seductively said, "Stay where you are." She came over and sat on the couch. Her beauty, and her small, warm butt next to my stomach brought back feelings from an age long forgotten.

Going from my comfortable early retirement to learning to scuba dive, preparing to search for certain gold treasure, and playing the best golf game I could remember had been energizing and exhausting at the same time. But right now I wanted only one thing, and my desire for Trisha was more than that of a husband of forty years.

The coffee table got kicked across the room as I rolled her from the couch to the hard floor. I climbed on top of her, ready for sex, and I could have done it right then and there. Something stopped me. I looked at Trisha's surprised eyes and apologized. Getting off her, I said, "It has been so long since I felt this way physically that I forgot how to make love."

I was thinking that Trisha would be more comfortable in our bed, and I reached out to help her off the floor. Her hand shot past mine and around my neck, pulling my face to her lips and inviting the wild animal inside me to rage on.

Lying on my sore back on the living room floor, too exhausted to move, I wondered who I was. No longer feeling like a contented old man, I became resentful of my sixty-one years of age. No amount of contentment, or gold, or excitement could give me the quality of life that the love of the woman lying on the hard floor next to me gave.

Just as I was about to drift off to sleep, Trisha's soft voice said, "I love you as much as I ever have, but I do like the new Wilbur." That woke me up, and I tried to think about how I had changed. My mind was getting sharper, and I was getting into better physical shape. My love life was rekindling. I was becoming more alive. I realized that I too liked the new me better than the path I had been taking to an old age. But I was also still full of fear in some ways. That nameless terror that I did not understand still threatened me sometimes when I went diving, and the robber that had attacked me had made me uneasy and fearful of strangers. Fortunately, though, fear was something that was not normal in my life.

Technical Diving

The next morning, Bernie was already at the boat when I pulled into the marina. The black sky had a shine to it, caused by a bright quarter-moon and a few billion distant suns dancing lively in their places. Bernie informed me that Shirley was in the marina's bathroom, getting cleaned up, and that he had to run up to his pickup truck to get some more gear. As Bernie passed me on the dock, I could smell his cologne. A dive boat is a crowded place, and I had never before noticed Bernie wearing cologne or aftershave. I started putting my diving gear together, and Shirley came back on board. She was cheerful as she asked me, "Hey, Wilbur, you know the enriched air that Mike had on the boat? Is it okay if we use it?"

I told her, "I imagine so, but frankly, I know nothing about using it. There are tanks in the storage behind the helm."

It turned out that Shirley already knew where they were, because she had done some exploring in her new home yesterday. I did not mind. I was thinking about the clear sky and the fact that there was no wind. *The diving should be great this morning.* Bernie came back on board with a green-and-yellow bag like the one Mike had in his storage box.

Bernie opened the hatch on the port side of the boat that exposed the cascade system and the oxygen tank. Looking up at Shirley, he said, "You're right! With enriched air, we can do some special diving. We're all set up for nitrox."

Bernie looked at me, but before he could ask, I said with a smile, "Shirley's in charge of that."

Bernie did not have to ask. Shirley squatted down next to Bernie as he explained how to use the charts to fill the tanks. Shirley grabbed one of Mike's tanks with a green-and-yellow "Enriched air" label on it. Bernie pulled out a long glass tube attached to a dive yoke and handed it to Shirley, who put the yoke on the tank. "Thirty two percent," Shirley said as she removed the air tester from the tank.

Bernie pulled a fill hose up from below; I had not noticed it when I had found the oxygen bottle. It took Bernie and Shirley a good ten minutes to fill the enriched air tank by turning valves and monitoring gauges that were hidden in the hold under the hatch. The second tank took half as long for them to fill.

Bernie was closing up the hatch when Shirley, in an excited voice, yelled, "Bernie!" She had been getting the other green-and-yellow bag out of the storage box and had found another bag and more equipment below the deck. Mike had cut out the deck under the storage box to hide more gear.

Bernie looked in the storage box and immediately stepped inside and squatted down. Shirley was piling up the gear all over the deck as Bernie handed it up to her. I started helping and realized that Bernie was standing on the hull of the boat, pulling gear out from under the deck. Shirley was pointing a flashlight into the area when Bernie said, "Here it is."

Bernie handed up a hard yellow case about the size of a shoe box. Shirley shone the flashlight on it and read out loud, "Underwater Global Positioning Satellite System." Excited, I thought that today we might dive on one of Mike's wrecks. Shirley looked around, held her finger to her mouth, and made a shushing sound.

Shirley put the GPS in her cabin and came up to start the engines. Bernie reminded her that Mark was on his way. Shirley asked, "Where is Mike's computer?"

Bernie said, "The sun will up in twenty minutes, and we'll find it then."

Our excitement would have to be contained until we were out in the seclusion of the lake. Bernie's excitement about the gear did not have to wait. He told me that there had to be at least five thousand dollars worth of technical dive equipment scattered on the deck. I was not sure what I was looking at and had to ask, "Wasn't Mike too old for technical diving?"

Bernie seemed a little hurt when he said, "Actually, Mike didn't buy his technical diving equipment, special tanks, and gear for really deep dives from my shop. He took a trip to New Jersey two years ago to take a course in technical diving. Mike was certified as a technical diver, but I didn't think he did any technical diving around here. With this specialized equipment, Mike could have been diving to depths as deep as three hundred feet," he concluded.

The thought of a three-hundred-foot dive terrified me.

Bernie said, "I've only read about technical diving myself. I never had the money to take the necessary training."

Shirley really shocked him then when she said, "Bernie, I want you to know that I am a tech-diving apprentice."

Mark showed up, and Shirley started the engines as Bernie ran up to help Mark with his gear. Mark had a small bag in his hand, and he reminded Bernie that he had left his gear on the boat. Bernie had the lines untied by the time Mark stepped on the boat. Mark looked at the tech gear on the deck and said, "Wow," before he could even say hi.

The boat jerked away from the dock, and Shirley said, "Sorry! I'd better keep it slow, so my wake doesn't anger people." Bernie took the helm as we finally greeted Mark, who was still waiting for an answer as to who the tech diver was.

I told Mark that Shirley was the tech diver, and with an astonished face, he used my expression, "Cool," and began getting his gear together. I wondered if Mark was being condescending, but then I just figured that the expression might be coming back in style. The latter was probably the case, as Mark seemed excited about diving and asked me if I was going to be his dive buddy. The boat was certified for eighteen divers and two crew members, but as the morning dawned, the boat appeared very crowded with all the tech gear scattered around.

Shirley waited until we had rounded the breakwall and Bernie had gotten the boat up on plane before bringing the underwater GPS up on deck. Bernie pointed to the helm as he looked at me, so I asked Mark, "Want to drive?" Youthful excitement sent Mark up to relieve Bernie, and I stood next to Mark as he took the helm. Mark's teeth showed through his smile and amplified the warmth of the sunrise.

Bernie and Shirley sat in the back of the boat, playing with the underwater GPS. Bernie had an instruction book out and was giving directions to Shirley. Mark looked back at the couple before turning to me and asking, "Where are we diving this morning?"

I had not given much thought about where to dive, because I was looking at the dead-calm lake and thinking it did not matter. I shrugged casually and replied, "I don't care." Mark smiled and seemed to agree.

We were a mile out, heading west, parallel with the shore, when Bernie told me very suddenly to turn left. Bernie and Shirley were right behind us, staring at the GPS. I watched the depth sounder decreasing from a hundred feet, and it felt good to think that Bernie had found one of Mike's wrecks on the GPS and that it was in shallow water.

Bernie was giving commands in compass headings.

"One seventy-five."

"One-seventy."

"One-eighty."

"Slow down."

Mark brought the boat to an idle as Bernie pointed with his hand. Bernie never took his eyes off the small screen as he guided us to an invisible location.

"Neutral!" Bernie barked. A moment later, Bernie's hand reached up and hit the anchor-release control, sending our heavy anchor down only forty-two feet to the hidden mystery below.

I could hear everyone's breathing as the anchor took hold and the boat swung to face the current coming from the west. Bernie was still staring at the small screen when Shirley broke the silence. "There is only one waypoint on the GPS, and this is it."

We looked at Bernie and waited for him to look up from the GPS. When he finally did, in a voice both excited and disappointed he said, "Unfortunately, Mike only has one waypoint on his GPS, and we are here."

I shut off the engines and listened to the peaceful quiet of Lake Ontario on a rare calm day. The sun rose somewhere through the gray haze that would darken our dive. Still, the thought of a forty-foot dive in extremely calm water eased any diving jitters I might have had. Instead, the idea of finding a shipwreck or some golden treasure drove my desire to get in the water.

Mark wore a black wet suit, while Bernie and I had matching black-and-bright orange dry suits that turned gray at the bottom. Shirley had a black dry suit with bright blue arms and shoulders. As we put our dive suits on, Bernie provided us with a dive briefing.

We were to get in the water and wait until everyone was ready to descend at the anchor line. I felt good when Bernie announced that I would be Mark's dive buddy. That meant that Bernie had enough faith in both Mark's and my diving ability that we did not need an instructor or a dive master with us. Mark confirmed his pleasure by saying, "Cool! No underwater babysitter."

Bernie continued, with a serious expression that demonstrated careful planning despite his obvious eagerness to get in the water.

"On the bottom, we will split up, with Shirley and I doing a search pattern to the north. You and Mark will do a series of square patterns to the south.

Each time you get to where the anchor line should be, just do a pattern that is larger than the first by the amount of visibility that we have."

We listened intently to Bernie as he explained how to signal by banging a dive tool three times on the back of our tanks if we found something. Then he explained that if we did find something like a wreck, we would be free to explore it, as long as we did not take any souvenirs.

With a look at the hazy sky, Bernie reminded us to take our flashlights, but warned Mark and me that because of our lack of experience in this type of underwater situation, we should not go inside of a sunken ship, even though we might see Shirley and him penetrate the wreck. With Bernie's last word, "wreck," on my mind, I suited up quickly.

Feeling alive and energetic, my young dive buddy and I did an extra-careful buddy check before performing back rolls off the side of the boat. A little water filled my mask when I dropped below the surface, but without any effort or discomfort, I exhaled through my nose, my left hand holding the top of my mask to my forehead. The exhaled air filled my mask, forcing the water out the bottom.

Bernie was on the boat, waiting for us to give the okay signal as we floated up to the surface. Once the signal was given and understood, Mark and I switched to snorkels and darted eagerly to the anchor line. I had my face in the water, hoping for a glimpse of some majestic shape on the lake's bottom.

I never heard the splashes from Bernie or Shirley hitting the water, but I lifted my head when Bernie's voice rang out, saying, "Ready?" I looked up and joined the other divers as we raised our inflator hoses above our heads and left the calm gray heaven for the seductive deep, with an excited anticipation of solving one of Mike's mysteries.

As the shadowy figure of the boat's hull disappeared from overhead, I could feel myself smile, knowing that we were getting closer to the bottom. The four of us descended slowly, exchanging thoughts, through our underwater eye communication, that only showed a comfortable existence in our surroundings, which most of mankind had never experienced.

A strange sound came from Mark's exposed mouth; it sounded kind of like, "Yeehahhh." Lake stones and sparse patches of green seaweed appeared not just below us, but all around us. Visibility was at least thirty feet, and we all gave fist "high fives" as we adjusted our buoyancy to float neutrally at five feet from the bottom.

Our underwater world was a beautiful combination of gray and brown rocks, with the patches of seaweed swaying in a mild current the way that wheat danced to the silent wind in a farmer's field. Bernie's suit lost its bright color at the depth, and the only sound was that of our exhaled bubbles moving upward past our ears.

Bernie checked his compass and pointed into the current, signaling Mark and me to start our search pattern. Holding our compasses in front of us, we started swimming west into the current. I was counting kick cycles, figuring that fifteen would cover the area we could see. Bernie and Shirley moved north, but we could still see their bright yellow tanks when they turned west about thirty feet from us.

At fifteen kicks, I added two extras to compensate for the current, before turning south. Mark was right next to me, and turned with me. I lost count of my fifteen kicks when a large lake trout darted in front of us. Mark was pointing to it as I looked at him to see if he'd seen it too.

I started counting from five as we continued moving south. Mark stopped and turned at my eleven kicks, and I guessed that he was keeping better count than I was. We swam east, and I began counting again. We began noticing small fish hanging around the seaweed patches. It seemed that the more comfortable I got underwater, the more I would see.

There were minnows everywhere, and a few crayfish were scampering on the rocks. As we turned north on our fourth leg, I noticed a pair of large drumfish following us. I pointed them out to Mark, who was busy reading his compass. The drumfish seemed to be enjoying the dive with us, when Mark stopped swimming and pointed ahead.

I expected to see the anchor, but I was astounded at what was peeking at us from ahead. Mark and I cautiously moved toward a bright white animal figure. I thought that maybe I was suffering (or enjoying) nitrogen narcosis again. Mark and I were three feet from the creature when we looked at each other with disbelief in our eyes.

Mike Moresby's Marine Park

I bent over to reach for my dive knife, but stopped when I heard Mark give the three loud bangs on his tank. I wondered whether Bernie and Shirley could hear the signal as I looked at the five-foot-tall reindeer. It was a freshly painted bright white, with only a few troublesome zebra mussels attached to it. The zebra mussels glimmered like the Christmas lights that had probably once decorated this lawn ornament.

I heard a faint three-bang knock in return. Mark gave the signal again, and the return signal was louder. About ten feet away was another figure. Mark and I swam closer and noticed more of what must have been Mike's idea of an underwater scuba divers' park.

A model airplane made out of some kind of metal was anchored to the bottom, with a square pad of concrete holding it in place. Mark banged again and the other dive team replied with three bangs that were much louder than before. A moment later, two divers appeared among the menagerie of figures on display on the bottom.

There were no eye gleams of disappointment at not finding a sunken ship with gold, but instead we gave congratulatory fist bangs as we explored the underwater park with enthusiasm and bewilderment. An underwater park that no one ever knew about was a strange but significant discovery.

As we swam over and around the displaced figurines, I saw that fish seemed abundant in the area. The figures must have provided some entertainment for the marine creatures as well as for us. Mark held his hand out in front of me to get my attention. He pointed to his pressure gauge and signaled that he had eight hundred pounds of air left. I checked my gauge and was a little surprised to find that I was almost out of air.

I signaled to Mark by holding up three fingers, indicating that I only had three hundred pounds of air left. I immediately followed with the thumbs-up signal to ascend. Bernie and Shirley were not in sight as Mark and I dumped our BCD air and managed a slow swim to the surface. Thinking of the underwater figures, I was only a little apprehensive as we surfaced without the aid of an anchor line.

We were in the area transiting from brown water to gray water, with only each other in sight. I watched my bubbles ascending faster than we were rising, and knew that we were all right. I checked my pressure gauge, but before I could read it, Mark's hand reached in front of me with his spare regulator.

I spit my regulator out and accepted Mark's spare. By the time I could grab his BCD to hold on, keeping us together, the gray water lightened and a clear area above us opened up like a round porthole to another world. I wondered how far we would be from the boat when finally broke out of the serenity and into a world I thought I was more familiar with.

I had enough air in my tank to fill my BCD as we broke the surface together. I let go of Mark's regulator and pulled my mask down to talk to Mark. Mark put air in his BCD and pulled his mask down as well.

I said, "That was great!"

Mark asked, "What were those things?"

"When did Mike put them there?" I wondered.

"Where is the boat?"

Looking at Mark's face, I knew he was okay, so I answered his question by saying, "Who cares?" Mark laughed, and as he turned around, he saw the boat twenty feet behind him. We slowly made our way to the boat without putting our masks on or using our snorkels.

The retiree and the college student were too full of excitement to worry about anything. We climbed on the boat and wondered where Bernie and Shirley were. Bubbles breaking the surface assured us that they were only forty feet behind the boat. Mark and I removed our gear and relaxed as Mark reminded me that experienced divers seemed to use less air than us beginners.

Five minutes later, Bernie surfaced together with Shirley, right at the ladder. Bernie took off his mask when he stood on the back of the boat next to the smiling Shirley. Slapping his forehead, he said, "It's an underwater GPS for finding locations when you're in the water! We were underwater. Why didn't I take it with us?" We all laughed and began talking about what we had seen.

Looking from Mark to me and back, Bernie asked, "Who saw it first?"

I said, "Mark." Mark just grinned.

"Congratulations!" Bernie exclaimed. "You discovered something really big, although I am not sure what it is."

Bernie had a way of making people feel good, and Mark was ecstatic as he announced, "Michael Moresby's Marine Park. Let's call it Michael Moresby's Marine Park!"

Shirley suggested that we do a second dive, asking, "Where do you want to dive next?"

"Here!" we all said simultaneously, and then laughed. Bernie said we could use the underwater GPS this time, but pointed out that the park was right under the back of the boat, making the luxury of an underwater GPS unnecessary.

Using Mark's recreational dive planner, I determined that we could dive for thirty-nine minutes if we suited back up and jumped in right away. Mark agreed, and Bernie approved our plan.

With fresh tanks on and still no fear, we entered the water from the back of the boat. Mark and I left the increasing haziness of the surface for our underwater world of youthful serenity and adventure. We descended at the back of the boat without the anchor line. It felt a little funny at first, but the bottom appeared and we landed next to a snowmobile with a sculptured-wire bear driving it.

I marveled at the construction of the exhibits in Mike's park as we counted twenty-one of the humorously designed art pieces that were mixed in with some plain old junk, like an exercise machine that still worked. Mark sat on it and moved the weight bar up and down.

Bernie and Shirley swam by us a couple of times, and it was fun to see other divers enjoying Mike's park. I checked my time and pressure often, so that I would not run low on air again. Thirty-five minutes into the dive, I was getting tired, and with a thousand pounds of air left, I signaled Mark to ascend.

Mark returned the signal, and we looked around one last time. A clown made out of wire and old car rims seemed to wave good-bye as we began our ascent. The ascent was the same as the first time, but it felt more natural. I was tired and ready to relax on the boat when we broke the surface.

Being forty-two feet up and hearing the sound of our own splashing were the only things that let us know we were on the surface. The hazy sky had fallen onto the lake's surface with a fog that blended gray water with grayer air. I reached out and grabbed Mark, so that we would not get separated. I became nervous and had trouble filling my BCD.

I still had my regulator in my mouth and my mask on when I noticed Mark smiling, with his mask around his neck. Somehow, having a dive buddy with me made me relax and fight off any panic that was haunting me from the blindness caused by the fog. I took a few deep breaths to calm myself down, so that I could assume the relaxed position that Mark was in. We held on to each other's vests as we slowly turned, looking and listening in every direction.

I was thinking about how young Mark was and what a tragedy it would be if we never found the boat, and just drifted out to sea, never to be seen again. Mark held up his compass and said, "Shore is to the south, and we are not too far away." *For a twenty-year-old,* I thought, *it might be feasible to just swim to shore, but I would just rather float until someone finds me.*

"*Kangaroo! Kangaroo! Kangaroo!*" The radio on the boat was on. *Kangaroo* was the name of another fishing boat from the Oak Orchard Marina. Someone was hailing it, and we could hear the call coming from our boat, but it was too difficult to tell where the sound was coming from.

Mark looked at his compass and said, "This way," pointing into the endless gray haze.

I had become physically relaxed, so I put on my mask and put my snorkel in my mouth. Mark saw me and decided to do the same, but he pulled his hood down to enhance his hearing. We swam slowly, trying not to make any noise in the water that would negate our ability to hear the radio.

Again the radio came to life, and it sounded like it was right in front of us. "*Kangaroo! Kangaroo! Kangaroo!*" Then silence fell upon us, but we swam a little faster, knowing that we were going in the right direction. I was concerned that we might swim right past the boat when I heard a clunk right in front of me.

Mark had swum right into a wall of white steel. We looked at each other and laughed, knowing that we had found the boat. Mark would not take his hand away from the boat as we tried to find the stern, with our ladder to safety. We made it to the ladder and felt our way up.

"Bernie? Shirley?" I called out to see if they were on the boat. They were not. Mark and I removed our weight belts and scuba units and sat quietly, listening for the other divers. A few minutes passed, and my concern was growing.

Mark called out, "Bernie? Shirley? Anybody?" But his calls were answered by a lonesome silence, broken only by the sound of our own heartbeats.

I was about to say something (or at least think something that would have created a noise, at least in my mind) when a nearby whistling sound broke the silence. The whistle was followed by Bernie's voice asking, "What did you guys do with the boat?"

I hollered into the haze, "It's right where we left it!"

We heard a few splashes, and then the ladder clanged, as if someone were climbing up it. Shirley's blue dry suit appeared from two feet in front of my eyes. She had to feel her way across the deck to take her gear off. Bernie appeared next and said that he was glad we had found the boat. We removed our gear and huddled in the helm area of the boat, barely able to see each other.

Bernie picked up the radio's microphone and hailed, "*Sea Dog, Sea Dog,* this is the *Gold Hunter!*"

Instantly the radio barked, "*Gold Hunter!* This is *Sea Dog!* Go to six-eight." Bernie set the microphone back on its hook and removed a microphone from higher up on the electronics box. He reached inside and turned on the other radio.

"*Sea Dog,* this is *Gold Hunter* on six-eight."

"*Gold Hunter!* What can I do for you? *Sea Dog* over."

"*Sea Dog,* I am anchored in forty feet of water and can't even see my nose. How is it where you are? *Gold Hunter* over."

"*Gold Hunter,* I am three miles out and enjoying clear skies and warm sunshine. There is a low layer of fog along the shoreline going west of Oak Orchard. *Sea Dog* over."

"*Sea Dog,* thanks much! We'll head north until we come out of the soup. *Gold Hunter* out!"

"*Sea Dog* out!"

Bernie hung the microphone up and said "Head 'em up! And move 'em out!" Mark and I went back and raised the dive ladder as Bernie started the engines. Shirley was somewhere in between, helping relay communications. We could not even feel the boat moving as Bernie headed north. Shirley was standing on the gunwale, looking ahead; Mark and I looked out abeam. It seemed useless to look for other boats when we could not even see across our boat.

Slowly, patches of water came into view, and finally we emerged from under the dark blanket of fog into the brightly lit morning with blue skies and silver water. We rearranged gear, and Bernie gave Mark the helm, telling him to keep it at idle for a while.

Bernie fished a gallon-sized plastic bag out of his BCD pocket. Shirley was right at his side when he carefully shook the water off the bag and opened it up. Inside was a sheet of paper that had a note from Mike on it, saying: *Whoever finds this place should share it with divers from all over.* It was written in Mike's handwriting and signed simply "Mike."

Mark was the only one that truly thought that Mike had left a treasure and that the statues made of wire and junk were that treasure. Glances from Shirley reminded us to keep quiet about the shipwrecks we had hoped to find. I did not like keeping Mark in the dark, but I thought that Shirley was looking out for his best interests, since she didn't want Mark to have to be involved in a criminal investigation.

The breakwall extended out of the fog, as if a guiding hand were showing us the port. Mark sat on the bow, ready to tell Bernie if he was about to hit anything. The fog was not as thick as it was on the lake, leaving patches of clear water around the boat. Shirley and I stood at the transom, directing Bernie into the slip.

The boat was still a mess of gear as we tied the *Gold Hunter* to its dock. Bernie was in a hurry to open the shop, and Mark had to get to class. Bernie explained that Mike used to lend him some tanks when they went on a trip like the weekend trip to Tobermory.

Remembering that Bernie was going to be gone for the weekend gave me a bit of an empty feeling. Bernie asked how many tanks I needed for the weekend. I shrugged my shoulders and said, "I don't know."

Shirley asked, "How many divers are in the group?"

Remembering Abraham Buffield made me wish that it was just Bernie, Shirley, and Mark diving for wrecks with me this weekend. "Abraham said that he was bringing three or four divers with him," I recalled.

Bernie looked up into the lifting fog and moved his lips as he counted to himself. "You'll need twenty-one tanks if you and Shirley dive and you guys do three dives a day. That means you have fifteen extra tanks." Bernie asked if he could borrow ten tanks for his trip. Looking at the equipment scattered all over the boat and thinking it would make the boat less crowded, I agreed and received an approving nod from the now-serious-looking Shirley.

Bernie sent Mark up to the parking lot to back his pickup truck closer to the dock. Mark hefted two tanks, one in each hand, and headed up the hill to the parking area. Shirley started sliding tanks on the dock, while Bernie grabbed two and started up the hill. I picked up two of the forty-pound tanks, and although I was feeling stronger than I had in a long time, it was a real struggle to carry the tanks.

Bernie met me on his way down the hill. He took the heavy tanks from me and asked if I could go get some coffee for him and Mark, because they wouldn't have time. I appreciated the help and the way he had offered it. Bernie's sensitivity to a person's capabilities was just as good on land as in the water.

I followed the wharf fifty feet to the steps that went up to the marina instead of walking up the eight-foot incline of the hill, so that I could catch my breath.

I should have carried one tank at a time. I considered the fact that Bernie was half my age, and then felt old, thinking that Mark was almost half Bernie's age.

I fixed the coffees in Styrofoam cups and put extra cream and sugar in the one for Mark. I put the lids on and dug into my pocket for some money. Bill Reed asked, "Find anything good?" letting me know that he was going to accept the money for the coffee this time.

Instantly, Mike's underwater park came into my mind, but I was getting so used to secrets that I just smiled and said, "Maybe."

The truck was loaded, and Bernie was putting tanks on top of wet gear, so that the gear would not blow off the truck as it dried on the way back to Batavia. I noticed the look on Shirley's face as Mark said good-bye.

"Call me Deb! My friends call me Deb." Shirley said to Mark.

"See ya later, Diver Deb!" Mark called back as he turned to sprint to his car.

Bernie looked at Shirley and then at me. I could tell that they wanted some time, so I said good-bye to Bernie and strolled down the hill to the boat. I looked back as I boarded the boat, and saw the couple in an affectionate embrace next to the truck. I liked both of them and felt happy at the idea that their friendship might blossom into something more. I could not think of any of my old friends who were not married with school-age children by the time they were Bernie's and Shirley's ages.

The fog had evaporated into the sunny blue sky, and I unwrapped a cigar. I lit the cigar and took a big puff just as Shirley climbed on board. The emotions that had filled her eyes a few moments ago had been replaced with the stern look of the investigator that hid behind the dive master I cared about as if she were my own daughter.

"Who drives white vans with red lettering on the side?" Shirley's question broke the serenity of the moment. I was thinking about her telling Mark that her name was Deb, and I was thinking that Shirley Tempest might be an alias.

Without much thought about the white vans, I said, "I don't know, but tell me about your name."

"Fair enough," she said, her stern look remaining dark and prying. "My real name is Debbie O'Hara. I had to use the name Shirley Tempest to infiltrate the ring of black-market precious-metals dealers—some of whom we will be meeting tomorrow." Her gaze eased a moment, and she continued, "You can call me Deb too."

I smiled at my correct assumption, and asked about the vans. Debbie explained that there was one at the point by the breakwall and another parked in an open lot three miles west of the point. They might be watching us, and they could triangulate our position on the lake from those two vantage points. There was also a white van parked at the far end of the parking lot. It sat inconspicuously next to a dry-docked boat with its name on the side blocked out

"Do you think we are being watched?" I asked, sounding disappointed. I really just wanted to talk about the dive site we had found, but I knew that Shirley's (or Deb's) investigation took precedence. Deb's eyes shifted in both directions before she suggested that we clean up the boat.

It took an hour to put away the tech gear that Mike had acquired for some deep diving nobody knew about. Then I hung up our BCDs and dry suits to dry. I was thankful for the distraction, because it gave us time to decide that it was a good idea to tell people about Mike's marine park. It would take suspicion away from the divers who would be looking for the treasure.

We decided that the gear would be safe from vandals or thieves, and left it hanging on the boat. Deb went with me to tell Bill Reed about the underwater marine park, and to ask him to keep a watch on our gear so we could go to breakfast.

Bill was both excited and surprised to learn that Mike had placed twenty-one "art objects" in a location on the lake's bed. He half-jokingly told us that he would have to start stocking diving equipment at the marina.

Lakeside Restaurant shared a parking lot with fishermen that fished off the breakwall, as well as people that used the county's boat launch next to it. I was shocked to see a white van with big red letters reading "Schmidt's Jewelers—Boston, Massachusetts" on its sides. The van was backing a fast-looking speedboat into the water with the name *Seaya* painted on the transom.

Deb said, "Don't stare," and opened her door to go inside the restaurant. We got a table next to the window that faced our earlier dive site. We watched two men load scuba diving equipment onto the *Seaya* while we ordered breakfast. Debbie ordered another fruit cup and coffee, but the smell of bacon was strong in the restaurant, so I ordered two eggs, over easy, bacon, and home-fried potatoes. Debbie looked at me with disapproving eyes, so I added whole wheat toast to my order, and a cup of decaf.

I recognized all five of the patrons in the restaurant and let Debbie know that they were all local people. She relaxed and said, "Wait until they find out about the Park." We both smirked as the fast boat headed out to our dive site. They were at the dive site by the time we were served our breakfast. We could see the red flag with the white diagonal stripe go up. They were too far away to see clearly. We both ate fast, agreeing that we wanted to drive up the shore to get a better look when they surfaced.

The heavy meal slowed me down and made me a bit drowsy as we left the restaurant. Debbie asked for the car keys, which I happily gave her. It took her a minute to adjust the seat before starting the engine. All she said was, "I want to see them surface." It was the girlish diver and not the serious investigator that peeled out of the parking lot.

I hadn't known that my car could move so fast. Debbie flew down Lake Shore Road until we had gone about the distance to the dive park. Debbie pulled down a lane, going slower to avoid raising a lot of dust. The lane ended between two cottages, and she parked the car. Debbie pulled a pair of binoculars from her purse, making me think that her purse must have a magical ability to produce anything.

The fast boat was anchored right in front of us, but there were no people in sight. Debbie was looking through the binoculars when she proclaimed, "I can see their bubbles." She handed me the binoculars and directed me to a spot off the back of the boat, about twenty feet away. Sure enough, there were divers' bubbles.

In total silence, we waited for the divers to surface, so that we could hear them talk when they broke the surface. We were too far away to hear anything, but with the dead-calm water and total silence around us, we hoped the flat water would carry the sounds.

Debbie was watching through the binoculars when I saw the first of the divers pop up. Silence. Then the other diver popped up, and within seconds, we could clearly hear two distinct voices talking angrily to each other. The sound was distorted, but one of them said loudly in an angry voice, "What the hell is this, anyway? It's just a bunch of statues underwater!"

The other one sounded equally enraged. "It's not my fault we wasted our time. I thought we were looking for gold, not an underwater Disney adventure!"

Debbie let out a little snicker as she enjoyed their displeasure. We hung around and watched them struggle up the small ladder on the back of the boat. One diver had to stay in the water and hold the other diver's equipment as he climbed the ladder. Once he was inside the boat, the equipment was handed up and pulled over the side before the other diver could climb up the ladder. I was thinking of Mike's dive ladder and thanking him for building such a large and comfortable one.

Debbie started the engine, and we drove back to the marina at a normal speed. Debbie said, "I think this is just the beginning. Tomorrow it will be a circus out there. A deadly circus!"

Back on the boat, Debbie decided that she should attend tomorrow's auction as Deb the dive master. She had intended to go as Shirley Tempest, the gold buyer, but her cover as a dive master would put her in the middle of the gold hunt. I liked the idea, because Shirley the investigator was not as much fun as Debbie the diver.

Bruce O'Connor's voice came from the river. "How's the diving?" We looked up and saw the sheriff's boat, with Bruce at the helm. I waved and quietly asked Debbie if she wanted to meet the local law. She nodded yes, so I hailed the deputy over, telling him that we had found something in the lake that morning.

He pulled the sheriff's boat into Captain Jack's slip, and Debbie and I tied his lines. Bruce's smile said a lot about his personality. He was genuinely happy, and this was the case this morning.

"This is Debbie, my new dive master," I said.

Bruce held out his hand to help her onto the sheriff's boat, and without waiting for me to introduce him, he said, "Call me Bruce!"

I climbed up onto the taller boat and sat on the gunwale next to Debbie. Bruce made a comment about what a good-looking dive master I had before asking what we had for him. I noticed his face became serious for a moment, and Debbie looked at me.

Not quite knowing how to start, I blurted out, "We found an underwater marine park with twenty-one figurines that Mike left on the bottom of the lake."

Bruce laughed and said, "Twenty-four." I exchanged shocked glances with Debbie, and we remained speechless.

Bruce explained that Mike had wanted to leave something behind that divers could remember him by. "We made the figures in my barn and took them out at night. People just thought we were practicing rescue maneuvers out in the lake."

Debbie looked inquisitively at Bruce and asked if he was a diver too. He said he was.

"What else do you know about Mike's findings in the lake?" Debbie spoke softly and scanned the marina once more. I could tell from the look Bruce gave me that he knew I had been holding something back when I reported the attack.

Bruce studied Debbie's face for a few seconds, but he wasn't able to read her, and he turned to me for an answer. But it was Debbie who broke the silence.

"Wilbur, do you trust Bruce?" I answered with an unhesitating affirmative, and Bruce's smile returned.

Debbie said, "I think that Bruce and I need to go someplace where we can talk about investigative matters in private." As Bruce started his engine, I offered to stay with the boat. I climbed down on the dock, untied the lines, and watched as the two cops left for the open waters of the calm lake.

It took an hour to fill the tanks. I had the compressor running when the sheriff's deputy brought Debbie back. I saw them coming up the river, and Debbie waved with a friendly salute that couldn't be mistaken for a distress signal. Bruce brought the boat up to the dock so that Debbie could jump off. I was happy to see the enthusiastic faces of two divers instead of the serious faces of professional law enforcers.

The first words out of Debbie's mouth confirmed the reason for the smiling diver faces. "Do you want to do a night dive tonight?" I had never dove at night and was exhausted from two dives already. Debbie must have recognized my hesitation. She explained, "Mike asked Bruce to keep the park a secret for a month after his death. But since we already found it, Bruce is excited and wants to bring two of his buddies to see the park."

Debbie was as excited as a little girl when she finished, "Some of the figures are painted with phosphorescent paint that glows in the dark." I was intrigued, and said that I wasn't sure whether or not I would dive, but I would at least drive the boat. Debbie smiled and turned to the waiting Bruce and gave him a thumbs-up. We were to meet at eight o'clock, she explained.

Bruce headed back out to the lake. "What did you and Bruce talk about?" I asked.

Smiling, Debbie said, "Well, we actually mostly talked about diving. But as for the investigation, you were completely right to trust Bruce. Our plan is that he'll watch the boat while we go to the auction in the morning."

"I want to go home and look over Mike's wreck journals again."

"Good," Debbie said. "And I want to call my office to bring them up to date on the case. I can do that in the cabin." She was cheerful when I left. The marina was a friendly place to hang out.

I was reading Mike's journal for the third time when Trisha came home. "Trish, I think I should let you know what I found out today. It turns out that Shirley's real name is Debbie. She works for the Bureau of Criminal Investigation and is looking into the possibility that Mike was selling gold on the black market. She met with Bruce O'Connor today to talk about the case."

"Wow! That's really something! She's such a friendly girl that it's hard to imagine her as a hard-nosed police officer too, but I guess that's what 'undercover' means. I hope Mike wasn't in any trouble, though." Trisha suggested that we take Debbie out for dinner before the dive. She also said that she wanted to go out on the boat for the night dive.

I called Debbie on her cell phone to ask about dinner. She responded with enthusiasm, and we agreed to meet at the marina in half an hour.

As I hung up, I tried to think of a time when Trisha had been so agreeable about doing the things I was interested in. Sadly, I realized that I had not asked Trisha to do anything with me for a long time. Trisha had not changed; I had. But now I was more alive than ever, and after resting, I was ready to dive again.

Lakeside Restaurant was an informal place to eat dinner. The restaurant was full of people at the dinner hour, but we still got a table with a good view of the lake. Fishing boats were coming back from the day's trawling for salmon or lake trout, and small cabin cruisers were heading out with people escaping their work pressures for an evening on the water.

A waitress hardly old enough to be out of school took our orders. Trisha ordered a broiled-fish dinner and nonfat salad dressing. I just ordered a salad, a bowl of French onion soup, and a fish sandwich. I did indulge myself by ordering a large glass of milk, though.

Debbie had had a busy day and must have decided that she would need plenty of nourishment, namely a jumbo cheeseburger, cottage-fried potatoes, and a large Diet Pepsi with a slice of lemon in it. She mumbled something about not having had lunch.

The conversation was lively, and Trisha seemed genuinely interested in scuba diving and in the way Debbie described how she pictured the underwater world. Debbie promised to show Trisha some pictures of the Caribbean and told us that she would take her underwater camera with her tonight. Listening to Debbie describe night diving to Trisha during dinner convinced me that I would dive tonight. The sun was glaring into the restaurant through the windows, providing a blast of welcome warmth before the August evening. It also signaled that it was time to head for the boat.

By seven thirty, Bruce and his two diving colleagues, Jim Beach and Cary Crane, were at the boat. We loaded up gear and headed out into the river. Trisha seemed eager to see the sunset. Using Mike's underwater GPS, we dropped anchor at the marine park just as the sun appeared to sizzle into the water.

Bruce opted to wait on the boat with Trisha. Jim was a forty-year-old sheriff's deputy who had learned to dive while on vacation in Puerto Rico. His short brush cut added to his military look and personality. He was going to dive with Cary, a pilot for United Transport who lived in Rochester, but who was born and learned to dive in the Bahamas. His Bahamian accent sounded almost British, which seemed funny coming from a face that was shaded by a New York Yankees hat.

That left me to dive with Debbie, and I was thankful for that, because I felt comfortable and safe with her and felt that she understood the nervousness that still came over me sometimes during a dive. We raced the sun into the water and beat it by the five seconds Bruce was counting down as we strode off the boat, one at a time. In the water, we checked our flashlights, then followed Debbie to the anchor line, where we descended together.

I had no fear of the dark, thinking that the bright stars would greet me instead of thick fog this time. It was also greatly assuring to have Bruce, an experienced diver and boat captain, waiting on the boat. We pointed our flashlights down so that we would not point them in each other's faces and give each other night blindness.

The bottom appeared, and this time we moved east and found the first figure, which was ten feet from the anchor. Shining my light on it made the wire model of a tugboat glow green with a red top. There were more fish than I had ever seen before on any dive. All sizes and kinds of fish seemed to move around the figures, as if they were in a museum, looking at art.

A big eel slipped through the hole on a wire pickup truck with real tire rims. I was hearing a strange sound, and I looked around for the source. Debbie made a signal with her hand that looked like a fish swimming, and then moved her hands, alternating up and down, as if she were holding something in each hand.

I finally realized what she was trying to tell me. *Drumfish.* I pointed my flashlight at a pair of them that seemed to be following Jim and Carrie. I looked back at Debbie, and she pointed her flashlight toward her chin, and with her eyes closed, she nodded in agreement. We never lost sight of the other divers, because the beams of their flashlights lit up the area all around them. Debbie showed me three small ceramic yard decorations that we had not noticed before. A green frog, a brown turtle, and a pair of squirrels were peeking out of a patch of short seaweed next to a wire lighthouse. The three figures did not glow in our flashlight beams, and they seemed to decorate an imaginary front yard of the lighthouse, which glowed blue with a ball of white in the center, where a light would have been. We were having a really good time on the dive, and I couldn't help but think of Mike and how pleased he would have been right then.

Debbie had me check my pressure gauge. Signaling that I had twelve hundred pounds left, I felt as if we had just got to the bottom, but I knew by the amount of things we had looked at that it was almost time to ascend. Debbie got her camera out and had all of us squish down in front of the lighthouse for a picture.

The flash was blinding, but I imagined that the picture would be worth it. By the time my eyes could see my surroundings, one of the other divers was pointing the camera at me, and I noticed Debbie's blue-gloved hand waving to the camera. She was right next to me. I closed my eyes for the second picture, and could see pretty well afterward.

Debbie gave me the thumbs-up signal and I returned it, acknowledging that I was ready to ascend. There was no white hole this time as we ascended the forty-two feet to the surface, but Bruce had the boat lit up with the anchor light on the roof and a spotlight that he aimed from the roof to the deck, making the boat stand out brightly in the darkness.

The familiar sound of excited divers filled the dark air behind the boat. I did not remember adding air to my BCD or pulling my mask down. I just relished in the conversation about the strange things we had just seen and heard. Jim claimed to have smelled hot electrical wires around the lit-up figures. We all laughed as we made our way to the dive ladder.

Bruce drove the boat back to Oak Orchard. Trisha seemed interested in hearing about Mike's underwater park, and I even thought briefly about taking her down to see it. But I didn't think she would be comfortable with diving; I remembered her reluctance years ago, when Mike and I first went diving together. Lakeside Restaurant was lit up with different-colored beer signs and lights, which made the harbor easy to find.

The experienced divers had loaded their gear by the time we reached the dock, and everyone was gone within five minutes. Debbie helped me stow the rest of my gear.

"Pick me up at ten," Debbie said as I helped Trisha up to the dock.

"Okay, and good night," I replied, escorting my beautiful wife toward the car.

Driving Trisha home, my mind was full of exotic scuba diving vacations, that Fiat Spider convertible I had wanted since college, and the thought of showering my lovely wife with fancy gold jewelry. In the silence, Trisha held my free hand, bringing my mind back to my teacher's pension that provided us with such a simple life. An image of piles of gold waiting in the clear, cold water filtered into my mind as I thought that tomorrow, after the Friday auction, I would find a lost treasure.

The Hunt Is On

Sheriff's deputy Bruce O'Connor was reinstalling the GPS that had been locked safely away at the sheriff's office when I picked up Debbie at ten o'clock. This gave us an hour to drive to the attorney's office. Debbie made me feel guilty about catching gold fever. She explained that the reason she had taken this case was to preserve the historical value of the wrecks and to satisfy the descendents of any who had perished in such tragedies.

An even greater excitement about finding the answers to questions about the final hours of many sailors and their vessels easily overcame my gold fever, but not entirely. We arrived at the attorney's office ten minutes early and were escorted into the larger conference room, where several bidders were impatiently waiting for the auction to begin.

Dolores gave Debbie and me seats along the wall in the back, because we would not be doing any actual bidding. Abraham Buffield saw us come in and immediately came over to greet us. He gave me a disapproving glance when I introduced Debbie as my dive master, but finally smiled at her and said, "A dive master will be very handy to have on the boat."

As Abraham went back to his seat, we noticed other bidders staring at us with unfriendly eyes. It was obvious that these people were in a fierce competition for the information that would lead them to Mike's treasure. I was trying to match faces with the voices from my previous phone calls when John Carski walked in.

"Everyone is here!" John announced as Dolores closed the door. She sat at the front of the group with a notepad, ready to document the events that were about to take place in the room. John Carski provided the rules for the auction, including the need to state your name and the amount of the bid each time you made a bid.

A list of lost ships was uncovered on a whiteboard at the front of the well-lit room. Packets of photos and written information concerning sixteen ships were to be auctioned off. Each packet included a pair of ships. The first was a schooner named the *Ontario*, which sank in 1780, and it was paired with an unidentified wooden steamer. John Carski announced, "Ten o'clock! Bidding may begin."

The first bid was for ten thousand dollars, made by an overweight, gray-haired man with a gruff voice. He identified himself as Richard Bailey. I remembered him from the phone as the guy from Chicago.

"Larry Plumber—fifteen thousand," rang out immediately after Bailey's bid.

The bidding went on until the pair of wrecks sold for forty thousand dollars. I was shocked by that large a sum for just the information on two wrecks, but the *Ontario* was known for carrying a large amount of wealth for a retiring British commander leaving Fort Niagara for England. Dolores wrote the name of the high bidder, James Donahue, on an envelope, which she placed on the table in front of her.

The next ship was the *Saint Mary's*, a British frigate that sank in 1772; it was also paired with an unknown schooner. An angry Richard Bailey won the bid at sixty-five thousand dollars. I remember Mike telling a story about how Golden Hill got its name from a ship called the *Saint Mary's*, which sank near Thirty Mile Point. I thought that might be the ship that would have the gold on it.

Next was the Viking warship, with an unknown date of sinking. It was paired with an American sloop of war named the *Tibet's*, which sank in 1715. Debbie looked at me and whispered, "No history buffs here," when the pair sold to Dale Schmidt for a meager ten thousand dollars.

An early propeller-driven ship called the *Young America* that sank in 1874 was paired with an unidentified steel ship. Displaying her knowledge of Lake Ontario history, Debbie reminded me that the first propeller-driven ship had been built just up the shore in Oswego, New York.

Abraham had seemed emotionless as he sat watching the other bidders. When the bid got to forty thousand dollars, it looked like Bailey was going to get another pair of wrecks.

"Fifty thousand," Abraham said in a voice that was deeper than expected from such a small man. Abraham had bought his first wreck, and I wondered if it would be his last.

It became obvious that each bidder had a time period in which he or she was interested. Abraham's was the early 1900s, as was proven when he paid ninety thousand dollars for the *Nisbet Grammer,* which sank in 1926. The ship was paired with an unknown schooner.

The most surprising low bid involved a World War Two German submarine and a 1956 tub called the *Cormorant;* it sold for a hundred dollars to the seemingly happy Dale Schmidt. Larry Plumber seemed to be desperate as he spent a hundred and eighty thousand dollars on the last four wrecks: two unknown schooners, a 1908 propeller-driven barge, and the *Wave Crest,* a schooner that sank in 1900.

"Bidding is over until all money transfers are complete. In the event that appropriate funds are not transferred, the bidding will begin again in fifteen minutes," directed John Carski. The five bidders broke out cell phones, and the room filled with a variety of beeping that reminded me of a space ship about to take off.

John's secretary, Dolores, brought in a cart with coffee. I helped myself, but the bidders were too busy for coffee. Then Dolores answered the phone and repeated the total for the auction. "Yes, $435,100.00 has been deposited. It is all there." The room went silent. Phones were pocketed as John Carski handed out the envelopes with the winning bidders' names on them. The sound of paper tearing seemed loud in the quiet room.

One by one, people began cursing Mike, because the latitude and longitude coordinates were in code. Abraham seemed to smile as he put his envelope in his suit coat pocket and headed for the door. "I'll see you in an hour," he said, looking at me with an expression of contempt. The man clearly didn't like me, and I didn't like him, but I agreed to meet him at the marina.

The others followed Abraham out, with their cell phones beeping. Richard Bailey gave me a particularly threatening look. Debbie patted my shoulder to signal that she had taken note of Bailey's threat. The room was clear except for John Carski, Dolores, Debbie, and me. Carski seemed to transform back into his normally friendly self as he reminded me that I would be getting a letter from Mike three days after the auction, explaining what I was to do with the half of the auction proceeds that had been left to me. I was so interested in the bidding process and the outcome that I had forgotten about that arrangement.

"One half of $435,100.00 is a lot of money," I said in surprise. "I guess I hadn't thought about the auction proceeds being so large."

Mr. Carski told me to give him a call after the weekend so that he could give me Mike's letter and make the necessary arrangements. We left the office as the sun was at its zenith, and we felt its full August warmth. As we drove back to the marina, Debbie was excited about seeing sunken wrecks that no living person had ever seen before.

Abraham was already on the boat with Bruce O'Connor and two other men when Debbie and I pulled up to the marina. Bruce seemed happy to see us, and pointed out the reason why when we approached the dock. The marina was full of small boats loaded with diving gear.

Bruce called the sheriff's boat to pick him up as Abraham introduced us to Jason Flint and Kenneth Eickenger. Debbie noticed the tech gear that cluttered the deck, and asked who the tech diver was. It was the taller of the two divers who spoke first. "We are all tech divers! You?"

Debbie smiled at his narrow brown eyes, answering, "Yes, I have done some tech diving."

Again I observed a commonality among divers in the friendly and enthusiastic way they talked about diving. Jason had a thinning hairline that made him appear to be in his midforties, but he had the muscular build of an active scuba diver.

Ken was younger and more studious-looking than Jason. Wire-frame bifocals stood out on his suntanned face, but his worn shorts and faded Yankees T-shirt gave him the look of having spent a lot of time on dive boats. Ken asked Debbie where to stow the gear, and she said that it was fine lying on the deck for now. Abraham was scowling and quietly looking around; still wearing his black suit from the auction, he looked even more out of place on the boat.

Bruce and Abraham were going over the charts of the area while the rest of us were talking about the dives. The sheriff's boat pulled in, and Bruce left with his usual friendly smile, saying, "Keep safe," in a voice that was friendly and authoritative at the same time.

Abraham motioned me over to see the chart, but first he gave the harbor a suspicious gaze. "You have to help me figure out this damned code," Abraham growled. He showed me the coordinates for the four wrecks. He had them listed vertically on a three-by-five index card. Debbie interrupted, suggesting that she take Jason and Ken on a dive while we figured out what we were going to do.

The divers seemed to glow. Abraham sneered and grumbled his agreement. Then he asked me for a ten-letter word that would have been significant to Mike. My experience as an English teacher gave me the answer right away, but I didn't really want to help this arrogant and unpleasant man who expected everyone to do his bidding. Abraham showed me what he had on his file card.

Young American	RNTGDOR DLOLGD HU	1-2-3-4-5-6-7-8-9-0
Unidentified steel ship	RNTODOG DLOLDO NL	l-d n t r
Nesbit Grammer	RNTOOHU DLOLHR EE	
Unidentified schooner	RNTOOGO DLOOHT DG	

I looked at the coded coordinates and at what Abraham had figured out from studying the chart. I allowed myself a victorious smile as Debbie excused herself to get her diving gear from the cabin that Abraham was blocking.

"I'm in charge of this dive, since I rented the boat, so I call the shots. You have to stay on the boat, and you will not be diving," Abraham sternly said to Debbie.

The hurt look on her face made me say, "I have the word you are looking for, but she gets to dive."

With icy coldness in his eyes and voice, Abraham said, "All right, have it your way." He stepped aside to let Debbie go below, and I told him that the word he was looking for was the name of the boat.

"G-O-L-D H-U-N-T-E-R," Abraham spelled out, filling in the blanks on his card. "It works," he said, looking at me with neither appreciation nor acceptance. Abraham has his puzzle solved, but his miserable attitude showed reluctance to believe that there was any treasure to be found.

Debbie came up from the cabin wearing shorts and a shirt and carrying a dive bag in her hand. I started the engines and headed out on the river.

Abraham was giving me directions to the location without entering the precious coordinates into the GPS. A half dozen smaller boats seemed to follow us like vultures. Colorful gear flapping in the wind showed us that they were other divers. Abraham suggested that we go to a site other than that of one of the wrecks. The underwater park was the first thing that came to mind.

Abraham and I stayed on board as other boats anchored about half a mile away and all around us. The noisy *Seaya* had passed us and anchored directly in front of us. I recognized Dale Schmidt from the auction on the *Seaya* and noticed that he had a wet suit half on and was ready to dive. I felt deprived as Debbie suited up and led Jason and Ken into the water. I would remain on the boat during the dive to keep an eye on Abraham. I really didn't trust him.

Abraham sat frowning on the bench, wearing his suit and tie. I jealously watched bubbles drift back and forth behind the boat in a pattern that showed the divers were moving from one figure to the next. Two small boats pulled right up next to us. Abraham pointed to the dive flag and motioned angrily for them to keep away from our divers.

The driver of the first boat made a hand gesture with his middle finger extended. I recognized the driver as Richard Bailey, the angry bidder who had given me such a threatening look. He dropped his anchor right on our divers and shut off his engine. Abraham was livid with rage and looked as if he was about to leap from our boat to the other, when our divers surfaced. They were all right, but the anchor had just missed Ken, and he was ready to punch someone. Bailey tormented Ken with an oar, which made him angrier. Debbie managed to get Ken to follow Jason back to our boat.

Debbie disappeared underwater, but surfaced at the dive ladder just as Jason followed Ken up the ladder. Jumping up the ladder in full gear, Debbie turned and pulled the ladder up, then said, "Get us out of here." I brought the anchor up and fired up the engines. By the time we began moving, we were within feet of Bailey's sinister face and I suddenly spotted his sidekick, who had a nasty black eye and a fresh scar over his forehead. I recognized him as my attacker from days before. I wanted to call Bruce, but I couldn't do it with Abraham hovering over me.

It was Debbie that kept everyone calm as we watched Bailey's sidekick go overboard in full gear. He was diving alone. A few seconds after he disappeared underwater, he was back at the surface holding the frayed end of the anchor line. We all looked at Debbie, who explained, "A dive tool comes in handy when you almost get killed by an anchor."

Jason and Ken cheered, but Abraham was studying the people in the other boats, realizing, as I did, that they were all watching us. We idled slowly away from Bailey, listening to him send his diver down to find the anchor. The diver obeyed and descended with the frayed anchor line. Debbie had seen the look on my face when I recognized the guy who had attacked me. While Abraham was distracted by what was happening on the other boats, she picked up the radio microphone and quietly called Bruce, who was already watching through binoculars and on his way.

Bailey started his engine and tried to move back through the current to where he thought the anchor would be. We heard the engine hit something and saw the silver tank surface behind Bailey's boat. The scar-faced diver's air hose was hissing loud enough for us to hear it from a hundred feet away.

I turned the boat toward Bailey and hurried to help the diver, who was lying facedown on the surface with his air hose swishing violently above him. Debbie jumped over the side as we pulled up next to the diver. A dark red area let us know that he was hurt badly. Debbie rolled him over as Jason and Ken moved to the back of our boat to help her.

The diver's neck had been hit by Bailey's propeller, nearly severing his head. Jason pulled his mangled body on board as Ken vomited over the side. Debbie agilely climbed up behind him. With the boat in neutral, we drifted away from the cursing Bailey as Debbie examined the diver.

Her eyes went wide and she exclaimed in a horrified voice, "This man is dead!" The blue lights flashing on the sheriff's boat let us know that he was only a minute away. I heard Bruce ask me whether there were still divers in the water. I told him there wasn't anybody else down there. Then Bruce pulled up next to us and could see Debbie covering the body with a towel.

Debbie opened her dive bag for a second to show me her .45 semiautomatic; she was ready for action. She stepped up on the gunwale, and without a word, leaped toward the sheriff's boat, as if she could fly through the air. She did fly, and she landed on the deck of the higher police boat.

Her conversation with Bruce was brief. They pulled up next to Bailey, and Debbie flew from the sheriff's boat to Bailey's boat. The large Bailey tried fighting Debbie, but with a spinning whirl, Debbie's foot laid the three-hundred-pound giant over the gunwale. She had Roger Bailey's right arm behind his back, and he screamed out in pain. She was as good at martial arts as at diving. She hadn't even needed to pull out the gun.

Bruce pulled up next to Debbie and handed her a pair of handcuffs, which she expertly put on Bailey. Bruce pulled him into the sheriff's boat and set him in the back corner. Debbie climbed back into the sheriff's boat. Bruce handed Jason a blanket and instructed him to cover the diver's body better.

An out-of-place smile came over Bruce's face as he asked me, "Can you do me a favor?" With all that had happened in the last ten minutes, I was in a little shock, but I nodded. Bruce asked me to tow the other boat back to the sheriff's dock, where he would be waiting for me. Debbie left with Bruce, and I kind of wondered whether Bailey would make it to shore alive.

I pulled up to the boat, thinking that I would rather get rid of the body in the back of my boat first. Abraham volunteered to get in Bailey's boat to grab a line for us to use to tow it back. Still in his suit, Abraham climbed onto the other boat and over the windshield to reach the anchor line. He tossed the line to Jason, who fastened it with a bowline knot over a cleat under the ladder on the *Gold Hunter's* transom.

The lake was calm, but I had to go slowly when towing the other boat behind me. Other boats that were watching seemed to have moved ahead of us and entered the harbor behind the sheriff's boat. Abraham had been going through the boat in tow, but stopped and just sat there, a grim, dark figure with the hot sun beating down on his black suit. I imagined that he had found Bailey's coordinates and hidden them in his pocket.

Deputy O'Connor was waiting at his dock for us with several other police officers. Bailey was in the back seat of a sheriff's car, and we saw him leave as we swung our stern around. Abraham tossed the officers a line as Jason untied the tow line from our boat. I backed the *Gold Hunter* into the slip on the other side of the sheriff's boat.

Debbie came with an ambulance and brought them to the boat. Ken and Jason got off the boat and met Abraham in a crowd of curious onlookers. I waited on board as a plainclothes investigator asked me about "the accident." Another investigator took pictures of the mangled body before the medical personnel loaded the body and left.

After the ambulance left, Debbie came over to me and asked, "Wilbur, are you okay? How are you doing?"

"I'm just fine. What about you? You really went into action, leaping onto the boat and pinning Bailey to the deck!"

She sighed, "You know, I feel a little guilty about having to give up my cover like that. I hope my boss won't take me off the case."

I felt lonesome on the water without Bernie and dreaded the thought of losing Debbie and spending my week with Abraham.

Debbie left for a meeting with her boss, and Jason and Ken went back to their motel for the afternoon, so Abraham was alone in the boat with me when I left the sheriff's dock. I asked him, "Did you get Bailey's wreck coordinates?"

Abraham would make a good poker player, because the question did not faze him a bit. He pulled out the envelope from Carski's office and showed me Bailey's name, saying, "The police don't need this."

Abraham's blunt statement bothered me, even though I knew it was true. A person had actually died in a meaningless accident, but from Abraham's point of view, all it meant was that there was one less treasure hunter to compete with. All he cared about was his continued search for treasure on two more wrecks. I understood that this cold man lacked any remorse for the death of the diver. When we docked the boat, Abraham surprised me by asking if I played golf. He knew that too many eyes were watching, and that none of the others had the code word. He wanted to kill time.

I was told not to clean the boat until Debbie got back, and lost my desire to dive. A game of golf sounded good, and it might provide an opportunity to find out more about the coldhearted Abraham Buffield.

"The golf course is about two miles down the road. I'll drive," I answered. Abraham got his clubs out of his Mercedes and put them in my car.

The course was quiet, giving us an instant tee off time. Abraham had a change of clothes in his golf bag. He looked more human in blue dress slacks and a white polo shirt and golf shoes. His game was as meticulous as he was.

I asked him what made him think that Michael had found a treasure. Abraham seemed no friendlier than earlier and he took his golf game too seriously, but he did provide a lot of information for me. His explanation took the whole nine holes and was thorough.

He cleared his throat and began his lecture. "You ask what I think Mike's treasure is? I think it's palladium. In 1803, an English chemist named William Hyde Wollaston first isolated palladium from platinum. About this same time, John Dalton was formulating the atomic weight theory and he took an interest in this new metal. Palladium was never as valuable as gold. Its white color made it valuable for white gold jewelry. Today, palladium has a more technical use as an ingredient used in the process for making hydrogen. Palladium is used for the lightweight car batteries in modern hybrid electric automobiles."

I knew of Dalton from my scuba book, and knew that he worked with gases, but had never known that he worked with metals too. Abraham was a walking encyclopedia of information, but he also shocked me with his knowledge of local history.

He told me, "My grandfather came to Oak Orchard in 1926 by ship to pick up a shipment of palladium. A miner that sold Medina sandstone to locations all over the world found a supply of ore and produced palladium at his foundry located farther up the Oak Orchard River in Medina."

"So what happened to the palladium from Medina?" I asked.

"When my grandfather was to meet the owner of the foundry at the mouth of the river to transfer the palladium to his ship, the plan went awry. The owner of the foundry was found dead, bitten by a rattlesnake, at the mouth of the river. The boat that he used to bring the palladium to the lake was missing and was never found. My grandfather figured that someone found the precious metal and made off with it."

"That's truly amazing," I replied. "How much palladium was lost?"

"Three thousand pounds of palladium were gone. The value on today's market would bring over nine million dollars, even more in the near future. However, the precious metal never surfaced."

"I don't get it," I said. "If it never surfaced, how did you find out about it yourself?"

"Last year, Michael Moresby brought me a few blocks of palladium to sell for him. Apparently, he had already sold some all over the country."

"Quite a secret! But now I'm wondering: wouldn't the metal have been ruined, having been underwater all that time?"

"No, not really. Like gold, palladium does not rust or deteriorate."

"I see." I remembered what Debbie had said about complicated ownership, so I added, "Of course, it might have been easier to ship the cargo on the Erie Canal, but I suppose that the discovery of the ore was kept secret for political reasons. The government could claim the palladium if it was found on a sunken ship. The descendants of the ship's owner or the country of the ship's origin could also claim ownership."

Abraham looked surprised that I understood the complexity of the situation. He went on, "Yes, if a so-called treasure was found on one of the wrecks in Lake Ontario, New York State, the United States federal government, and the Canadian government all could claim ownership to any such treasure. It would become prohibited to scuba dive in the area if a known treasure was found, and it would take years of international court time that would eat up the value of any treasure found." With a sinister note entering his voice, he concluded, "But the metal is needed now, and quietly."

I was thinking about my earlier imaginings of shiny golden bars on the lake's bottom, but now the more dominant thought in my mind was diving again. Golf just couldn't hold a candle to diving. I three-putted on the ninth hole, losing to Abraham by twenty strokes. I offered to buy him dinner.

We stopped at the boat, only to find that Debbie had cleaned it up and Bruce was waiting there with her. Debbie was famished and joined us for dinner. Bruce stayed at the marina to watch the boat.

The restaurant was full of new faces as we walked in for dinner. Debbie had already talked to Trisha and told her about the diving accident. Bernie had also called to see if we had found a wreck yet. I didn't have to suggest a night dive, because that was our unspoken plan anyway.

As we were eating, Captain Jack walked over to our table and asked what we had found. I described the underwater park that Mike built. Snatches of conversations throughout the restaurant included references to my answer, and dismay because no treasure had been found.

With our dinner finished, I spoke loudly and suggested a ride out to see the sunset, so that other divers listening in would think that we weren't diving tonight. We left the restaurant to find Jason and Ken waiting at the boat. We left to the west and traveled twenty miles to the farthest wreck.

The wreck was an unidentified schooner a mile and a half west of Shadigee in forty-one feet of water. Abraham stayed on board and said he would bang on the ladder five times if danger approached. I was excited to dive with Debbie as my partner again. Jason and Ken dove together as dive buddies.

The lake was calm and inviting as the sun was just beginning to set. I felt no anxiety as I strode off the back. With Debbie beside me, I swam around to the anchor. As we passed the side of the boat, I remembered the propeller damage to the diver earlier that day and became a little fearful. We waited by the anchor for Jason and Ken. They were going to do a search pattern to the north while Debbie and I searched the south.

We descended the anchor line, but a search was not necessary. Large wooden masts lay right in front of the anchor. In the beams of our lights, a grand figure grew at the large end of the masts. The large wooden schooner was badly broken up on the lake's floor. I was astonished by the size of the wooden parts and marveled at the idea that these old ships were built with only hand tools.

Ken's light hit a bright object on an upper deck section of the schooner. Jason picked it up and showed it to us. It was a large coin that appeared to be gold, and it was in a plastic bag with a handwritten note tucked inside it. Since I didn't think this was the treasure ship, I just enjoyed the rest of the dive and spent my time looking at a variety of fish and marveling at the ship's construction.

A chill ran up my spine as I imagined the storm, or even cannon fire, that might have caused the sinking of the schooner. We circled the entire wreck and were at the masts again. Following them back to the anchor, we noticed more fish than we had looking for the wreck. Jack perch were bountiful among small minnows, and zebra mussels were everywhere. An occasional bass slowly scattered the minnows, clearing the view of the bass.

All four of us ascended the anchor line together. Abraham met us at the stern, but disappeared when Jason handed up our find. We exited the water up the dive ladder and removed our gear, talking about the dive as if we knew we would never find more than the historical value of the wrecks.

Abraham announced that there was no treasure on this site. He held up a note from the plastic bag and read, "Not this one—Mike." Abraham put the note down and held up the coin, saying, "The gold in this coin is worth about a thousand dollars, but the coin is probably worth ten times that to a collector."

I thought, *Gold coins and the white palladium are hiding somewhere in the lake.*

We headed back east, but decided not to dive again that night. It was after midnight, and we wanted a good night's rest before we dove on any deeper wrecks. The guiding stars were bright, and other than a tanker about ten miles out, there were no other boats in sight. A midnight fog filled the calm river as we made our way to the dock.

It was too quiet at the marina, and I did not want to leave Debbie on the boat alone with all the strangers in town. After Abraham and his two divers left for their motel, I was about to offer to stay with Debbie. A familiar voice said, "Go to sleep, already." I turned and saw Deputy Bruce O'Connor's grinning face on the bridge of the *Sea Dog*. I left for home, confident that Debbie was safe.

Friday's auction and night dive left me exhausted. It was eight in the morning when my eyes opened from another all-night sleep. Saturday was Trisha's day off, so she drove me to the marina. Weekends at the marina were busy. The fishing boats were gone, leaving the *Gold Hunter* quietly alone at the dock.

Sitting on a lawn chair at the end of the dock was the deputy, Jim Beach, in his marine uniform with the Orleans County sheriff's insignia. Jim held a fishing pole and was staring intensely at a ripple in the water when Trisha and I startled him by stepping on the dock. He explained that Bruce had got him some overtime to work the marina this weekend, so he was keeping an eye on the *Gold Hunter*.

"Has anyone been around?" I asked.

"No, not really, Wilbur. I've been here since six or so this morning. There were fishing boats in the early morning, but since they went out, it has been quiet."

Bruce had called in, though, and reported a few dive boats with divers in the water. He said that the weekend water skiers and jet skiers wouldn't start zipping around until noon.

"Okay. Thanks, Jim." I wondered where the divers were this morning. The cabin door opened and Debbie stepped out with a bag in her hand. With her face down to hide a just-woken-up look, she made her way to the marina's bathrooms.

We invited Jim to join us for breakfast, but he had already eaten. Unsure of when Abraham and the divers would show up, Trisha and I waited for Debbie to join us for breakfast. In only five minutes, she returned, looking refreshed and ready for breakfast.

Abraham pulled up in his black Mercedes as we were leaving. With his window down, Abraham said, "I need to talk to you." I asked him whether he'd had breakfast.

"Just came from Lakeside Restaurant," he proclaimed. I got out of the car, telling Trisha and Debbie to have breakfast without me. Trisha offered to bring something back for me.

"A sausage sandwich would be great," I said. With a cynical grin, Trisha slid into the driver's seat and drove away.

Abraham told me that at the restaurant, he had heard that divers were already in the lake. Jason and Ken were finishing their breakfast and would meet at the boat in a few minutes. I recognized urgency in Abraham's voice, and felt the same need to be out on the water.

I gestured toward the boat, saying, "Boat's ready." The treasure hunter had brought a leather briefcase that was too dressy for his tan-colored safari outfit. I had to smile as he headed for the boat, because I had never seen such neatly pressed shorts; they even had pleats in them.

Trailing behind Abraham, I noticed how with each step, he coordinated his hands to open the briefcase, rearrange papers, and remove the gold coin as he stepped onto the deck. He showed me the coin and explained how he had faxed a copy of the coin to his New York office. The unique markings engraved on the coin proved that the coin was one of six hundred that had disappeared with the British ship called the *Ontario*.

"This explains the presence of James Donahue and Dale Schmidt," Abraham said. This was just another surprise that seemed to add to the hidden knowledge that Mike took to his grave. There was *gold* in the lake, as well as Abraham's palladium. I wondered how many varieties of treasure actually existed in the hidden solitude beneath the day's calm watery surface.

Abraham told me that he wanted to dive the *Nisbet Grammer* first, because it was the most obvious wreck on which to find the palladium. The ship had sunk in 1926, just two weeks after the loss of the palladium from the mouth of Oak Orchard.

Jason, Ken, and Debbie got back from the restaurant, ready to dive. Abraham was in a hurry to get started.

The familiar sound of the twin diesel engines took us out of the river. There were two out-of-town boats with dive flags at the underwater marine park. The extended dive flags meant that divers were in the water. I smiled to myself, thinking that the divers would enjoy the figures placed on the bottom, regardless of the lack of precious metal treasures.

Abraham led us to the site of the *Nesbit Grammer*. It was two miles past Shadigee, and much farther out from shore than any diving we had done. We anchored in ninety-nine feet of water. We agreed on our normal search, in which Jason and Ken would do a rectangular pattern to the north and Debbie and I would do a rectangular pattern to the south.

Debbie looked at the recreational dive planner and told us that we had only twenty minutes from the time we began our descent until we would have to ascend without having to make a decompression stop.

"If you have enough air!" she added.

We suited up, and feeling confident, I entered the water first. Jason followed, with Ken right behind him. Debbie was being extra cautious in helping the divers in the water. Jason and Ken left for the anchor line, while I waited for Debbie, who made a big splash entering over the side of the boat. All four of us descended the anchor line together.

I felt very comfortable until we were twenty feet down and I looked at my dive computer. Seventy-nine more feet seemed a long way to go. At forty feet, I was enjoying the solitude of seeing just my three companions and the diagonal line leading to the anchor that rested on the bottom. Fear seemed to come for no reason, but before the fear overcame my emotions, it would vanish, like a glimpse of the occasional fish that meandered past us.

At eighty feet, Ken pointed behind me. I turned and saw a wall of darkness that sent terror throughout my body. When I saw the other divers approach the darkness, I followed, for fear of being left alone. The darkness became clearer as we swam closer. With the realization that we were next to the pilot house of a steel ship, my fear departed and excitement took over.

The thought of future riches was far from my mind. The sheer excitement of the present adventure filled me as I followed Debbie to the pilot house. Jason and Ken descended farther down and disappeared through a dark hole on the deck. I watched as nothing but bubbles came from the hole. Debbie beckoned me toward the open door of the pilot house. I followed her inside, but kept my hand on the door frame.

It was dark inside, even though the room was all windows at the top half of the walls. There was no glass in the windows. Two large trout moved through one window and out another. Debbie seemed to disappear in a growing cloud of dust that arose from the movement of her fins. I looked up, seeing my bubbles grow across the ceiling, and noticed more dirt moving off the overhead area.

I backed out the door and moved back about five feet, seeing a cloud of dust where the dark door had just released me. Debbie appeared from in front of the windows. I figured she had swum out a window when the dirt had gotten stirred up. I followed Debbie down to the deck where Jason and Ken had entered a hole a few minutes earlier.

I was happy that Debbie swam past the hole toward the bow. The hole seemed dark and uninviting; a cloud of green-brown particles oozed from the confines of a hidden darkness. I followed Debbie, but as I swam past the hole that had swallowed Ken and Jason, I felt as if a prestigious invitation floated up with the scattered particles. The word "enter" rang in my mind.

I looked toward Debbie and saw her watching me look at the hole. She held her pointer finger up and waved it back and forth, like a mother scolding a child. The hand signal meant no in the diver language that I was becoming familiar with. Debbie recognized the unequivocal lure of exploring a wreck.

The scolding finger changed into a pointing gesture, showing me the bubbles escaping from small cracks and openings on the deck. Debbie was following Ken's and Jason's bubbles, and beckoned me to follow with her. Obediently, I followed until the bubbles came out of a large open hatch. We saw the beam of flashlights as the two divers emerged from the darkness.

Still lingering in the dust, Jason shone his flashlight on his clenched hand. I stared as he slowly opened his hand, revealing another gold coin in a plastic bag. Debbie checked her console and pointed away from the wreck. I checked my dive computer and pressure gauge and discovered that I had twelve hundred pounds of air left and plenty of bottom time.

An urge to drop down into the hold quickly dissolved as the other three divers swam away. Not wanting to be left alone, I followed the colorfully clad divers to the anchor line. The sun must have been straight above us, because it brightened the anchor line, and at fifteen feet, a dancing white glow formed directly above us.

Jason was looking at the gold coin as we held on the anchor line for a three-minute safety stop at the fifteen-foot depth. The time went quickly as the thought of glistening treasure brightened my mind. Debbie looked at my computer and gave me the thumbs-up signal. She ascended with me, leaving Ken and Jason on the anchor line. They had gone deeper than Debbie and me, so they needed more time to decompress, or eliminate nitrogen from their blood to avoid "the bends."

Transforming from underwater diving to surface snorkeling was natural as we made our way to the back of the boat, where Abraham was waiting for us in a glossy black dry suit. As I followed Debbie up the ladder, I noticed several different-sized tanks with different-colored regulators attached to them on the port side of the deck.

Debbie told Abraham that Ken and Jason were making a decompression stop and that they would be up in a few minutes. His dark eyes stared through the young girl, as if waiting for more information. Debbie seemed to get a kick out of making him wait. She turned her back to him so he could help her out of her scuba unit.

"Another gold coin in a bag," Debbie said, with her back to Abraham, allowing a smile at making him wait for the tidbit of information.

Expressionless, Abraham set Debbie's gear on the deck and looked at me with a glint of disgust for her delayed response. Clearly, he wasn't satisfied with Debbie's report, and he wanted to see for himself what else was down there.

"Can you leave your gear on and help me suit up in the water?" Feeling very comfortable and even a bit exhilarated after the dive, I agreed. I put some extra air in my BCD and reentered the water.

With my mask around my neck, I watched Abraham heft his double-tank scuba unit over his head, dropping it perfectly in place and buckling the harness. He sat on the corner of the bench to put his fins on. He connected the carabineers that held a large Pelican flashlight, two reels of bright yellow polypropylene line, and a spare mask. Abraham was a lot stronger than he appeared to be.

The splash was intense as Abraham's overladen frame stepped off the back of the boat. He surfaced and gave the okay signal before pulling his mask around his neck and barking orders to Debbie. Debbie handed me the extra tanks one at a time so that I could help Abraham attach each piece of equipment to his harness.

Abraham had an array of seven tanks, but he seemed comfortable with all the extra equipment and hoses. He waited for Ken and Jason to surface, so they could explain the layout of the wreck before he let them climb on the boat. I slipped my mask on and put my snorkel in my mouth so that I could watch the tech diver descend into a blur before disappearing, one color at a time, into the depths of Lake Ontario.

White Treasure

With Abraham gone, the atmosphere on the boat was very relaxed, allowing us to talk about the wreck. I was hotter than I realized as I pulled off my dry suit. I had been sweating in the forty-degree water, yet I was quite cozy on the dive. We all stripped down to shorts and T-shirts to wait for Abraham to surface.

Water quenched my thirst and tasted better than anything I could remember drinking, and the store-bought peanut butter cookies tasted almost as good as Trisha's homemade ones. One of the advantages of diving, I realized, was the heightened sensitivity to such simple pleasures.

Ken explained the layout of the wreck's insides and concluded, "I'm guessing that it'll take an hour to cover the whole area."

Debbie sounded worried. "I really don't think that Abraham should be down there alone."

"He always dives alone. He's definitely a skilled diver, but he makes a lousy dive buddy," Jason blurted out, making Ken laugh. Debbie just looked at the water for bubbles.

Seagulls appeared from nowhere, prematurely announcing Abraham's return. Squawks were heard circling above the bubbling surface, which must have looked like a school of small fish to the birds. After ten minutes of circling the seagulls, must have figured out that the bubbles were not fish, because they disappeared into the blue sky.

Abraham was gone for an hour and a half before he surfaced at the anchor line. Jason dove in the water to help him remove his cumbersome equipment. On the boat, Abraham removed his hood, showing, for the first time, that his hair could get messed up. However, his eyes were expressionless when he said, "Nothing on this ship!"

Abraham opened the plastic bag with the gold coin and read the note: *Not this one.* He looked at Jason and then Ken, saying, "An extra thousand dollars for each one of these you find." Then Abraham saw the stern look on Debbie's face, and holding the coin up, he asked, "What do you think this is worth?"

Debbie gave Abraham a penetrating stare for a few seconds before responding in a deep, serious voice. "The coin is historically priceless." It was the first and only time that I saw Abraham smile. He handed the coin to Debbie and instantly turned his attention to me.

"Six miles west," was all he said.

It was good to be underway again. The breeze melted the August's midday heat as we motored west toward Thirty Mile Point. Debbie was still holding the coin when Abraham directed me to the next dive site. We dropped anchor in seventy-three feet of water a half mile from shore. The boat swung northwest as the anchor line became taut. There would be a good current on this dive.

Jason and Ken were already suited up by the time I shut the engines down. I hurried to get my suit on, because I wanted to find the next gold coin. Abraham told us that this was one of the unidentified schooners from his list. He would wait on the boat.

Jason and Ken entered the water and descended immediately. Debbie and I had to change tanks before we geared up, giving the guys a fifteen-minute head start on us. The wind was picking up from the east and waves were growing. I had to fight the current to get to the anchor line with Debbie. I was breathing hard from gearing up in a hurry when we left the surface.

Five feet down the anchor line, I was relaxed again. At sixty-five feet, the massive oak frame of a two-hundred-year-old wooden schooner appeared directly underneath us. Its timber was scattered on the rocky bottom, but the aft section was intact and lying on its side. I felt like I had gone back in time as I followed Debbie to the ship.

Ken was waiting by a large hole in the ship, watching Jason's bubbles escape through the many crevices on the old ship. The current took the dust particles away, leaving visibility good outside the wreck. Ken motioned us over and showed us that he had already found the plastic bag that we expected Mike had left. This time there was no coin in the bag, just a note.

Disappointment that I did not find the bag quickly left as I read the word on the note through the plastic bag. *BULLSEYE* the note simply read in large letters. A burst of bubbles left Debbie's regulator as she looked at the note.

Ken was holding the end of the yellow line, with Jason on the other end inside the wreck. Debbie followed the line through the tight opening. I looked at Ken, who held his hand out, signaling me to enter.

A new excitement filled me as I took out my dive light and kicked my way into the darkness. I had one hand loosely around the yellow line as I followed Debbie's dust trail. A few feet inside the wreck was a long, dark, metal object. I felt along it with my flashlight hand until I reached the end and realized that it was a cannon.

A thousand questions entered my mind at once. Was this ship sunk on purpose in a war? Did men die when she sank? All of a sudden, I could feel the spirits of the brave crew who must have sailed on the ship. I looked up and saw my bubbles hitting the ceiling above me. There were old wooden tables and benches and boxes.

The line in my hand started to tug, so I turned around and swam the ten feet to the hidden hole where I had entered. Ken was waiting with a smile that was concealed by his regulator, but glistened in his eyes. It was good to be out in the better visibility, where I could see the shell of the ship that had met its unknown fate hundreds of years ago.

Debbie and Jason were making their way out, creating the tugging I had felt on the line. I was not ready for what I saw when the divers came out. Four hands were pushing a dark object out of the murky hole. It was a *treasure chest!*

It was dark-colored and had metal corners and a latch, just like the one Trisha had at the foot of our bed, but this one was smaller. The latch was open, and when Debbie and Jason were outside, Jason lifted the curved lid, revealing hundreds of brilliant, shiny gold coins.

Jason closed the chest lid as Ken went to work wrapping the chest with the spool of yellow line, adding a growing glow to the exterior of the long lost treasure. Debbie helped Ken move the line reel around the chest as Jason and I lifted one side and then the other to completely cover the chest in line, making a loop at the top each time the line passed over.

The chest was only about twelve inches square and eighteen inches long with a curved top, but it seemed awfully heavy for its small size. With the polypropylene line around it forming a loop at the top, Ken pulled a bright yellow bag about three feet long from the inside of his BCD.

I had never seen a lift bag before. It had a carabineer that Ken hooked to the loop on the top of the chest. We all checked our air supply, and I had eighteen hundred pounds left. Jason took his regulator out of his mouth and held it under the bag. As he purged his regulator open, the air came out and filled the bag, making it look like a hot air balloon about to float upward.

Ken gave Jason his alternate regulator to breathe from while the lift bag was being filled. I was waiting for the bag to raise the treasure chest to the surface, but the more air Jason put in the bag, the slower and more careful he was. All of a sudden, bubbles filled the area. I knew what a free flow was, but had never seen one before now.

Ken's regulator spewed out air uncontrollably and at such a force that his regulator flew from his mouth. Jason had to take out Ken's alternate regulator. Jason replaced his own regulator in his mouth. Debbie was quick to give her alternate to Ken, and she reached around behind him to turn off his air supply. The massive force of air escaping upward returned to the now-excited breathing of the four divers.

Pressure gauges were instantly checked, revealing that Jason barely had enough to make it to the surface. Debbie must have turned Ken's air back on, but he only had a hundred pounds left, which would not give him enough air to surface. Ken continued to breathe from Debbie's alternate regulator and seemed more relaxed than I was.

We all gave the okay signal to each other, which lowered my stress a bit. Jason gave me the signals that indicated he was low on air and needed to share mine. I reached down and unhooked my alternate air source and handed it to Jason, who accepted it eagerly.

I was thankful that Bernie had made me perform an alternate air source ascent a few days ago. But as I mentally prepared myself to do it for real, Jason signaled to get closer to the chest. Jason squeezed his head under the lift bag to let his exhaled air fill the bag.

It was uncomfortable to lay on the bottom, holding onto Jason, with my face touching the rocks on the bottom. A little brown crayfish peeked out from under a light tan–colored stone and waved its tiny claw at me, as if to say, "Get out of my area." The threat was so minute that it brought an inner smile to me and relaxed me in my awkward position.

Jason pulled me off the bottom and back to reality. Debbie and Ken had hold of the chest, which was six inches off the bottom. We checked pressure gauges and decided that Debbie and Ken would continue buddy-breathing, but that Jason would use his own air.

The anchor line was visible about twenty-five feet from us. We began our ascent with Debbie holding onto Ken and Jason and me carrying, or floating, the lift bag and treasure chest. It was a slow ascent, with Jason carefully releasing air from the lift bag to keep it from running away to the surface.

Abraham's expressionless face met us at the back of the boat. He had no problem lifting the chest onto the deck. Ken had enough air to fill his BCD, but Debbie had him go up the ladder first, followed by Jason. I waved for Debbie to go up the ladder and looked at my pressure gauge as she did. I was shocked to see that I only had two hundred pounds of air left. That would have only lasted me a single minute on the bottom. It was too close, and I vowed to plan better and leave room for problems on my next dive.

Debbie was the first to speak on the boat. Her interest was clearly in the ship and its history. The fact that Mike called it an unidentified ship came to my mind as I remembered a name marked on the cannon that was inside. ONTARIO had been printed in small print on the barrel of the large gun. I said the word out loud and realized that Debbie had seen it too when she said, "Please join me." Even Abraham bowed his head with the crew of the *Gold Hunter* as Debbie continued.

"Lord have mercy on the souls of the brave men and women that suffered from the sinking of the *Ontario*."

"Amen."

The prayer was short, but emphasized the historical significance of the men who fought in the many wars that took place on Lake Ontario. We took our gear off in a relaxed mood without acknowledging the gold. With the deck straightened up and our gear stowed away, it was time to look at Abraham's gold.

Jason and Ken carefully unwrapped the chest, as if their line was more valuable than the gold inside the chest. Abraham made a call on his cell phone. Debbie talked to me about the ship's construction. She said, with amazement in her voice, "The making of a ship like this was quite a feat, especially considering that all of that massive timber was cut with only hand tools."

I remembered seeing the wooden pegs protruding from some of the wood. I added, "To make matters even more difficult, they didn't even have nails in those days, and so they fashioned wooden pegs instead to hold the timber together." Jason and Ken were listening with interest, and agreed that another dive to the wreck would be great.

We had maxed out our dive time for the day and there would be no more diving. However, my mind was on a steak dinner.

"It's ready," Jason's tired voice sounded out as he looked at his employer for the approval to open the chest. There was a nod from Abraham, and the chest opened. Jason stood back as the sun peeked over the gunwale and lit up the gold coins with a bright, blinding light.

Abraham pulled one of his unused nitrox tanks out of the tank rack and laid it down next to the treasure chest. Jason and Ken seemed to know what to do without being told. Jason straddled the tank and held it tight as Ken turned the boot that protected the bottom of the tank. The boot came off, as did the bottom of the tank.

The specially redesigned tank had a cloth lining inside, containing canvas bags that Ken pulled out. The tank was made for smuggling. Abraham was reading some notes from his briefcase as his divers transferred the gold. Debbie watched carefully before she looked at Abraham and said, "On behalf of the Bureau of Criminal Investigation, I am confiscating this gold."

Everyone's attention was on Abraham as he set his notes down and turned to address the crew.

"There were several ships named the *Ontario* that sank in the Great Lakes, but only one was believed to have been carrying gold specie, or coins, on it. The *Ontario* that we just discovered was built on Carlton Island in 1779 as a twenty-two-gun sloop of war for the British Royal Navy. She sank a year later with a crew of three hundred souls, with no survivors to say where she went down."

Turning his head to Debbie, Abraham asked, "Do you know whose gold this is?"

"It belongs to the state of New York," said Debbie.

"And to the federal government," Abraham added.

Debbie was adamant that she should take the gold, and Abraham seemed to sense her feelings as he continued, "The Canadian government and the real owner of the gold, Britain, will tie up the courts for years, leaving the gold to be wasted on lawyers."

When Abraham added, "No one will be able to dive on the wreck until this is settled," Debbie seemed to cave a little. Abraham recognized the right moment to tell us that he would see to it that the gold was divided up among the survivors of the crew without any legal problems.

Debbie asked, "Will you melt down the gold?" All eyes were on Abraham as he explained that the coins, at a little over two ounces each, were worth about a thousand dollars melted down, but that they were worth ten times that to collectors.

The coin in Debbie's hand drew her eyes, making them shine for a moment before she handed it to Abraham, saying, "I have your word that you won't melt them down?" Abraham handed the coin back to Debbie and explained that in treasure hunting, a single coin is of extreme value, because it is proof that the final resting place of lost sailors has been found.

Debbie took the coin. Then Abraham walked over to the chest, bent over, and picked up three more coins, handing one to Ken, one to Jason, and one to me. I looked at his black eyes and saw a dark victory hiding in them, but I accepted the souvenir, hearing Mike's laughter of approval in my mind.

Ken finished filling the sacks with the rest of the coins and screwed the boot back onto the tank. Then Abraham put some lead diver weights in the chest and sent it over the side with a splash. His interest in hiding evidence saddened me as the historical chest disappeared. We pulled anchor and headed back east to Oak Orchard.

Three miles east, we passed the *Seaya* with a dive flag up and kept our distance. Debbie was watching with her binoculars and said, "They must be under." Two other boats with divers were anchored as we passed them at a distance. The cry of seagulls circling divers' bubbles let us know that the divers were down.

The falling sun combined with the wind had dried our gear, and we were packed up by the time we reached the mouth of Oak Orchard. Debbie was driving the boat so I could fill air tanks on the way. With the boat in order and the tanks ready for Sunday morning's diving, I joined the rest of the crew in watching the weekend activities along the river as we headed for our dock.

Debbie backed the boat in successfully, and Jason and Ken tied the dock lines for us. Two men in suits approached the boat. Without saying a word, Abraham handed up his special tank. As one of the men bent over to take the tank, his gun peeked through his jacket, letting us know that they were Abraham's security people. That must have been the call Abraham had made from the boat.

I wondered what would become of the gold coins as the duo loaded the tank into the back of an expensive-looking SUV. Debbie was watching too, and she wrote something down in her notebook. I guessed it was their license plate number. I got Mike's cell phone out of the electronics box and called Trisha to see whether she wanted to have dinner at Lakeside Restaurant.

Trisha said she could meet me at the boat in fifteen minutes. I invited Debbie, Ken, and Jason to join us for dinner. I asked Abraham as well, but he declined because he had too much work to do.

As the five of us squeezed into Trish's car and left for the restaurant, I wondered what kind of work Abraham had to do. Dinner conversation revolved around the history and the discovery of the *Ontario*. Trisha asked for more details and exclaimed, "I never realized how exciting this kind of adventure could be or just how much historical information is contained in a sunken ship and its artifacts."

Ken explained, "We could see quite a bit about the construction of the wreck, because the entire massive wooden ship was lying on its side, exposing the handiwork of the many carpenters that had constructed it so long ago."

The subject of gold never came up at our table, yet I knew it was on everybody's mind, along with further explorations. Debbie said, "Tomorrow we'll dive the *Young American*." Everyone laughed. But being reminded of this other wreck in particular excited me. Mike's journal described the *Young American* as one of the first wooden propeller-driven ships built in Oswego about fifty miles east of where we were diving. It was in only fifty-six feet of water, which would make it an easy dive, with a lot of bottom time to allow for thorough exploration.

We finished dinner just as other boaters were filling the restaurant. Outside we saw Deputy Bruce O'Connor talking to the crew of the *Seaya* as they were pulling their boat out of the water at the boat ramp. I recognized Dale Schmidt, from the auction, driving the truck that towed the fast boat. His two divers wore the bottom halves of their wet suits as they helped secure the boat to the trailer.

James Donahue, the gruff-speaking man from Buffalo, was pulling his boat up to the dock, awaiting his turn to pull it out. One of the local fishing boats that agreed to take divers out was letting Larry Plumber, from Providence, Rhode Island, off at the dock. Then Abraham's black Mercedes pulled into the parking area.

I was shocked to see Richard Bailey get out of the car with Abraham. I thought that he would be in jail for a long time. I wondered whether Abraham had bailed him out, and if so, why. We sat at a bench at the end of the breakwall and watched as the entire group we had met at Carski's office eventually climbed into the back of Schmidt's van.

Fifteen minutes later, the van doors opened and Donahue stepped out, putting an envelope in his pocket. The others followed, with Abraham the last to exit.

Debbie's voice broke the silence as we watched. "He bought them off!"

"Why? He found the gold." I wanted to tell her about the palladium, but I had promised Abraham I wouldn't talk about it.

I wondered whether Jason or Ken knew about the palladium. By the expressions on their faces, I guessed not. Bailey got in the car with Abraham and left. Bruce stopped Plumber and had a short conversation with him before walking toward us.

"The treasure hunt is over," the tall deputy said, with a big smile of relief.

"Buffield bought the coordinates from all the others." It was Ken that spoke up first, demonstrating the desire to continue diving. We all felt the same. But I knew that the hunt for palladium would continue.

We drove back to the boat to find Abraham there, waiting. Bailey was nowhere in sight. Abraham told us to be ready to leave the dock at six in the morning. Sighs of relief came from his divers. He confirmed what Bruce had told us and added that gold wasn't the only treasure out there. He looked at me and said, "It is okay to tell them about the palladium, but no one is to tell anyone else about it. Tomorrow we are just exploring wrecks."

Ken and Jason left with Abraham. Trisha invited Debbie to stay with us instead of on the boat. Debbie seemed a bit embarrassed when she declined the invitation, stating that she liked sleeping on the boat. Trisha reached out and held my hand, telling Debbie to have a good night. We left for the car to go home. Holding Trisha's hand stirred some familiar feelings, and I was happy that Debbie was staying on the boat.

I got to the boat early Sunday morning to find Debbie sitting on the deck, talking on her phone. I decided to grab a cup of coffee from Bill's marina. I brought a cup back to Debbie, who had finished her early-morning phone conversation.

"Bernie says hi," Debbie said as she held out her hand for the coffee. "He wishes that he could be here with us."

"I do too," I said.

Debbie seemed very relaxed, and I could tell that she had been up for a while, because she was all cleaned up and had her hair loose so it could dry. "You know something, Wilbur? I really want to explore each of the shipwrecks. Each and every one of them."

"Yeah, me too. Did you tell your boss about the coins?"

"Well, in a way. When I reported to my office, I explained about finding the single coins Mike left on each ship."

"What about the chest that was filled with gold coins?"

She smiled demurely and whispered, "I didn't mention that yet."

Captain Jack greeted us as he was heading out with a group of eager fisherman. I hailed him back and wished him luck as he fired up the engine on the *Sea Dog*. We watched the boat shrink down the river on the clear, cool Sunday morning. A pair of white swans was swimming upstream, demonstrating a gracefulness that perfectly complemented the calm start of our day.

Abraham arrived with Ken and Jason, and they boarded the boat, ready to go. As we headed out to the lake, Abraham was busy adding all sixteen sets of coordinates to the GPS. When he was done, he instructed me to head for waypoint number nine, and I did.

Ken and Jason suited up for the first dive. Debbie and I agreed to do the next dive and alternate, so that we could cover more wrecks. The guys were ready to enter the water, and I felt a little left out because I could not go. I wondered what condition this wreck would be in.

Ken and Jason entered the water at the same time. The big splash was cold as it hit my face and arms, but just as the water settled back down, a sliver of sun appeared behind the boat, giving me a warm feeling about the day. The two divers left the surface empty as they began their dive.

They surfaced, excited about the wreck. It was the Viking ship that Mike had written about in his journal. I felt really bad that I could not have seen it, but enjoyed the fact that Debbie felt the same way when she said, "We'll have to come back here."

Ken drove the boat to the next dive spot so that Debbie and I could suit up. Seconds after the anchor was dropped, Debbie and I were in the water and eagerly descending to our wreck. I felt good all the way down and was not surprised to see a wreck just south of the anchor. All of the wrecks we had visited so far had been just a few feet south of the coordinates. Mike must have done that so that the wrecks could avoid any damage that might be done by dive boat anchors.

This wreck was another wooden sailing ship. It was half the size of the *Ontario*. We followed the planks that were skewered along the bottom of the lake. The largest part that was in one piece was the massive oak rudder. The masts were broken off, probably by a storm before the ship sank.

I was disappointed not to find the name of the ship anywhere, but I marveled at the workmanship that went into building such a ship. Pieces of black coal surrounded the ruins, revealing that the ship was probably carrying a cargo of coal when it sank. A large salmon darted by our side, and I looked at Debbie, who was peering under a long piece of oak about ten feet in front of me.

Visibility was close to fifty feet at the sixty-foot depth of our dive. I had lost track of time when Debbie approached and pointed to her pressure gauge, signaling "up." I looked at my gauge and saw that I only had seven hundred pounds of air left, so I returned her "up" signal.

We had made it all around the ship and were right back at the anchor line. A quick prayer for the sailors of the crumbled wreck was in my mind as we made our way up the anchor line. We made a three-minute safety stop at fifteen feet before finishing our ascent to the calm of the surface. There was no current and there were no waves, making the surface feel like a swimming pool.

The other divers welcomed us as we swam to the back of the boat. Debbie was describing the wreck to Ken and Jason as I climbed up the ladder. Ken helped me get my gear off, while Jason helped Debbie up the ladder and helped her get out of her gear. Abraham watched for a second before he lowered his eyes back to the sheets of paper he was studying.

The sky was pure blue without a single white puff of a cloud in it. The sun was well above the eastern horizon and delivered welcome warmth as we removed our suits and compared our morning dives. The next dive was a forty-foot dive on a steel tugboat. Ken and Jason did the dive and spent a whole hour under water.

Abraham was interested, and wanted to make sure that the divers looked in every nook and cranny inside the boat. He reminded us that we were looking for eight-inch bars of white palladium that would fill the deck of the *Gold Hunter*. Satisfied that the palladium was not on the tug, we left for the next dive site.

The last wreck was the *Young American*, which lay in fifty-six feet of water. I was anxious to see this wreck, but I felt a little claustrophobic about going deep inside the ship to search it thoroughly. Debbie was in the water before me and had to wait for me to adjust my BCD so I could enter the water. Satisfied that my gear was okay, I stepped to the back of the boat and raised my left foot to the air, leaned forward, and splashed into the water.

I switched to my snorkel and led Debbie to the anchor line. We signaled to descend, deflated our BCDs and switched to our regulators. It was eight-eleven on my dive computer. Three feet down, I became eager to see the wreck. The water seemed colder than at the first dive, and there was a mild current pushing us northeast from the anchor line.

A thin layer of thermocline with a hazy white appearance met us at thirty feet. At thirty-five feet, we broke out of the thermocline and saw the propeller-driven wooden barge in its entirety. Visibility was the best I had seen all week. There were as many different species of fish swimming around the wreck as there were rocks on the bottom.

Large lake trout tormented the smaller jack perch that swam in schools and disappeared into the wreck when a trout came too close. Sunfish the size of my hand decorated the upper deck of the ship. Bass traveled in pairs, looking for crawfish on the bottom. The drumfish were quiet, but greeted us inquisitively as we settled next to the ship.

I saw the plastic bag hooked on the hatch handle and swam to it. I unhooked the bag and looked at the gold coin in it before triumphantly turning to show it to Debbie. She helped me put it in my vest pocket before pointing to the hatch door. We slid the hatch open and looked into the darkness. Debbie tied the end of her reel line to the hatch as I fumbled for my flashlight.

Debbie rolled out some line and swam carefully into the darkness. I followed a moment later. The hold was huge, and we were able to see the bare walls all around us. The cargo area was empty. Debbie descended to the floor and stirred up a lot of dust as she moved the floorboards. I held my light so she could see under the floor, but again there was just emptiness.

Debbie signaled to go up, so I turned and followed the line back to the hatch. A dimly lit area displayed the opening through the dust we had stirred up on the floor. I got my hand on the opening but could not move upward. Something had caught my tank and was holding me down. I started to struggle and felt the hold grabbing me tighter. Mike's voice sounded in my head, saying, "Relax, relax." I stopped moving and took a deep breath and felt something tugging behind me. It was Debbie, working to free me. She pulled me back into the darkness before pushing me back to the hole. I was free and could swim out.

Outside the hole, I swam about ten feet to get out of the floating dust before turning to see Debbie right behind me. She gave me the okay signal to see if I was all right. A bit embarrassed, I returned the signal. Debbie went back and got her line reel. She attached the reel back to her BCD and pointed to the pilot house.

I swam to the pilot house and found the door was openable. I opened the door, but moved back to let Debbie inside the small pilot house. I swam around the small glassless windows on the outside, watching Debbie explore the inside. Dust started pouring out the windows before I met Debbie squeezing through the door on the other side.

I had checked my air before Debbie came out, and signaled to her that I only had a thousand pounds left. She checked her gauge before pointing to the railing on the top of the deck, following with her finger around the ship and to the anchor line. I understood that she wanted to take a swim around the wreck before heading up. I gave the okay signal and swam to the rail.

We enjoyed the last look at the small ship before heading up the anchor line. We did another safety stop at fifteen feet. We could see the silhouette of the boat above us, so we left the security of the anchor line and made our way to the back of the boat before surfacing.

Ken and Jason were jealous as we described the excellent condition of the *Young American*. Debbie looked at Abraham and said, "It does warrant another look."

As we climbed up the ladder, the pale-faced Abraham simply said, "Tomorrow."

It was nine o'clock, and I realized that we had been down for almost an hour. I felt good about my conservative air consumption, but I was embarrassed about the way I had panicked when my tank had gotten caught on the hatch hinge. Debbie was gracious when I tried to apologize for panicking, telling me that I only had panicked for a second and that I had gained my composure very well. I did admire this skillful diver.

Jason started showing scratches on his equipment from times that he'd gotten hung up, and Ken laughed and said that it was a good thing he had been there to help, or Jason would be part of a wreck now. Then Ken showed some scratches, making Jason laugh. I realized that wreck diving was a lot more dangerous than following fish around, and I vowed to relax more around wrecks, while being alert at the same time.

Removing my gear, I remembered the coin in my pocket. I pulled it out with all the pride of a high school freshman scoring his first touchdown. I was immediately cheered by everyone except for Abraham, who was still working with his notes. I asked him, "What are you working on?"

"My algorithm," he answered.

"What's an algorithm?"

"Humph."

Debbie spoke up, explaining that an algorithm is a model, in this case a set of technical specifications for deep tech diving. Abraham said, "Waypoint thirteen next." I put gear away and started the engines. The anchor came up, and we left for a site in a hundred and sixty-five feet of water. It was about a mile from the lighthouse at Thirty Mile Point. Abraham suited up, with Ken helping him attach equipment in the water. Ken got back on the boat as Abraham followed the anchor line down alone.

Jason said, "We will be here for an hour and a half before he comes up."

I went to the cigar box and grabbed a handful of cigars, offering them to Jason and Ken. They each took one, and Debbie said, "Is this a celebration? Where's mine?" I handed her a cigar, and we all lit up. The boat must have looked like an old-time steamship with all the gray smoke rising from the four tiny cigars on the deck.

Conversation was great. There is no age, race, or sex gap with scuba divers, only humble recounting of experiences and modest boasting. The ninety minutes went fast before Abraham surfaced. It took all of us to help get his equipment into the boat before he climbed in.

On the deck Abraham opened his dive bag and pulled out a brick of white metal about eight inches long and two inches square. "Wow!" Jason exclaimed. "So that's what was down there! What in the world is it, anyway?"

Ken seemed as baffled as Jason. He shook his head and added, "It isn't gold, because it's so white. Bright white—not like snow, but like light itself."

"But it is a metal all the same," I added, suddenly feeling pretty knowledgeable.

Debbie explained in some detail what palladium was and talked about its history and its present value. "It's a sort of white treasure, wouldn't you say, Abraham?" she concluded.

"Right," he said, totally expressionless. Then he said, "It's time for lunch. We'll come back later."

We pulled anchor and headed back to Oak Orchard River. It seemed odd that there were no other divers on the lake. It was a perfectly calm and sunny day, with plenty of unexplored wrecks just waiting for divers to reveal their mysteries to. Even Mike's underwater park was deserted. Jason seemed quiet on the way back, as if something were bothering him.

Abraham left us at the dock, ordering us to be ready at five o'clock to go back out. That gave us six hours to relax before diving again. Ken got out a deck of cards and suggested a game of euchre. I enjoyed the game and agreed, as did Jason and Debbie. First I called Trisha and asked her to pick up a pizza and bring it to the boat for us. Then I lit up a cigar and offered them around. I asked Jason how he was feeling, and he expressed his concern that Abraham was a dangerous dive buddy. I asked what that meant.

Jason gave Ken a glance before telling us, "Abraham had a partner he dove with that never came back from a tech dive off the Jersey shore. Abraham always dove alone after that. Then a dive master insisted on diving with Abraham on a German submarine. Two days later, rescue divers found the dive master's body tangled in some steel piping inside the wreck. They never proved that Abraham had just left him there, but there was a lot of suspicion. Especially when papers found on the sub surfaced in the black market two months later."

Ken added, as if he felt we deserved an explanation, "Abraham pays us well, including buying all our tech gear and travel. We have dived some great wrecks, but nothing like the variety of historical wrecks that are here."

Ken was a good euchre partner, and we beat Jason and Debbie ten to two. Debbie asked for another round, but Jason reminded us that they had to fill the technical diving tanks for the next dive. They carried the tanks up the hill, and Jason backed up the pickup truck. When he dropped the tailgate, four large storage tanks were revealed that had been hidden under a false floor.

They laid the tanks on the ground and started working on planning the dive. With my limited diving knowledge, the terms were alien to me. "Wings," "can," and "end" were words used differently than I was used to hearing.

Trisha showed up with the pizza, and we enjoyed lunch on the deck of the boat. Bernie had called Debbie, and she seemed excited about him returning. Jason and Ken continued to plan their dive. Debbie got out Mike's tech gear and started planning a hundred-and-sixty-five-foot dive as well. Trisha and I took a walk over to the marina.

Bill Reed was all questions about the wrecks he had heard about. I assured him that it was true that Mike had found several wrecks and kept them secret, and that we were exploring them. Bill's concern—or rather, hope—was that divers would come from all over and boost his business.

Trisha and I walked outside for a half mile to the point, where we sat and watched people fish and boats pass by. It was a pleasant afternoon, and I really enjoyed Trisha's company. As we walked back, I noticed a line of gray clouds moving in from the south and wondered if a storm was approaching. I made a mental note to check the weather channel when I got back to the boat.

The divers were still busy planning their dive when we returned. Trisha decided to go home, and promised a good dinner when I came home. I walked her to her car, thanked her for the pizza, and gave her a real kiss good-bye.

Abraham was at the back of the pickup truck, filling his tanks. He had a kit with two tanks labeled with the green-and-yellow sticker saying "Enriched air." He had a small glass tube-like instrument that he used to measure the gas mixture. On the ground was a green tank with large letters reading "Oxygen." A very small yellow tank that read "Argon: Do not breathe" was with his gear. It was way too complex for me to understand, so I just got on the boat and grabbed another cigar.

Debbie stopped me before I opened it and explained that some of the tanks were pure oxygen and would explode if I lit the cigar. I put the cigar away and turned on the radio, switching it to the weather channel. It reported a chance of a thunderstorm with gale force winds arriving late in the evening. I was happy that I was not diving and would keep watch on the boat.

The Rescue

It took another hour for everyone to have their tech gear ready and on the boat. Abraham brought some extra lines and three large baskets that looked like lobster traps. He explained that they would be used to bring up the palladium with the boat's davit system, a crane-like device for lowering equipment, which he hooked up while the others filled their tanks with the strange gas mixtures.

At five o'clock on the button, we were ready to head back out on the lake. The wind increased as we headed for Thirty Mile Point. Waves remained small, with the south wind coming from offshore. The sky stayed blue, but there was a darkening row of cumulonimbus clouds lining the southern horizon.

I agreed to wait on the boat as a safety man while Jason and Ken dove together and Abraham dove with Debbie. I was concerned about the stories of Abraham being a poor dive partner for Debbie, but she winked at me, letting me know that she could handle the dive.

The long ride to Thirty Mile Point gave everyone plenty of time to assemble their gear, go over their dive plans, and check slates and computers. The eighteen-passenger dive boat seemed full with only four tech divers and the massive amount of gear they would need for the dive.

We anchored in a hundred and sixty-five feet of water at the site. Jason and Ken attached the two wire cages to the anchor line with carabineers and a heavy line that sank as they unrolled the line. With the cages on the bottom, Abraham and Debbie were to dive first. Jason and Ken were to wait until the cage line was tugged three times. They were to pull the first cage up and then they could enter the water to start a descent to the bottom.

My job was to help on the surface and wait. I thought the waiting would be the hard part, because the total time for the dive would be an hour for each team. Still, I was comforted by the fact that Jason and Ken could look out for Debbie in the event that Abraham failed to come to her aid if needed.

Abraham was first in the water, wearing his double tanks, followed by Debbie, with Mike's double-enriched-air tanks on. Jason was in the water, helping the two divers attach the rest of their gear. It was a lot of heavy work to hand the equipment to the divers, and it left me exhausted by the time Jason climbed back in the boat.

I watched as Debbie followed Abraham to the anchor line and disappeared beneath the surface. Jason and Ken moved their gear to the back of the boat, while I felt the cage line as the divers descended.

Ken took over watching for the signal from below. I decided to put on Mike's wet suit so I could get in the water and help when Jason and Ken were ready to gear up. By the time I was suited up, Ken announced that the three-tug signal had been received. I helped pull the line up through the davit pulley. It took a good five minutes before the filled cage broke the surface. I was astonished to see the glistening white cargo, dripping with water. Palladium was a lustrous silver white metal, and a stack of bars like this was an impressive sight indeed. Here was just the first shining load of Mike's precious white treasure. We swung the davit to lower the cage onto the deck. A slate with a penciled note said to send the cage back down. We unloaded about forty pounds of the palladium from the cage before I attached it with the line and sent it back down the anchor line. Jason was in the water with Ken, waiting for me to hand them the rest of their gear.

I was overheated from the wet suit and eagerly got in the water with the divers to help them fasten the extra equipment. I waited for them to descend before I got back on the boat. The water cooled me off, and I felt better while I waited on the boat.

The wind had swung around and was coming from the east, increasing the waves to a foot and a half. The clouds were darkening, growing upward, and coming closer. The storm was coming a lot sooner than the weatherman had predicted. I became nervous, and put my fins on and pulled my mask around my neck, in case I needed to get in the water to help Debbie and Abraham when they surfaced.

The sky darkened as the first droplets of rain increased my anxiety and the waves began rising up menacingly. I wished for a way to signal the divers, and remembered the five bang signal on the ladder. I used my dive knife to strike the ladder five times. Ten seconds later I signaled again.

It was hard to see any bubbles with the increasing waves, but I noticed a set getting closer to the boat. Somebody was ascending the anchor line. I was eager to see Debbie and Abraham and hoped that Jason and Ken were coming with them. The bubbles seemed to stop moving, because the divers were probably making a decompression stop on the anchor line.

Suddenly the surface exploded with bubbles. I wanted to leave the boat, both to get out the impending storm and to hurry the divers along. One set of bubbles moved closer to the boat as the other set disappeared. The bubbles close to the boat were probably in only twenty feet of water, but there were too few of them for more than one diver.

I grabbed my scuba unit and set it on the back of the boat, just in case I needed to go in. I turned and looked to see the bubbles moving closer. Abraham surfaced. I remembered the stories about Abraham losing his dive buddies before and became extremely worried about Debbie.

"Where's Debbie?" I cried out, but Abraham did not answer. The extra equipment did not seem to slow Abraham down. He made it to the back of the boat and used the waves to help him throw his gear in the back of the boat. I asked again, "Where is Debbie?" and he still did not answer me. I helped him climb the ladder and asked once again, but he shoved me away and removed his tanks.

It was hard to get up with my fins on, and by the time I did Abraham had pulled a .45 out from his equipment bag. I was facing the open end of the barrel and looking into the cold eyes of Abraham Buffield. I knew that I was about to die. Surprisingly, death did not scare me, but the thought of Debbie in trouble angered me and gave me the strength I needed to lurch forward at the gun.

A wave dropped the stern of the boat, making Abraham's first shot go over my shoulder. I felt the warmth of the bullet pass my ear just before I knocked the gun from Abraham's hand. I landed a left hook on the side of Abraham's face, sending him to the floor. Unfortunately, the boat rocked from the increasing waves, and I fell over the ladder and into the water.

I was quick to reach up and grab something on the back of the boat, but Abraham had found his gun and I was again looking in the barrel. Above the barrel I saw the evil eyes of a killer, and above that was a bolt of lightning. All I could do was to fall back in the water. My hand was on the BCD strap of my scuba unit, pulling it into the water with me.

I had no air in my BCD, so the unit took me under just as the loud bang of the gun went off again. Sinking, I was blinded from the lightning and deaf from the gunshot. Still, I found my regulator and gasped for a breath of air from it. Relieved by the first breath, I headed under the boat to escape the bullets penetrating the water from above. As my senses came back, I found my mask and put it on. The engines started.

I managed to put my vest on. The calm serenity of being underwater helped me sort out the situation. If I surfaced, Abraham was sure to use me for target practice. Debbie had not surfaced yet. I decided to look for Debbie. It seemed that I was descending too fast, but looking at my depth gauge, I realized that the anchor and cage line were going up.

Then I saw some bubbles and left the anchor line to find the source of the bubbles. At a hundred feet, I looked at my gauges and figured that to surface was sure death, and to continue down without the requisite training and equipment was suicide. I heard a voice that seemed to be inside me say, "Help me!" It was not my conscience, and not even Mike's voice; it was Debbie, calmly asking for help.

Maybe it was telepathy or something, or maybe it was a sound being carried up from one of Debbie's bubbles. I was committed to going all the way as I put my depth gauge away at a hundred and thirty feet and followed the bubbles. My head was hurting from not having a hood on, as if a thousand pins were being pushed into the skin. I was freezing in the thin wet suit, and I missed my dry suit.

The water became dark as a sure storm blackened the surface and concealed the sunshine. The only things I could see were the bubbles. Then the colorless shape of a scuba unit came into view. It was sitting next to the wreck, but no one was wearing it. The bubbles were coming from an opening in the wreck. I thought it was Jason and Ken.

I hit the bottom and looked inside the wreck to see Debbie breathing from a hose connected to her scuba unit. I fumbled for my flashlight as I closed in on the flashlight beam that Debbie was shining on her face. There were no smiling eyes this time, but a look of sheer terror was on her face as I closed in on the young girl.

I shone my dive light along Debbie to see that a steel beam was holding her legs down. I started to move her legs to free them, but Debbie's hand spun me back to face her. She gave me the "share air" signal, so I reached for my alternate air source. Then Debbie's hand hit my face, with her regulator pointed at my mouth.

In an instant I realized that breathing pure air at this depth would give me oxygen toxicity, so I took two breaths from her deep-diving air and handed it back to her. We did this several times before I put my own regulator back in my mouth and turned to her legs. I could not budge the steel beam.

I took a deep breath and tried again. This time the beam moved a smidgen, but it was enough for Debbie to pull her legs free. A cloud of dark liquid emerged from her leg as she moved. I dropped the beam as soon as her fins moved out from under it.

I was exhausted from hefting the beam, but made my way the three feet to the wreck's exit behind Debbie. She gave me her regulator again and took mine in her own mouth. We both relaxed for a minute. I turned to her leg and saw a three-inch tear in her dry suit. There was blood oozing from the tear. I was about to try to find something to wrap around it when a hand grabbed my arm.

It was Jason. He reached in front of me and tied a piece of rope around Debbie's leg, about six inches above the cut. Then he folded the material from the dry suit over and tied another rope around the tear. He was trying to keep the dry suit from leaking cold water into it.

I turned and was handed a regulator by Ken. We began buddy-breathing as Jason helped Debbie into her scuba unit. Jason and Debbie were also buddy-breathing when we began our ascent into the darkness. It was hard to stay in a group with the four of us passing a regulator back and forth. I watched Debbie as she started to shiver from the cold.

Numbness had replaced the extreme discomfort I had felt from the cold on the way down. Jason and Ken looked at each other's computers and at mine and Debbie's. We seemed to stop going up. I looked at my depth gauge and saw that we were at sixty feet.

Jason helped Debbie change to one of her green regulators. Ken changed to a green regulator too, then turned to me and signaled to buddy-breathe. I obeyed as I watched Jason buddy-breathe with Debbie. I realized that I had no clue what was happening. Watching Ken and Jason write on the slates and look at computers, including mine, helped pass the time, but I was getting anxious from buddy-breathing. I wanted my own air.

I looked at my pressure gauge and saw that I had eleven hundred pounds of air left. I knew that that was plenty to get me to the surface. I signaled to Ken that I wanted to use my own air, and he handed me my regulator. Ken wrote something down on the back of his slate and turned it over so I could read it: *30 min of deco time w/my air, but several hours left with yours.*

Then Ken made the signal to buddy-breathe again. I did not want to buddy-breathe, but realizing that I was going to survive this ordeal if I did as instructed, I spit out my regulator and tried to relax as well as I could.

It did not seem like thirty minutes when the signal to go up was passed, but I was happy to be moving. We continued to buddy-breathe up to twenty feet, where Ken showed me his slate. *18 more*, it said. At twenty feet, we changed to the smaller green tanks marked "Oxygen." This time I took turns buddy-breathing with Ken and then Jason.

It was pitch black all around us, but I could feel movement. A current must have been pushing us along. We could see each other swaying back and forth from the waves only twenty feet above us. I began thinking of the surface. Would Abraham be waiting for us with his deadly gun, or would a storm swallow us and leave us on the bottom with one of Mike's wrecks?

I thought about Mike's underwater park and how serene I felt diving there. I really wanted to see the Viking ship and the wrecks that Mike found. A physical stirring entered my body as I thought about my wonderful wife, Trisha, and I longed to hold her in my arms just once more.

Another look at computers, and Jason signaled to ascend. Ken gave me my own air, and I was ecstatic as I signaled to ascend with Ken and Debbie. We started the short ascent to the surface, but the daylight didn't dance on gentle waves above us. Instead we surfaced in total darkness, with waves tossing us about, making it near impossible to stay together.

Wave motion was the only way to tell the surface from underwater, because the rain was so heavy. A clap of thunder reminded me of Abraham's gun for a moment, but I was too terrified to care which was which. At least I was warm. Debbie was having trouble staying on the surface until Jason disappeared under the surface for a moment. When he resurfaced, Debbie seemed to sit higher in the water. Jason must have let her weight belt go.

I overinflated my BCD to stay above the water, only to find that I had to time the swells and breathe as we came down the waves. We held onto each other, because we could not see three feet away. Jason and Ken had their masks around their necks and were talking. I could not hear what they were saying, but I could see that they were looking for the boat.

I did not tell them about the fight with Abraham or the gun, because I did not want them to give up hope. Debbie seemed weak and cold, but she managed to keep one hand on my BCD and the other on Jason's. I was holding Ken, who was holding Jason. We formed a tight little square.

Breathing during the storm was more difficult than buddy-breathing underwater. We waited for each lightning blast, hoping that the light would show us a boat. I was anxious and tired, so I reached into my BCD and released the integrated weight system. I rode higher in the water, so I let some air out of my BCD, making it more comfortable to breathe again.

Time was measured by the little successes when we did not have to spit out water before we could swallow breaths of air. Despite her weak state and the difficulty we were all having breathing, miraculously Debbie found the energy to start singing in a raspy voice, "We all live in a yellow submarine." She couldn't really sing more than a line herself, but it brought laughter to the dismal situation, so the rest of us took up the familiar song and sung it with as much spirit as we could manage in the choppy waves. The singing must have appeased the Lake Ontario storm gods, because the rain seemed to let up somewhat as we sang, although the waves were still pretty rough and potentially dangerous. The rain slowed down, giving us a better view of the area. We could not see the shore or any boats. The current was moving us away from shore. We had been an hour underwater and another hour on the surface. We looked about desperately.

Jason was the first to hear the sound.

"Listen," he said, and we became dead silent. The sound of wind whistling through the air and water being blown from wave crest to wave crest made it impossible to hear what Jason was hearing. Then, in a state much like delirium, I suddenly heard the faint echo of our song.

"We all live in a yellow submarine, a yellow submarine..."

Ken started singing back. We all did. Then we became silent again. It was someone else singing. We started yelling. A face appeared above us, like a god from the heavens. It was Bernie Kloch. He was on the front bowsprit of a boat, and he threw us a line. The boat rose up on the next wave and we swam back so it would not crush us as it came down. When it did come down, the words *Sea Dog* welcomed us to its port side.

Jason filled his BCD and dropped his weights as Ken held the line from Bernie. Then Jason dropped his weight belt and removed his equipment, pushing it behind him and away from the boat. The boat rose again, and Jason was ready. The boat dropped, and Bernie and Mark held out their hands to catch Jason.

The boat rose out of sight with Jason slammed against its side. When it came down again, Jason was gone. Ken helped Debbie out of her gear as I held onto the line and onto Ken. Debbie had her mask on and her snorkel in her mouth as Ken guided her to the thrashing vessel. Again Bernie and Mark appeared, hands outstretched, and Debbie disappeared.

It was my turn. I felt that the storm was not as bad as getting near the pounding boat, but I filled my BCD and let the waves carry it off, thinking, *How will I find it again?* Ken was holding onto the line and onto me as I watched the boat crash down again. I timed it as the boat was high and raised my arms and kicked with my fins. The boat came down.

My arms were pinned to the side as the waves pulled the boat upward. I thought that my arms were going to come out of their sockets, but as the boat fell back into the swell I was rolled over the gunwale. I rolled onto the deck to find Jason asking whether I was okay. I nodded, and Jason helped me get out of the way for Ken, who came rolling in with a big smile.

Sitting in the back of the *Sea Dog*, I could not even see Captain Jack on the bridge, but I heard him tell Bernie, "That was all of them." The storm was horrific. We bounced around in the small cockpit of the fishing boat. Bernie slid across the floor to Debbie and looked at her leg.

Debbie shivered uncontrollably. Bernie untied the rope around her leg. I had to hold Debbie as Bernie peeled her dry suit off. The coveralls she wore underneath were sopping wet. Bernie pulled them off, wrapped a blanket around her, and took her below to bandage her cut leg.

Mark sat next to Ken and told him what had happened. "Abraham ran the boat into the dock. Two men helped him unload his diving gear and a bunch of some stuff that looked like white gold. Then Captain Jack asked him several times where they had gone, but he refused to answer.

"Bruce was out helping another boat when the storm hit, so we came out looking for you," Mark continued. Deputy Bruce O'Connor had watched everything that happened along the lakeshore and told our rescuers that we were diving near Thirty Mile Point. It was Captain Jack who had used his radar to find our equipment on the surface.

Mark had met Bernie at the dive shop when the group returned from the dive weekend. Bernie had suggested a ride to the point, and Mark jumped at the chance to dive with us. That was when Captain Jack had decided to look for the abandoned divers.

I left Mark with the other divers and climbed the slippery ladder to the bridge. Captain Jack was busy negotiating the waves. He had me help by calling Deputy O'Connor on the radio to let him know that we were safe. Looking out the window, I was not so sure that we were safe, but I called Bruce, who sounded happy that we were on our way back to Oak Orchard.

Seasickness set in about a mile from the river. I was too nauseated to climb down the ladder to the cockpit. I held out as long as I could, but I finally had to lean out the flybridge window and let go. I wasn't the only one who was seasick, because just as I let go, I noticed Ken leaning over the gunwale. It was too late, and my vomit hit Ken on the back of the head as his vomit spewed into the raging waves.

I was embarrassed and too sick to pull my head back inside. I realized that Ken had not noticed, and I thought I might not get caught getting sick on Ken. My mental comfort was shattered when the grinning face of Mark peeked around the corner and spotted my green face. He took a pail, scooped up some water, and doused Ken, who barely flinched.

Captain Jack used his electronics to navigate the narrow entrance between the invisible breakwalls of Oak Orchard River. I knew the breakwall was there, because the whitewater sprayed over the barrier and into the calmer river. My seasickness subsided as we docked next to our deserted dive boat. I finally had the chance to thank Captain Jack, who shrugged and said, "You would have done the same for me."

I thought I did not have the ability to do what Captain Jack had just done, but vowed to myself to help whenever I could. The rain was hard as we docked, but it felt good to stand on solid ground, even in the pouring rain, with my fellow divers. Jack said good night and went below. Bernie drove Debbie to the hospital to get her leg looked at. I invited Mark and the boys to come home for dinner.

I locked up the boat before driving home with the divers. I brought Mike's cell phone and called Trisha from the car. She had been worried about the storm, knowing I was still on the water, and she was very relieved to hear my voice again. She said that she'd be delighted to have the divers over for dinner, but she was disappointed that Debbie wasn't coming with us.

Before we made it out of the parking lot, the sheriff's car pulled in. A hand stuck out the window, waving us down. I stopped next to the car and rolled my window down. It was Bruce, and he wanted to know where the divers were. I told him that they were with me, and we were going to my house for dinner and some warmth. "All except Debbie, who is on her way to the hospital with Bernie," I concluded.

"Is she okay?"

"I think so. Just a cut leg and the chills."

"Get warmed up, but don't let anybody leave until I get there," he said.

I told him, "It'll take hours for us to warm up."

"Good. I'll see you in less than an hour."

Rain pelted the car. I drove slowly, still feeling the motion of the waves. Mark turned my contemporary music off and we sang "Yellow Submarine" all the way home. I felt young with my dive buddies, and enjoyed the camaraderie.

Trisha had a fresh pot of coffee waiting when we four drenched men sashayed in the back door to the kitchen. She always yelled at me if I did not take my shoes off when I came into the house, but she pulled out chairs for us and told us to sit at the kitchen table. She poured us coffee, and put cream and sugar on the table.

Then she brought some towels in for us to use to dry our heads and told us that she was getting some dry clothes for us. Five minutes later, she came in with a basket full of clothes and instructed us to change in the kitchen and leave our wet clothes in the basket so she could wash them for us. Trisha said, "Holler when you're done," and left for the living room.

I had always taken pride in my physical condition, but as these divers dried off and slipped into some of my old clothes, I was a bit embarrassed because all my pants were way too large for the guys. "Got any suspenders?" Ken joked, before looking at me apologetically. Everyone else laughed, and even I had to laugh, looking at Ken holding the trousers out in front of him, with room to spare. Ken smiled when he saw me laugh too.

I took the laundry basket full of wet clothes to the laundry room next to the kitchen as the guys tied knots to hold up their pants. I felt better when they had to roll up the legs and I realized that I was taller than any of them. We wiped up the chairs with the towels that Trisha had given us, and I mopped the floor to dry off the mess we had made when we came inside.

We were sitting at the table and enjoying our hot coffee when the front doorbell rang. I got up, but then I heard Trisha's voice rise two octaves in friendly surprise. "Debbie! What in the world did they do to you?" The gang followed me in to see Debbie standing there in crutches, wearing a wet man's shirt that made it obvious that she was not wearing a bra. Her bandaged leg was exposed.

Debbie looked at the oddly clad guys and laughed. It was good to see her laugh. Trisha chased us back to the kitchen, saying, "Get out of here until I can get her dressed!" We ran like scolded little children back to the kitchen, where Bernie was coming in the back door.

"Trisha told me to come in the back," our courageous rescuer said. He was still wearing the wet clothes from hours ago, but had a bag of dry clothes in his hand. I sent him to the laundry room to change into his dry clothes. I had a cup of coffee for him when he came back to the kitchen; he accepted it eagerly.

Conversation about Mike's wrecks filled the room until Trisha brought Debbie in. She was wearing one of Trisha's sweat suits, navy blue with white stripes down the sides of the arms and legs. Jason quickly got up and offered her his chair, which she took, proudly saying, "Five stitches," as if they were an award of some kind. One of Trisha's hair clips held Debbie's blond hair behind her tiny neck. She became the center of attention.

After raising her leg up to the table to show her stitches, her face became stern. She looked at me and said, "What were you doing on the bottom with just air? Don't you know that you could have gotten into real trouble from oxygen poisoning at that depth?"

All eyes were on me, and I realized that nobody had any idea what had happened. Trisha was getting folding chairs from the closet, and I waited for everyone to sit down before I started to explain. I opened my mouth to speak, but then the doorbell rang again.

"It must be Bruce, and I'm sure that he will want to hear this too." I got up to answer the door, and Trisha got out another chair. Bruce came in, and Trisha gave him a cup of coffee and sat him down. I began telling about the afternoon's adventure, starting with the impending storm and my concern for Debbie when Abraham had surfaced without her.

I felt like Samuel Clemens while telling the story, because everyone was so interested. Ken and Jason filled in the reason for the explosion of bubbles I had seen. Abraham had cut one of their air hoses and tried to stab Ken with his dive tool as he ascended past them on their way down.

Concerned about Debbie, they had descended the anchor line and redone their dive plan to determine how they would find Debbie and still make it through their decompression dives with enough air. When the anchor line started moving, they had just descended to the wreck. It had taken a while for them to find it without the anchor, and they were shocked to find me there, because they knew I had no special gear for diving that deep.

Debbie said, "I really want to thank all of you from the bottom of my heart for the collaborative effort that saved my life: Wilbur, for finding me and the steel beam and getting me out of a tight spot; Jason, for your tourniquet and for taking off my weight belt at the right time; Ken, for the buddy-breathing and equipment checks that got us above the waves; Bernie, for hearing our song and singing it back to us and for being there at the right time; and Mark, for helping us back on board."

We were all pleased and embarrassed by her gratitude, and then Mark broke the silence by saying, "That's what's so great about scuba diving, you know? It's not just about your own experience of beauty and underwater challenge, it's about being a team, diving together."

We all heartily agreed and then I added a light note. "Hey, Debbie," I said. "That's a lot of thanking, but aren't you going to thank the Beatles for the song about the yellow submarine?"

"Thanks to Ringo, Paul, John, and George," she replied with a smile.

"I haven't any questions to ask, but I can add to your story," Bruce said. "Those two men who were helping Abraham are now in custody. Unfortunately, Abraham himself slipped away. Also, I found a bullet hole in the side of the *Gold Hunter* after Captain Jack called in the mysterious arrival of the dive boat without its skipper or crew."

Jason spoke up next. "It turns out that the SUV had a hidden compartment in the back, so the gold was probably still there."

Bruce said, "We have the vehicle, but two bars of some strange white metal were all that we found in the back."

"Palladium," I explained. Bruce made a note in his notebook.

Debbie spoke up, asking, "Only two? We brought up forty bars in the first cage and twenty-two in the second one."

Bruce's eyebrows shot upward, and he said, "Interesting." Bruce made another note in his notebook before asking to use our phone. Trisha led Bruce to the living room to make his call.

With Bruce out of the room, Debbie whispered, "I think the palladium must have been placed in the wreck after it sank." Everyone stared at her in eager anticipation as she continued, "I don't think Abraham realized it." Mike had left another tease, which meant that there was still valuable treasure to find. The windows lit up, and three seconds later, a clap of thunder rocked the window panes. The storm was not over. Treasure was still hiding quietly somewhere in the serenity of the depths of Lake Ontario.

Bruce came back in and said, "We put out an APB on Abraham Buffield and received a report that he got on a plane in Rochester headed for Puerto Rico."

"Damn!" said Debbie. "He is out of my jurisdiction."

"Mine too," said Bruce. "But we can have him picked up and extradited back for attempted murder, with your testimonies."

Jason spoke up next, looking at Ken, "We have been working with Abraham for almost a year, off and on. We have been waiting for proof that he was selling on the black market and is connected with a terrorist group."

Ken looked at me and said, "We work for United States Department of Defense."

Jason got up and said, "I need to use your phone. Abraham must have transferred the palladium already." Jason left to make his call. Another lightning bolt, followed by two seconds of quiet before another clap of rolling thunder, shook our confidence.

Ken said to Bruce and Debbie, "I have something else to add, which may come as a surprise to the rest of you. Abraham is not to be apprehended. If you hear anything, let me or Jason know. This information is highly classified. Please make sure that it doesn't leave this room. Understand?"

Bruce replied, "Yes," but Debbie gave Ken a penetrating stare.

"Understand?" Ken asked, looking at Debbie.

"Ya," was all that Debbie uttered.

Trisha broke the tension when she asked if anyone was hungry. I got up and opened the refrigerator door. Debbie yelled, "Hand me that Diet Coke!" Ken reached in and grabbed the single can of Diet Coke and handed it to Debbie. The refrigerator became a traffic area as the politics of police work gave way to a group of happy divers.

Solving the Riddle

Trisha was helping the hungry divers get some serious snacks. I watched a week's worth of groceries disappear. When the human feeding frenzy was over, Bruce thanked Trisha and left for the night. Trisha announced that the guys would sleep upstairs in the kids' rooms, and Debbie would sleep downstairs in our room.

The aroma of Monday-morning coffee made its way upstairs, reminding me that I had slept the whole night through. I hurried to get into the bathroom before the other guys woke up. A hot shower felt good after yesterday's dive in the forty-degree water with just a thin wet suit on. Diving was on my mind as I went downstairs to find Trisha fixing breakfast. Fifteen minutes later, the four divers came down, freshly showered and wearing clean clothes.

Trisha seemed to really enjoy fixing breakfast with Debbie's help, and the guys enjoyed eating it. Then Trisha went to get ready for work, and Debbie sat and ate with us. Bernie walked out the back door with his coffee, and I could smell the night's rain, but the thunder no longer boomed. A dreary gray light lingered outside the windows.

It took two minutes for the guys to clean up and do the dishes before we could leave for the marina. Jason made a phone call and came back with some news that terrified me.

"Abraham Buffield used his credit card to purchase a ticket to Puerto Rico last night, but it was Richard Bailey that got off the plane in San Juan." The room was quiet.

Jason continued, "Bailey was followed to Fajardo, where he took a ferry to the island of Vieques on the southeast side of Puerto Rico. There he met with a former Navy Seal and gave him a bar of the palladium."

Bernie scratched his head and said, "Wilbur said last night that the strange white metal was called palladium, but I never heard of it before. What is it? What's it used for?"

Debbie told Bernie, "I'll explain on the way to the boat." She got up and carried her crutches to the door.

The rest of us took our time getting ready to go to the boat. I figured that last night's storm would make it impossible to dive, and for the first time, I wondered what had become of the equipment we had ditched during the treacherous storm.

Mark sat in the front of the car with me, and I explained as much as I knew about palladium. Jason and Ken listened from the back seat. When we got to the marina, Bernie was waiting in the parking lot. Deputy Bruce and Debbie were searching the boat for something.

Debbie finally waved for us to come to the boat, and Bruce told us that they were checking for any explosives that Abraham might have placed in the boat. "Abraham!" I said out loud. Even though I'd heard about the Puerto Rico switch, I was still surprised and frightened at the thought that he could still be here at the marina. Bruce said that he figured Abraham must still be around, but assured us that the boat was safe.

Bernie suggested that we take the boat out and check the lake conditions, and maybe look for our equipment. Jason and Ken seemed eager to go at the idea that we might find our ditched gear. The sky was a dozen shades of gray, but not one was as dark as yesterday's storm clouds. We departed for the lake.

Two-foot-high chocolate-colored waves gently moved the boat up and down as we rounded the breakwall. I was astonished by how calm the lake was so soon after a storm. It even looked like I could dive a few hundred yards out from shore, where the chocolate-colored water turned to a gray that made a pleasant background for the white seagulls that squawked overhead.

Bernie drove the boat slowly and close to shore. We studied every speck of storm-delivered debris that decorated the rocky shoreline, trying to single out a piece of colored diving gear. Due to the lack of wind, the waves just rolled gently, and they seemed to be shrinking in size as we went along.

An hour into our search, the radio squawked, "*Gold Hunter. Gold Hunter. Gold Hunter.* This is the United States Coast Guard. Over!" Bernie picked up the radio's microphone and answered the call. The Coast Guard had a boat heading west to Oak Orchard and wanted us to meet it. Bernie agreed and hung up the radio.

Speed made the waves disappear as we throttled up and turned east to meet the Coast Guard cutter that was headed in our direction. As we got to the mouth of the river, we could see the cutter about a mile to the north, headed our way.

Bernie hailed them on the radio and made plans to raft up beside the cutter a half-mile offshore. Bernie turned the boat to port, and we headed straight for the big Coast Guard ship, which was a shade of gray different from the grays in the sky and in the water.

We were out of the chocolate-colored water when we tied up to the Coast Guard ship. A pair of uniformed Coasties told us that they had talked to the Orleans County sheriff, who had let them know that we'd surfaced in a storm and had to ditch our gear. The Coast Guard returned our equipment with no further questions, but gave us a warning to watch the weather.

The gear was wet and torn, so we decided to head back to port to clean it up. The dreariness of the day and a warning from the Coast Guard about the chance of another storm took away my desire to dive. On the ride in, the serenity of the rolling lake was broken by the sounds of cell phones ringing, mixed with the cry of a watching seagull that followed us, looking for scraps of food in our wake.

Jason got a call telling us that Richard Bailey was back in Rochester. Debbie got a call from her chief, who requested that she return to the office in Lockport as soon as possible. Deputy Bruce called Mike's cell phone, wanting to see me when we got back to the dock, to talk about Abraham Buffield. Mike's wrecks would have to wait another day to be explored.

Deputy Bruce helped us tie the *Gold Hunter* to the dock. He helped Debbie out and talked to her for a few minutes while we secured the boat and turned off the engines. Debbie said good-bye to us and gave Bernie an affectionate hug.

Bruce said, "Wilbur, how about a cup of coffee?"

I looked at Mark, who said, "Go ahead. We'll take care of the gear." I went to the marina with Bruce, where we got our coffees and sat at the damp picnic table outside.

Bruce explained that Abraham had been seen in the area, and suggested that we stay away from the boat until he was apprehended. I figured that we were not going diving anyway, so I agreed to stay away from the boat. The steam from my coffee seemed to mix with the developing fog that was sneaking around the corner of the marina's store and covering the ground before it moved out to the river.

The tops of boats tied to their docks remained visible through the engulfing grayness that seemed to match the dreary color of the sky. Green trees and colorful boat tops turned to what looked like a black-and-white movie, with distant people moving in slow motion.

Bruce left after promising to call me when any information became available. I stepped into the two-foot layer of fog, careful not to trip over any unseen objects hiding under the moving fog. It was eerie to walk on the hidden dock to get back into the boat. Gear was spread out everywhere and hung over the gunwale of the boat. Mark said, "Everything is hung up, but it won't dry in this stuff."

Jason and Ken carried their gear up the hill to their truck and yelled, "See ya later!" from the top of the hill, obviously not too interested in making another trip down the fog-covered hill. Bernie and Mark said that they would like to try diving the next morning, and I agreed to meet them at the boat at six o'clock.

I was alone on the boat, and I remembered my promise to Bruce. I sat there watching Mark get swallowed by the fog as he walked up the hill, and then I saw him reappear five feet away from where he had been. I was not too eager to get up and negotiate my way through the fog again.

Within a few minutes, the world disappeared altogether as the fog thickened and completely engulfed the boat. The fog brought a dampness that sent a chill from my face to my toes. I could barely find the cabin door to escape the cold. I felt my way down into the cabin and locked the fog outside.

An electric light provided ample heat in the tiny cabin as I sat on the cleaned-up bunk that Debbie had been sleeping in. The peacefulness took my thoughts back to the good times I'd had with Mike, and the discussions we had shared about his underwater world.

Mike's voice was reciting his poem in my mind. *Forward the sun sets/An opposing zenith/Bigger the oak gets/All my secrets/Treasure begets/From beneath.* The poem made no sense to me as I drifted off to sleep.

Crash, boom, bang! The cabin lit up. I jumped up off the bunk. It took a moment to recall where I was. Another lightning storm. I peered out the porthole; the fog was gone. I climbed the narrow steps to the deck, and there was no rain. A distant clap of thunder that lasted for ten whole seconds echoed down the river and made the boat tremble. I looked to the western sky as a bolt of lightning shot from the sky to the ground somewhere miles away.

The lightning lit up the silhouette of the old oak tree that sat high up on the western bank of the river.

> *Forward the sun sets*
> *An opposing zenith*
> *Bigger the oak gets*
> *All my secrets*
> *Treasure begets*
> *From beneath*

Mikes poem made sense all of a sudden. "Forward the sun sets" was looking forward to the west as the boat was at rest or at its dock. "An opposing zenith/Bigger the oak gets" meant below the tree, under its roots. "All my secrets/Treasure begets/From Beneath." I knew that the treasure was under the oak tree.

There was not a soul around in the afternoon dark. I donned my scuba suit and rolled off the side of the boat. I raced the approaching storm the three hundred feet across the river to a spot directly under the oak tree. I switched from my snorkel to my regulator and dumped the air out of my BCD.

As I sank in the black river water, I confidently reached into my vest pocket and grabbed my underwater flashlight. Turning it on just before I hit the muddy bottom, I began looking for a cave in the underwater bank. There was no cave, but there was a small wreck.

It was a wooden barge that was only two feet high. A modern hatch was freshly bolted to the top of the barge. I opened the hatch to find that the barge was filled with bars of palladium. I swam the length of the barge and saw that it was over twenty-six feet long. It was like an old-fashioned canal barge that used to carry cargo down the Erie Canal to other parts of the world.

I decided to keep Mike's secret to myself as I took a compass heading east to get back to the dock without having to surface. It was black all around me, and the flashlight barely provided enough light to read my compass. I made it to the ledge that would bring me up the other side of the river.

I ascended slowly with my hands above my head, to avoid running headfirst into the bottom of a boat. I was directly in front of the *Gold Hunter* as I reached the surface. I started swimming around the side of the boat to climb up on shore. Another crack of thunder vibrated the water.

Three seconds later, a blinding flash of lightning lit up the area with an unnatural-looking white light. The dark silhouette of a small man was on the shore in front of me. A pair of black glowing eyes told me that it was Abraham. The light disappeared, leaving a blurred darkness.

The only thing I could see was the flash from the gun in Abraham's hand. I sank quickly as the sound echoed between the boats. My head hit the bottom of the boat, and I knew I was safe from bullets hiding under the boat. Michael's voice rang in my head again. "Ditch the gear," he said. I took off my scuba unit and hung it on the propeller shaft of the port engine. A piece of seaweed got caught in the regulator, making it look like I was still breathing from it.

Holding my breath, I came up the starboard side of the boat. Abraham was leaning over the port side, looking at the bubbles, his gun pointed at them. A rumbling thunder started. If only I could climb on board without him hearing me I could push him over and run for help. The thunder got louder, and something inside me said, "Now!"

I climbed over the gunwale unheard and looked for a weapon. I grabbed a tank from the rack in the center of the boat, but I made enough noise that Abraham heard me and turned. I pushed the tank at him as the gun swung around with an echoing bang. I felt warm as I dropped to the deck and lost consciousness.

The rain was coming down hard as I heard a familiar voice above me. It was Captain Jack. He'd heard the gunshots and come out of his boat. "You all right?" he kept saying. I struggled to sit up and felt myself for a bullet hole. There was no wound. I looked over to where Abraham had been standing a few minutes ago and saw the scattered remains of his lifeless body.

His own bullet had hit the scuba cylinder, making it blow up. The percussion had knocked me down, but the tank had exploded in Abraham's direction and torn him apart. Captain Jack helped me to my feet, but the ringing in my head made me sit back down on the bench. I was warm from the wet suit, and unzipped the front.

Bill Reed came running down from the marina's store. He stopped next to the boat and saw what was left of Abraham, then asked whether I was okay. I nodded, almost speechless with shock. Bill and Jack helped me to the store, where Bill gave me a hot cup of coffee and told me that he had called the sheriff's deputy, who was on his way.

I had finished the coffee when Bruce walked in. "I thought I told you to go home," Bruce said, with a smile. I shuddered a bit, and he said, "Stay here while I look at the boat." My head was still pounding, but I felt good, having defeated my attacker. Bill and Captain Jack had a lot of questions, but I did not feel like answering then, and simply enjoyed the care and concern they gave me.

Deputy Bruce came in and used Bill's phone to get an investigator to come down. Then he called Debbie at her office at the BCI and told her what happened. Bruce poured himself a cup of coffee and sat in a chair across from me.

Bill and Jack were quiet, waiting for Bruce to start asking the questions that never came.

Bruce took a long sniff of his coffee before he took his first sip. Then he looked at me with his stern eyes and said, "A patrol car picked up Richard Bailey speeding in Abraham's Mercedes about a mile from here. He is telling the officers everything that happened. You are very lucky to be alive."

I put my hand to my aching head and agreed. Bruce asked, "Do you need an ambulance?"

"No," I quickly replied.

"Why are you in your wet suit?"

"I'm not sure," I said, with a purposefully dazed look.

He said, "Debbie is on her way."

Bruce got up and took his coffee outside to meet the red flashing lights that had just entered the parking area. Bill and Jack went outside to watch the activity.

I could see through the window that it had quit raining and was getting lighter outside. The storm was passing as quickly as it had moved in. Ten minutes later, Debbie came in, wearing a tan pantsuit with her badge pinned to the blazer. She looked older and professional, but I felt relieved when she spoke to me as a diving buddy rather than a police officer.

I got up and went outside with her. My headache was gone, and I watched them carry Abraham's remains away in a black bag. Debbie turned to me and asked, "So! What happened?"

I told her that I would explain in the morning, then I asked, "Are you diving with me tomorrow?"

She smiled and said, "Now I am, crutches and all."

Debbie brought my clothes from the boat and told me to change in the marina's bathroom, which I did. When I came out, I saw the sun setting through the oak tree. A rainbow extended from beyond the massive oak to a point out in the lake somewhere. I thought to myself that there was a pot of gold at the end of the rainbow.

Debbie hung my wet suit on the boat for me and insisted on driving me home. Bruce followed in the patrol car, so he could bring Debbie back. Trisha came out into the driveway just as the patrol car pulled in the driveway behind us. She looked sexy in her work clothes.

"What is going on?" Trisha asked as I got out of the car.

"I'll explain inside."

Debbie just waved hi, exchanging looks with Trisha, and climbed into the waiting patrol car. Trisha and I walked inside as my friends left. I explained everything, including the ship full of palladium, to my wife. We ate dinner in silence as Trisha let me ponder whether I would tell anyone else about the treasure, and if so, how.

I slept through another night without waking up. I felt energized and even youthful as I dressed for another day on the *Gold Hunter*. Trisha beckoned me back to bed for a kiss good-bye. I was a little late when I arrived at the boat. Debbie was holding Bernie's hand as they sat on the back of the boat. Jason and Ken were at the picnic table, drinking coffee and listening to Mark tell a story that must have been funny, because they all laughed when he finished.

The sun was hiding just over the eastern horizon, its glow reddening the calm sky. Captain Jack waved as he headed out for a day's fishing. I stepped on the deck of the boat and said, "First, we'll dive the Viking ship." A few minutes later, the six of us were headed out to the lake.

The water was silver this morning, without a trace of gray. The sky turned blue, and the only white to be seen was that of some distant seagulls searching for their breakfast. We anchored at the dive site. Mark and I were first in the water, and we descended before Jason and Ken entered.

As expected, the Viking ship was just north of the anchor. Mark and I swam around it, marveling at the craftsmanship that had gone into building this misplaced piece of history. We met Bernie and Debbie, who were holding hands, even underwater, as they passed over the dragon's head at the bow. I could see the bubbles from Jason and Ken as they maneuvered over the center of the ship, accompanied by a school of small fish.

My air pressure was down to five hundred pounds, and I did not want to return to the surface, but I signaled Mark anyway, and we ascended. We climbed the ladder just as Jason and Ken surfaced, talking in excited voices that demonstrated the understanding of only six people still alive, who knew that Norsemen had discovered Lake Ontario long before Christopher Columbus was even born.

Debbie and Bernie surfaced as Jason and Ken climbed the ladder. I helped everyone on board and out of their scuba gear. We sat for a half hour, talking about the dive, Vikings, and American history. We did not have time for another dive. Jason and Ken had to get back to New York, but vowed to come back next summer.

Debbie had to go to work, and Mark was helping Bernie open the dive shop at ten o'clock. We idled back to the river, with the sun brightly shining above the horizon. I had just witnessed real treasure as my divers experienced something that only a few people would ever experience or even see.

Gear was unloaded and put into car trunks and trucks. Jason and Ken left first, with heartfelt good-byes. I lit up the last of Mike's cigars and put the empty box in my trunk for Trisha, who always appreciated Mike's empty boxes. My eyes caught the *FOR SALE* sign I had made for the *Gold Hunter* a week and a half ago. I picked up the sign, carried it over to a garbage can, and disposed of it. I was going to keep Mike's boat and take people out to his marine park, and a select few divers that earned my trust would get to see a sloop of war or an old wooden tugboat.

Mark and Bernie were ready to go, but I asked them to wait. Debbie was on the boat, and we joined her there. I recited Mike's poem to my now-captive audience:

> *Forward the sun sets*
> *An opposing zenith*
> *Bigger the oak gets*
> *All my secrets*
> *Treasure begets*
> *From beneath*

No one seemed to understand the poem, but they all believed that it held a clue to the rest of the treasure. The group was silent as I pointed to the big oak tree on the bluff over the *Gold Hunters* bow. I watched as their eyes dropped from the tree to the water below and then looked back to me. Without waiting for any questions, I simply said, "Yes, it is there."

"You've seen it?" Bernie asked.

"What is it?" Mark said.

"That explains the wet suit yesterday," Debbie said.

I sat at the helm and took a long drag on my cigar. All eyes were watching me when I began to speak.

I knew from Mike's letter that his wish concerning the auction proceeds was to protect the sunken ships for others to explore, enjoy, and learn from. So I said, "A pile of white metal is useless to me. It is the protection of the wrecks in the lake that is important to me, as it obviously was to my friend Michael Moresby." I looked at Debbie before continuing.

"If revealing the existence of this palladium to governmental authorities might someday help the environment by powering cars that don't need to burn fossil fuel, then that is good, I guess. But if the money from a secret private sale of the treasure would protect the wrecks of Lake Ontario so that we may learn from them in the future, then we should sell the palladium."

No one spoke as I took another puff on the cigar. I felt like Mark Twain again as I concluded, "It is up to you, my fine friends. Decide among yourselves, and let me know what you think."

Debbie spoke first. "The treasure belonged to a Medina family that owned the foundry that produced it. The state will claim it as its own, and the federal government will make it so we can't dive on any wrecks if they think there are valuables on any of them. This needs to be our secret."

"I'm with Debbie," Bernie added in a melancholy tone.

"And I'm with Bernie," Mark said.

"Then we are all in agreement," I said as I stood up, dismissing my friends. They all got up and took a look at the water underneath the oak tree before exiting the boat.

"Anyone up for a morning dive tomorrow?" I asked.

Bernie smiled and said, "I'll be here at six."

"Me too," said Mark.

"I can't make it until the weekend," said Debbie, with more than a hint of disappointment.

"Tomorrow at six. And Debbie, I'll see you this weekend," I said to the group, looking at the sad eyes in Debbie's face. I watched them leave for their jobs, and sat on the boat enjoying my cigar and watching the smoke swirl upward in a windless sky.

A young voice broke into my tranquil existence.

"Ahoy, sir. Are you Captain Bone of the dive boat *Gold Hunter?*" I turned to look at where the voice had come from and saw two young couples. The one speaking was wearing a PADI dive hat.

"Call me Wilbur," I said, with a strange new confidence.

The young man said, "We learned to dive with Michael Moresby and wondered if we could go out today."

"Get your gear. I leave in five."

"Alright! Yeehah! Okay!" the four young divers replied as they scrambled to get their gear.

While I was helping the divers load their gear onto the boat, one of the young girls asked, "Have you found any sunken ships yet?"

I just said, "Nope," and prepared for a morning on the lake.

I took my group of divers to Mike's underwater park and really enjoyed their excitement as they surfaced, babbling about the figurines on the bottom. I wondered how many more divers would come just to see Mike's underwater park and hoping to discover a sunken ship.

Epilogue

Trisha retired a month later. We bought a winter home that looked over Blackbeard's old stomping grounds off Saint John's Island in the Caribbean. I come home every summer to take divers out in Lake Ontario. Occasionally we stumble on a wreck—if I like the divers enough. Mark finished college and became a scuba instructor. He works for a dive resort on Saint Thomas, a few miles from our front deck.

Trisha learned to dive, and we go out with Mark occasionally. He still talks about the wrecks in Lake Ontario, and he is one of only six people to have seen all sixteen of them. Trisha likes the warm-water diving in the Virgin Islands better than the cold water back home.

Debbie married Bernie, and Peter Digs is flying them down to visit us for a week in January. They just bought some kind of new hybrid-electric car. Debbie no longer works as a police officer. She became a dive instructor, and now works with Bernie in their new dive store. The store keeps them busy. It has a specially built swimming pool right inside for instruction.

I heard that no one ever showed up at Abraham Buffield's funeral, which even to me seems sad. Roger Bailey was convicted of involuntary manslaughter for killing the diver that he ran over with his boat; he's serving time in Attica Prison. Bruce O'Connor ran for sheriff and won the election by a landslide, but still spends his summers patrolling Lake Ontario.

I no longer worry about my teacher's pension lasting. Instead I just enjoy every day, and look forward to my next dive with my wife, Trisha. I sent plane tickets to all my children, who are coming to Saint John's for Christmas. I am looking forward to seeing my first grandchild. His name is Wilbur Michael Bone.

The End

Another R. Jack Punch book published by iUniverse
The Barrister
When Rory McDonnell, the only son of power attorney Michael McDonnell, learns of his father's unethical business practices, Rory is faced with a difficult decision. Will Rory follow his heart? Or is he headed down the same immoral path as his father?

Rory walked in. Michael looked surprised, maybe even a bit embarrassed. Rory asked outright if his father had just committed collusion at the expense of a trusting client. Michael tried to dignify his answer by justifying the collusion with reasons. Rory had always thought of his father as perfect. Realizing that his father was less than perfect, even downright dirty, Rory simply turned around and walked out of the office. Michael did not try to stop him, thinking that time would aid in the realization that the world is not a perfect place.

Rory left the building realizing that his father's office was not as large or as grand as he remembered growing up. He remembered how intimidated he was by his father when he had worked his internship at the office. In fact, the whole world seemed a bit smaller to Rory. Family guidelines embedded a set of values that had imploded in Rory's mind. Were Rory's values based on those of a hypocritical father?

978-0-595-36575-3
0-595-36575-2

Printed in the United States
R2211000002BA/R22110PG48146LVSX00004BA/4}